AND WE SHALL PERISH

Book Two in the 12 Series

ALSO BY JEFFREY MARCUS OSHINS

12: A Novel About the End of the Mayan Calendar.
The Eye of the Archer (movie version of 12: A Novel About the End of the
Mayan Calendar)
Hippies in the Andes/Freedom Pure Freedom
Women in Politics

JEFFREY MARCUS OSHINS

DeepSix Publishers
Santa Barbara, CA

AND WE SHALL

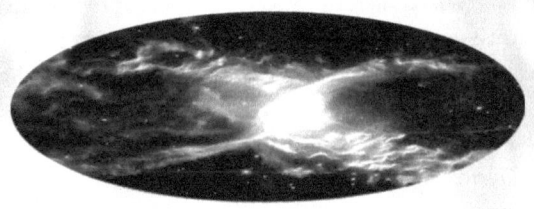

PERISH

Thanks to Gia Esola, Bernard Baycroft, and Erica Konieczny

Every 25,800 the Sun makes a reverse cycle through the Zodiac and rests in the eye of Sagittarius (the archer). At this time the temporal and celestial planes touch creating a portal through which gods enter the temporal plane to battle for the elemental nature of the Earth.

The following is the story of the Water god, Tatya-Masi, who passes through the eye of Sagittarius to destroy the Age of Man and bring forth the Fifth and Final World of Water.

An account of the battle for the Sixth and Final World of Earth.

CHAPTER ONE
THE ORPHANS OF FIRE

The rains came a week before the god was to appear. How could Anta not know the date of *Tatya-Masi's* return? Her father's devotion to *Tatya-Masi* was what had gotten him killed; why twelve-year-old Anta, her twin brother Koya, and her little sister Ati had been left without a father in the slums of Quesada.

The clouds swept in from the eastern jungles and beat various rhythms on the roofs of Us'me, a squatter camp behind the Quesada city dump. If you were fortunate enough to have a metal roof there was a pleasing resonance to the rainfall. To those with only cardboard over their heads there was a dull plop and soon a drip as rain seeped in.

Anta rolled over and tried to find a dry spot beneath the loose cover of cardboard, wood and plastic, but Death was looking for her little sister Ati.

Uma, their mother, pulled the three-year-old onto her lap. "Spit, spit." She slapped an urgent beat on Ati's narrow back.

The tiny girl gasped for air and her eyes widened in panic.

Uma shook her. "Spit."

Koya reached over Uma and hit Ati hard between the shoulders. Her small head shot forward and a foot-long roundworm fell from her mouth onto the newspapers bedding.

His thin lips pressed tight with anger, Koya spoke in the dialect of the street where there was no time for wasted words. "No eat dump food."

The city garbage dump gave them a place and a way to live, but you had to know what green mold could be knocked off a piece of bread or fruit, what meat could be boiled clean of worms and other things that could kill you. Anta blamed herself for not making enough money or finding enough good food for Ati.

Uma held Ati against her shoulder, massaging her back. "Light," Uma said.

Anta lit a candle she'd stolen from a church. The flame flickered over the broken chair and crates; clothes and tools pushed against the upper wall to thwart thieves.

No going back to sleep now, Anta carried the soiled bedding outside and threw the still-glistening white worm into the embers of their cooking fire.

Street lamps lit the city spread out below the mountainside dump. Anta's eyes were drawn to the distance where an electric snake with fire wings flapped atop a tall building. Always the fire snakebird flap-flapped but never rose, stuck like she was. She silently cursed the pitiless gods who'd put them here.

Like every day, Anta thoughts were on how she'd make the money the family needed to beat Death one more day. The first garbage trucks would be arriving at the dump in two hours. There hadn't been enough rain to fill the water buckets, so she had to buy the day's water before starting her hunt for things to sell.

Clothed in a man's shirt tied with a belt and a pair of knock-off athletic shoes that Koya had stolen, she moved down the muddy hill. The empty paint buckets knocked against her skinny knees when she jumped over the open sewer that ran behind their shack.

Their neighbor, a woman who made her money reading cards, called from the open window of her kitchen. "Dear Anta, bring one water."

Anta picked up an empty bucket and wondered why she didn't wake her lazy son, Gypsy, to stand in line.

"*Tatya-Masi* protects you," the card reader called after her.

Anta shuddered and stared into the dark. She wanted nothing to do with the god *Tatya-Masi*. He was the reason the red-eyes had killed her father.

For a year, the family had traveled the countryside while her father had preached to groups of *indios* that the god was coming and this world was going to end. One night while camping on the side of a road, the family had awoken to what sounded like monsters clearing their throats to swallow you.

"Shraaaa." The voices of the red-eyes echoed from the bottom of their graves. "Let no man say the name *Tatya-Masi*." Three red-eyes took their father in their skeletal hands. One last shriek and Death took her father.

Anta ran the bad thoughts from her brain. Fear made you weak. The weak and stupid died first in Us'me. Demons were near everyday. She needed to think about paper and metal, a few centavos to pay for some Top-Ramen.

A half-hour to dawn, a line of women and girls carrying plastic containers stood by a white wall. They endured the rain in the open with the dumb acceptance of cows and horses. A bird's nest of electric wires ran over their heads.

Something–though Anta could never say what or why–made her feel a better life was waiting for her than standing in line to buy a few cans of water. By the time she'd hauled the water up the hill, the sun was out. She fixed the coffee Koya had brought home last night and poured the first serving into a jar for him. No taller than Anta at five feet, he took the coffee without a smile or thanks. Her brother was a gangster.

They stood outside by the cooking fire in front of the shower curtain that covered the entrance to their hut. The bare ground was littered with scraps of wood and discarded wrappers. A company of parrots complained from the spiral branches of ciebas trees in the hillside forest.

"Have one sugar." She poured the white grains from the packet she'd found behind a restaurant yesterday.

"I feel in one good way today," Koya said after a sip. "Tonight I go by Rosas' store."

Was he joking? Why would the richest man in the world have a store? Rosas had a country, this country–New Granada.

"Need I help?" Anta asked. Sometimes he let her go with him to whistle if trouble came.

He ignored the offer and gazed down the mountain at the city.

She wanted to ask more about Rosas' store, but the day was getting old.

* * *

Koya kept an eye on his sister until she disappeared behind the shacks. If things went right tonight, he would do a job that would make him rich enough to take Anta and the family away from Us'me. They'd drink coffee at a café from white cups with as much sugar as they wanted. Maybe they'd go north to Los Angeles where they made the movies and the shirts and caps with the pirates and red bulls on them. He knew a world beyond this hard life. He'd seen it in the DVD's at Emilio's, the fence who bought what Koya stole. Guns that fired flaming rockets, tanks, grenades, cars that always survived when the ones chasing you crashed; men who kept fighting when they had been hit and kicked so hard they should be dead. Tough guys like him.

He liked his sister all right. But he didn't show it. Anything you liked would get taken from you. He couldn't spend all day protecting her. Anta could take care of herself.

* * *

The rotten-egg and burning-flesh smell of the dump grew stronger as Anta reached the bottom of Us'me. Dark-winged vultures and crows sat amongst the piles of paper, old food, plastic bags, and everything else the *ricos* didn't want. *Indios* waited to be the first to meet the arriving trucks. Children with bloated bellies and the red hair of those too far gone to live long ate whatever they could find.

Anta concentrated on collecting metal, newspapers and magazines not too wet from the rain. She found a metal sign, filled two bags with aluminum cans, slung them over her back and walked for a half-hour to where the streets were paved and the electric buses ran.

Nura, the junk lady, lived behind a white wall with broken bottles cemented on the top. Inside her open gate were cleaned backpacks, washed foam rubber for mattresses, tires, auto parts, forks, knives, spoons, tops of jars, glasses. The *mestiza*, fat from beans and lard, did business behind a wooden counter. She had brown teeth and a dirty mop of stringy hair that hung around her shoulders. As usual, she insulted Anta, telling her that she stank and was filthier than her dog Pepe. Anta pretended not to hear, wishing that she could eat as well as Pepe, a strong black brute who slept in the corner with an eye open.

Anta put the aluminum cans on a scale. There would be no haggling over that. She hoped she might get a good price for the sign and set the square piece on the counter.

"What is this?" Nura used her fat lips to show how much she didn't like something. "Why do you bring me this useless trash?" Nura lifted a corner of her lip toward her ear. "You know what it says? Course you don't. Says stupid girl. So I know it's your sign. Ha, ha." The fat *mestiza* looked at her dog to share the joke.

Anta's expression remained blank like she really was a stupid girl. She was smart enough to know that Nura was going to give her some money for the sign.

"I'll give you five *centavos* for it." The lip twisted over brown teeth.

"Ten."

"How many people you think need a sign says stupid girl, stupid girl?"

They settled on eight *centavos*, and fifteen more for the cans. Nura gave her small round brass coins, enough for the day's water and some bread. Anta would have to carry ten bags of cans to Nura to earn enough for beans or rice for the family's dinner.

She made three more trips to the junkyard, getting an extra thirty *centavos* for a part of a car and a dry book she found behind a school.

Near evening Anta crept into a garage where boxes of vegetables were put into trucks. Some squashed tomatoes lay on the ground behind the trash. Anta rushed to pick them up, but was chased away by a *mestizo* who hollered, "Dear god, why are these filthy people on the Earth?"

A thousand poor were lined up at a church waiting for bread. Anta knew better than to stop. A hundred would be lucky to get a few rolls. Better to find candles in churches than bread. Sometimes there would be rows of burning candles and without anyone looking she could steal ones that still had plenty of wax.

The trashcans outside restaurants where the *gringos* ate were best for bread and other food, but you had to be quick and know when to be there. Otherwise you could be in for a beating from the *gamines*, the orphans who lived on the street. They smoked *basuco*, coca paste, their eyes wide, skin drawn tight on bones, giggling idiots. Last week, Anta had seen five of them dead in the dump with bullets in their heads.

Anta cut off the day's work to go home, knowing Ati would be waiting for the packages of dried noodles she'd bought in the *indio* market on the other side of the dump.

Uma had a bone boiling with corn and a soft carrot. Ati waited by the fire, her eyes never leaving the food. The worm had left her hungrier than ever. When the soup was done, Anta let Ati have more than she took.

Karla came over looking for a meal. She sat on a wooden crate and held Ati in her lap. "Do you know what day it is?" Karla asked her.

Wide-eyed, Ati shook her heads.

"The twelfth month. *Tatya-Masi* is coming." Karla began to hum, and then sing softly.

"Move, move to *Tatya-Masi*

Twelfth month, Water washes the Fires away

Move, move to *Tatya-Masi*

The twelfth quarter moon

Move, move to *Tatya-Masi*

To the Temple-By-The-Sea

Move, move to *Tatya-Masi*."

Uma pulled Ati by the arm away from Karla.

"What be the matter, dear Uma?"

Uma looked about to make sure no one was listening. "No words by these things."

"But this day be one better day for all us La'ku," Karla said.

Uma took Ati inside the hut.

Karla sang louder to bug Uma.

"Move, move to *Tatya-Masi*

Twelfth Month Water washes the Fires away

Move, move to *Tatya-Masi*

Tatya-Masi of the *Water*

Move, move to *Tatya-Masi*

Tatya-Masi, the one truth

Move, move to *Tatya-Masi*."

Anta saw the fire snake growing brighter in the distance. There is only one truth she thought, Death–Death always there, waiting for you to slip, to get sick, to be too weak to run, to fall into the dark hole. The rats lived better than they did. How could they ever *move-move* to *Tatya-Masi* or anywhere else?

Koya came out of the hut. He had extra plastic bags in his rear pocket.

"Where go by?" Anta asked.

He pulled his lucky pirate hat tighter over his head. "Go by I-work," he spoke in the slang of the barrio, and sauntered down the hill.

Anta followed him. "I come?" she asked.

"No job for one little girl," he said, as if they were not the same age.

Anta didn't follow until he'd cut through a row of shacks on the dirt path to the city. He might be a better robber, but she was more careful. Last month she'd stopped him from snatching a purse just as a cop who would have shot him had walked around the corner. She was better at following people too. She hid behind walls and peeped around corners to see where Koya was going. Every time he checked over his shoulder, she was hidden. She tracked him from Us'me to where the land flattened and *ricos* lived in brick houses covered in white plaster. Paths became roads. Electric lines ran across the streets. The smell of cooking pork on hot coals came from a market where sometimes Koya would buy her cooked meat and sweet drinks when he had good luck. Cars and trucks blew dark smoke from their exhausts. Drivers sped a few feet, honked, and cursed when they stopped.

Anta saw a street orphan use an old trick to steal a watch. The *gamín*, younger than she was, stuck a lit *cigarillo* on a taxi driver's left arm. When the driver slapped the burn, the kid lifted the watch off his right wrist and ran. The cursing *mestizo* yelled, "I'll find you and when I do..." He did not have to finish the sentence. The *mestizos* and cops hunted *gamines*, shot them and left them in the dump or the river.

The distraction caused her to lose sight of Koya. She hurried in the direction he'd been traveling, past a blonde *gringa* on a big sign that told *ricos* what to buy. In an alley near a store with windows, where plastic people showed dresses and suits, Anta had to pass up a cardboard box that would have been just the thing to repair the hole in the shack's ceiling.

By the central market was a place with a fountain in its center where *mestizos* and *indios* sold blankets and other native clothes, weavings, and carvings to *gringos*. Deformed young begged here. Sometimes, Anta wished that her feet grew out of her ears so the *gringos* would leave *centavos* on her blanket.

She reached the *Plaza de los Mártires*, the oldest part of the city, and still could not see Koya. He'd said something about robbing Rosas, so she went to the side of the plaza where the General lived.

* * *

Koya's street sense told him he was being followed. He ducked behind a vendor's stall, and saw his sister moving through a group of *mestizas*, young schoolgirls in their uniforms. They were a chattering flock of birds in blue skirts and white shirts, the kind he'd rob just to make them cry. If one of the *mestizas* were his sister, he'd not let her walk alone on these streets. He hated the *ricas* schoolgirls. What did they know about life? Anta was better than any of them. After tonight when he was *rico*, Anta would go to a church school and be a happy, empty-headed, weak, *niña* in a blue skirt.

* * *

Anta stuck her head around a corner in case Koya had seen her following him. But he wasn't in the alley that ended at the rear of a government building.

A hand fell on her shoulder. She gasped and tried to spin away, before seeing it was only her brother.

"Why be here?" Koya pressed his face close to hers.

She leaned away from him. "Rob I Rosas store."

"Quiet. Want all cops in the Quesada to know where we go?"

We, he had said *we*. He was going to let her in on the job.

Koya hesitated and then smiled. "Come by me."

She loved it when he smiled at her, but kept her expression serious so he didn't change his mind. She followed him a hundred steps up the alley to a store with dark windows.

Koya reversed his hat on his head, and went to work on a heavy padlock on the door. He fit two shims he'd cut from a can around the top loop and worked them until the lock popped open. He had more trouble with the door lock. She watched him carefully put a straight piece of metal into the keyhole, take it out, shave off more of the metal with a file.

Her heart beat loudly in her ear and her arms trembled. He was taking too long. The alley was a dead end with nowhere to run. She turned her back to Koya. People were walking past the entrance to the alley. Cars drove by on the boulevard. This was the center of the city. They couldn't just spend all night breaking into a store, particularly if Koya was right and it was Rosas' store. With a click the lock opened.

"Move," Koya said.

They stepped inside the dark store and Koya closed the door behind them. What if there was a dog or an alarm? Why had Koya said this was Rosas' store? Someone who lived in a palace would not work here. Maybe Koya had it wrong or she didn't understand. She peered over his shoulder to see the shapes of machines and rolls of cloth stacked on shelves.

Koya lit a candle and held it high.

In the glow of the flickering wick, she saw a machine with cloth lips. They'd have a great night of stealing if they could carry that away.

"There be one door here," Koya said and ran his hand along a wood-paneled wall.

Anta saw nothing but a wall.

"Locked." Koya cursed.

"Rob one thing and move from here." Her voice quavered. They'd be killed if anyone, especially General Rosas, found them.

Koya put his hands on his hips and thought out loud. "Be on street last night. One man walk by. See I big *jefe* Rosas. Follow Rosas down one alley, keep I very small and quiet. Rosas look round and then move by this place. I come by window and look in. There be one space to see inside."

Steel bars covered a blackened window. She hoped nobody could see them through whatever space Koya had been able to see Rosas through. How did Koya know Rosas was not here now or about to come in the door?

Koya's thin shoulders tightened. "It be Rosas. There be one door behind this wall."

Was Koya *loco?* Rosas lived in a palace guarded by *Fierros* and red-eyed skeletons who'd killed their father.

"I no move in when he be here," Koya said.

Anta saw a big pair of scissors on a table. She could get 30 *centavos* for them.

"Rob these one time." She picked up the scissors.

"That be!" Koya said. "Rosas move by these. Rosas pull down one time by this."

Koya reached past her and closed the top of the cloth mouth machine.

To her amazement the wood-paneled wall opened to reveal another door. Koya handed her the candle and put the two points of the scissors into two holes in the wall and twisted. A door opened before them. "Oh Anta, I be so happy you come by here."

Anta blushed at the rare compliment. Koya took the candle and stepped into a dark hallway. Maybe if she'd been thinking less about compliments and more about staying alive she could have said something to stop him.

She followed him along a cement wall, trying not to make noise but their feet echoed in the hollow space. A gust of wind blew past them and caused the candle flame to flicker. She smelled oil. Ahead the darkness ended. Please stop, she wanted to beg him, but followed close as he crept forward to the edge of a garage. Koya put the candle in his pocket, and boldly stepped forward.

"Whew, whew," he whispered. "I told you this be Rosas place. Sure be one Rosas place."

Bright bulbs shined on a small tank and a fat-tired racing car that looked fast enough to fly.

Koya walked toward the car in a trance, and ran his hand along its red side. "Whew, if I could rob this one," he muttered.

Anta didn't know he could drive.

"How Rosas move car and tank by here?" he asked. "How go by street? Sure there be one more secret door."

She'd seen tanks before in the parades, daddy tanks to this puppy.

Koya walked around the tractor wheels. "One time we move by this," he said. "You drive. I shoot."

"Shoot?" Anta asked.

"Shoot machine guns, rockets and one big gun."

Koya was in a dream. Nothing could make him leave this place without the tank or car.

"Move by here, rob and move," Anta said and kept her eye on another doorway behind the tank.

Koya also saw the other path. "Rosas be by here. One truth now!" Koya said. "Move that way to the palace under the plaza."

He walked to a pair of open steel doors. "See we move by here under the *Plaza de los Mártires*. This be Batman place. This be way to Rosas Bat Cave. Stay by here."

Koya lit the candle and stepped into the dark passageway.

If somebody closed the doors, Koya would be trapped. Anta hurried after him.

"No move by I," Koya said over his shoulder.

She ignored him and stayed close to him and the candlelight.

With his hat brim facing back, Koya walked fast like he knew where he was going. The sound of their steps seemed as loud as shouts to Anta.

The long stone hall slanted down, taking them deeper. Anta imagined the Cathedral of the Apostles and the Presidential Palace over their heads. After a city block, the tunnel flattened. Ahead was another bright room.

Koya pressed against the wall and glided forward. Anta rocked on her feet ready to run. Koya stepped into another room as big as a store.

"Whew, whew," he said.

Anta stayed close to him. What was this place, a house, police station? Tubes ran across the ceiling. There was a bedroom, a glass shower stall, and guns, lots of guns. Soldiers and red-eyed skeletons would be near to so many guns. Anta studied a table with a big lamp over it. Beside the table was a barber's chair with leather straps. Drills and sharp metal tools hung on a wall. This Bat Cave was one scary place.

"Be fire rockets. Be grenades." Koya pointed to things hanging off the wall and in boxes. He lifted a heavy pistol and held it like the gangsters in the movies.

Anta studied four small video monitors on a desk that showed the stone hall they'd come through, the inside of an elevator, and rooms more *rico* than a hotel lobby. She searched for a camera. Somebody could be watching them.

On the far side of the room was another pair of open steel doors. Three underground tunnels, steel doors everywhere, what kind of place was this?

"Rosas' palace be up there." Koya looked for a button on the wall, and then pulled on the shiny doors of an elevator. She was glad he couldn't make it open.

"Look by there." Koya examined a narrow slot at the side of the elevator. "Be one money machine elevator."

"Rob one thing and move by here," Anta again pleaded. The gun alone could get them enough for the family to eat for a month. Nura would pay a lot for the tools.

Koya pulled his ear. "We rob by Rosas Bat Cave more times."

I hope not, Anta thought, but didn't say it.

Koya opened a center drawer in the desk that held the monitors. "Whew! Whew! This sure be the money machine elevator card. Rob I Rosas palace by this." He pulled out a piece of plastic hanging from a necklace. His eyes glistened like he had a fever. Anta hoped the credit card wouldn't open the elevator, that they could grab some loot and escape this cave.

Koya pushed the thin plastic into the slot. The door opened with barely a sound.

"No go by I," Koya said. "Move back one time for you."

She sidled through the small gap as the door closed.

Koya scowled at her and pushed the top button sending the elevator up so fast her stomach rose to her throat.

"Why come?" Koya shivered. "No place for one girl."

She pushed herself into the corner, Koya the other.

They stopped rising. The door opened. Anta was sure this was no place for a girl or a boy.

CHAPTER TWO
ROSAS' JEWELS

Why had he let Anta come? If Rosas or a *Fierro* tried to capture him, he'd kill them with his new gun or be killed. But what about Anta? He didn't want her to die. The job would be that much harder, but he wouldn't stop. Heroes never stopped.

His guts twisted as he stepped from the elevator and swept the gun in front of him. He'd been right. The cave was only the beginning. This was Rosas' room. He knew it.

Rico clothes hung from bars. Shelves held enough shoes for a department store.

At the end of the clothes room was a closed door. He pushed it a crack and peeked out to see a *rico* bed as big as a house. That had to be Rosas' bed.

There was a movement. Koya retreated and motioned for Anta to duck behind hanging clothes.

A boy as tall as Koya but twice as wide, wearing only underpants, his *tetas* jiggling, came in the clothes room.

From behind a curtain of dresses Koya recognized Enrique, the son of Rosas. How could he not recognize him? Enrique was the prince. Every boy in New Granada wanted to be Enrique. He was always on television having so much fun, winning at soccer, riding a horse, playing with all his *ricos* friends.

Enrique took a dress off the rack, almost exposing Anta's hiding place.

The prince was a princess. Koya watched him step into the gown and tie a pink sash around his waist. Enrique reached with a flabby arm and spun a dial to open a wall safe. He took out a handful of jewelry and went into the bedroom.

Koya peered from his hiding place, could not see Enrique, took a deep breath, and went to the safe. He stood on his toes to reach inside and pulled out a thick wallet. Rings and necklaces followed. He was glad Anta was there to help him carry so much loot. They loaded their plastic bags as fast as they could.

The last thing to come out was a beautiful box. Jewels in the eyes of *Tatya-Masi* sparkled on a gold lid.

The box glowed. Was he crazy? He felt stronger, could hear and see things better.

"Cruuuuuu."

Koya twitched at the faint sound. His sister was shaking. Was it an alarm? Was a camera moving to see them? He couldn't take his eyes off the carving of *Tatya-Masi* on top of the box. He put the gun down and held the treasure in both hands.

"Put in, now!" Anta said and held open a bag.

Her voice broke the spell and he slipped the box into his plastic shopping bag and picked up the gun.

The door to the closet opened.

Enrique squealed and ran the other way. The high-heeled shoes he was wearing caught in the rug and pudgy boy fell on his face.

Koya went after him. "Quiet one time," he said, waving the gun.

Enrique whimpered and pushed himself along the floor, but didn't say anything.

"No move," Koya warned. What should he do with him? Tie him up? Hit him over the head with the gun, or shoot his way out?

The bedroom door opened and a woman screamed. Koya recognized *Señora* Rosas followed by General Hernando Rosas.

Koya was too scared to use the gun. He ran through the clothes room to the elevator where Anta was waiting.

"Push the button," he shouted.

The door was closing too slowly.

Rosas, worm-lips twisted, eyes burning with rage, lunged and grabbed Koya by his red bull shirt.

"Run." Koya tossed his loot bag to his sister.

* * *

The last thing Anta saw of her brother was Rosas dragging him through the closing gap of the door. She pressed her elbows against her ribs. Her mouth opened in a silent scream. Why had they ever come here?

As the elevator carried her down she sobbed. Her brother was dead. The plastic bag he'd thrown was heavy with loot. Maybe if she gave it back to Rosas they might only get a beating. Her hand reached for the up button, but she didn't press it. Who would help their mother care for her sister if both she and Koya were in jail or killed, a couple of *gamines* left in the dump?

Koya's last word to her was to run. When the elevator door opened she fled toward the tunnel to Rosas' store.

Steel doors on both sides of the Bat Cave shut. She was trapped.

On one of the small monitors, she saw Rosas coming down in the elevator carrying a rifle.

Anta set the bags of loot on the desk and pushed as many buttons as fast as she could. The door at the rear of the Bat Cave opened.

Anta swept up the bags and ran past the elevator door just as Rosas stepped into the room. She raced by him carrying a plastic bag in each hand, through the rear door and into a hallway carved from rock.

This new tunnel was the scariest one yet. Lamps set in the floor and ceiling shined on holes in the wall where skeletons with dried skin, long cobweb hair and yellow-curled fingernails stared down at her. If she was not already as scared as she could be she'd have run.

"Put-put-put!" Firecracker sounds snapped in her ears. Pieces of rock flew near her head. Each breath punched from her lungs. Fire ran up her legs. She didn't care about the dead bodies dried up like old rats or carvings of monsters. Her pumping feet carried her through the underground graveyard.

The rock passage came to a room with a round stone roof. In the middle of the floor was the top of a head. Anta ran downstairs along a wall that wrapped around a statue of *Tatya-Masi*. She heard Rosas' heavy breathing and saw his black boots two steps above her. The stairs ended at a rock wall. There had to be some way out of here. A six-inch crack in the rock was the only place she saw to go. She twisted sideways and forced herself through the narrow break until there was no room for her head.

"Vermin," Rosas shouted.

Anta pushed with all her might until her head felt like it was being crushed, and squeezed through into a dark space where she was blind. Rosas' gun blazed. Flashes of fire lit the crack in the rocks. Bullets made whining noises as they flew by her. She retreated another step and there was nothing to stand on. Her arms whirled with bags of loot in each hand, but she couldn't keep her balance and fell backwards into a deep hole.

She gasped. Her head hit the ground causing a pain that shot up her spine into her eyes. Koya's bag fell from her grasp. All she could see were spinning stars, and then nothing but darkness—darkness blacker than the darkest night.

"Cruuuuu."

Ghostly light rose from the ground in a blue-green cloud filled with small bubbles.

Something was with her, a spirit. Had she fallen into the underworld? Her fear had discovered new limits. Her breath came in gasps. She felt weak and wanted to cry.

"Cruuuu."

The sounds and light were coming from Koya's bag. She reached out and touched the plastic. What was in there? Her racing heart slowed until she could think. She felt stronger. Her fear quieted and she could breathe again.

Grateful to have anything to see with, she took out the box. A picture of *Tatya-Masi* was outlined in burning gold on the lid. The god's eyes shined with inner brightness. Warmth radiated from the metal.

"Cruuuu."

The calling surrounded the box.

"Cruuuuu."

Her shaking hand carefully lifted the lid.

"Cruuuuu."

A cloud with its own light the color of sage wafted from the box. Inside each drop within the haze was a winged frog-faced monster the size of a bee. She'd heard about them from her father. These were *chacs*, water spirits that brought the rains.

The magical shower lit a gold *tunjo* inside the box. A pendant of *Tatya-Masi* was attached to a silver necklace and lay on a bed of woven *indio* cloth. Jewel eyes of *Tatya-Masi* shined with their own brightness.

Rosas would not stop trying to get back his treasure. She would trade the box for Koya.

Then there was a new sound—a mixture of a growl and hiss that took her back to the night the red-eyes had come for her father.

"Shraaaaa."

In the dark, two red-eyes, then four, and then six moved toward her.

The red-eyes had come for the necklace holding the pendent of *Tatya-Masi*. She closed the lid and bent over, trying to shield the box with her body.

"Shraaaa."

The eyes of the *tunjo* darkened as if to help her hide.

"Shraaaa."

The nightmare wail lessened. First one pair of red-eyes blinked closed then the others.

Great magic and danger were inside the container. She should leave it and run as far and as fast as she could. But what would she trade for Koya? She put the magical container inside the bag and set about finding a way out of this dark place.

Using her hands as her eyes, she felt her way along a slime-covered stone wall. Rats ran over her feet. Water dripped into puddles she waded across.

Hours passed. She inched forward until she heard the flushing sound of a river. The echo of whatever was ahead made it hard to judge the distance in the underground night. Where was she? How could she get out of here in the dark? Should she use the *tunjo?* No, she'd gotten this far with her own eyes and ears.

She held out her foot and felt nothing. There was no way forward and she wasn't going back. She pressed against the wet wall and felt with her hand that she was at a corner, reached around with her foot, and stepped onto a narrow ledge. She swung around the sharp bend and crept onto another path.

She kept moving until her outstretched hand felt cold steel on the wall. It was a ladder. Climbing up, she heard a car splashing a puddle, smelled the fresh scent of rain. So close to escape she could see the car lights through small openings in the steel manhole cover. Pushing up with her shoulder and hand, she tried but could not lift the lid.

The ladder shifted beneath her, pulling free from the wall. She didn't move, willing her body to be completely still, took a breath and then with as much balance as she could find on the teetering perch, stepped down, shifting her weight in tiny increments to keep the ladder from tipping until she stepped on the ground.

There was nothing to do but keep going along the path, shuffling her feet, running one hand along the wall and holding the bags of loot in the other until she found another corner with her hand and stepped around with her face pressed against the wet, cold wall.

A foul smell filled her nose with every breath. At least she thought she knew where was she was going now. The sewer came out in the river where the poor washed their clothes. Would Rosas and the red-eyes be waiting there for her?

She moved toward the sound of rushing water. Drops flew up to her face. What if she had to swim? She'd drown if she fell in.

At last there was a change. At first she thought the light was something in her mind. Then she could see that she was on a narrow ledge in a pipe carrying stinking water. When she came to where the sewer flowed into the river, the night air smelled as sweet as a rose. She stayed in the pipe and scouted for signs of the red-eyes or Rosas. A soft rain was falling. Everything sounded quiet and peaceful. She guessed that it was an hour before dawn. A stabbing pain in her heart quickly replaced the joy of her escape from the underground world. Koya had been with her when this night had begun. How was she going to save him?

* * *

Koya was strapped to a table in the gunroom beneath the palace.

Rosas showed him the cruel claws of a pair of pliers and slowly lowered them toward Koya's tied hands. Koya sucked in his breath and waited for the pain.

"Where is the *tunjo*?" Rosas demanded.

"No I *tunjo*."

"Who was she?"

He wasn't going to tell him. He would not rat Anta, but then another of his fingernails was pulled out.

"I-sister."

"Where do you live?"

"Us'me, on first hill, by dump. Go I, find I-sister." He blubbered like a girl.

Koya didn't know if Rosas believed him but the torture stopped.

Koya hated himself for being weak. He'd betrayed his family. Better to die, to end this pain—in his head, in his hands. No! Do not give up, he told himself. Be a hero. Find strength. He would say no more, no matter what Rosas did to him. His life was now dedicated to one goal—to survive and have his revenge. Anything Rosas did to him would only be added to his debt.

His eyes were nearly swollen shut from the beating he'd received, but he could see Rosas at the desk with the monitors, talking into a phone.

"I want a construction crew," Rosas ordered. "Take the wall down behind the underground temple. Tear it apart from top to bottom, every crack. I want a family named Raymi brought in. Turn the dump barrio upside down for them. Just do it!" Rosas ordered.

* * *

All was hopeless. Koya was gone. The weight of his loot was heavy in Anta's hand. She found a dark doorway and opened Koya's bag.

"Cruuuuu."

The lit cloud plumed from the beautiful box with *Tatya-Masi* on the lid.

"Cruuuu."

The sound was here and nowhere, up and down. She checked the street for a sign of the red-eyes. She wanted to see the necklace again, to feel the strength she'd felt when she'd held the *tunjo*.

She opened the lid.

The verdant steam billowed upwards. Anta gasped and reflexively closed the top. *Chacs* flew out of the cloud into the night sky. Rain fell harder.

Here was deep, old magic. Koya had stolen a great treasure.

She put the box in the bag and took out the fat wallet stuffed with money, not *centavos* but *gringo* dollars–the best kind of money. There must be hundreds of the bills. With this, they could eat steak and potatoes for the rest of their lives. They had more money than a drug dealer now. They were rich. Koya had made them rich.

All her life she'd thought that if only they had money, she'd be happy, but now felt only sadness. Should she save Koya first or protect the family? Koya would tell her to make sure the family was safe. Rosas would be coming after the family. She had to take them where Rosas couldn't find them. Then she would trade everything: the box, the money and jewels for Koya.

She had dollars but no *centavos* to pay for the family to escape. What was she going to do with the box? The magic cloud would tell Rosas where she was.

Hurrying through the dark city, shivering and dripping from the soft rain, Anta came to the junk woman's closed and locked gate. She didn't have time to wait for Nura to open for business. If Anta made too much noise, she might get caught. If she tried to climb over the wall, she'd cut herself on the broken bottles, and if she made it she'd be attacked by Pepe, or shot by Nura.

Anta hit her fist against the metal door.

Pepe barked, wanting to bite her.

"Nura!" Anta called softly.

Pepe barked louder.

"Nura!" Anta shouted.

Other dogs on the block began to bark. A light came on at the end of the street.

"Nura! Wake now." Anta called more loudly.

"Who is it? What do you want?" Nura shouted from inside.

"Have one good thing for you," Anta called.

"Come back later. I'm closed for business."

"No. Have one good thing now."

More lights shined in windows on the street. Every dog in Quesada now seemed to be barking. A door opened down the block.

"Move now Nura," Anta called.

"I have a gun," Nura warned from behind the gate.

"Nura, be Anta stupid girl. Know you stupid girl."

A view hole slipped open.

"Stand where I can see you," Nura said.

Anta stood on her tiptoes.

"You? What do you have?"

Anta held up one of the bills.

"What is it?" Nura asked. "Paper?"

"Money. Dollars," Anta whispered.

"Are you alone?"

"Only I one time."

There was the click of a lock being opened and the metallic complaint of a latch being pulled.

The gate opened slightly and Anta slipped through.

Pepe wasn't the lazy dog that slept in the corner during the day. His back was arched and his teeth bared. Nura held him in one hand and an umbrella in the other. The dog pulled free and shot forward.

Anta shrank from the dog.

Pepe didn't bite her, but barked and kept his snout aimed at her throat.

Nura locked the gate from the inside. "*Hijo de Dios*, you smell worse then ever."

Nura led her into her office, closed the umbrella, and turned on the light. "Stay there near the door where I don't have to smell you."

Even to Anta, used to the scents of filth, she reeked worse than dead bodies in the dump. She didn't care.

"Give me the money," Nura said.

Anta reached across the space until her arm was almost completely outstretched. She hoped the light or spirit sound didn't come from inside the bag with the box and loot.

Nura took the bill from her and examined it. Her narrow-set eyes bulged over her fat cheeks. "That's a hundred dollars," Nura said. "Where did a dump rat come by dollars?"

"One *gringo* move dollars by I."

"What do you want me to do with it?"

"Make *centavos*."

Nura's lips twisted around her yellow teeth. "You stole it. I know you did. I should give it to the police. I should have you arrested."

Anta tried to keep her expression blank. "More dollars again."

Skin rolls deepened on Nura's forehead. "How many more?"

"Give some *centavos* and move I more dollars by you."

"What is that in the bags? You have more here, don't you?" The junk woman leaned across the counter.

Anta couldn't stop herself from swaying. She was ready to run if

Nura came around the counter.

"Give *centavos* for dollars." Anta kept her voice firm.

Nura's lips twisted. "You stole these dollars. You know you stole them. What keeps me from keeping it all? I'm one nice lady when I give you two hundred centavos."

"Four hundred. One book bag."

"A backpack? All right, a nice backpack and three hundred for the dollars and then you're lucky."

"And one large plastic bag," Anta said.

It was like they were arguing over an old tire, but this was more than all the tires in the dump. Anta knew how far Nura would go and settled for three hundred and fifty.

The *mestiza* made Anta wait beside the old boards of her counter as she held an umbrella over her head and hurried among the piles of junk. Bending over to hide her secret places from Anta, she collected money from old cans and bags of coins hidden in different places in the junkyard. She brought Anta a plastic bag heavy with bills and coins and another larger empty plastic bag.

Anta peered inside the moneybag.

"It's all there," Nura said. "Here's your backpack." She picked up a bag that Anta had found in the dump a few weeks ago and sold to Nura for 10 centavos. It was pink and on the outside was a picture of an angel with a magic wand.

Anta could tell by way the junk woman's thin smile that Nura had given her far less than three hundred and fifty, but still it was more money than Anta had ever seen. She gripped the bag of money at the top and took the backpack.

"You have more?" Nura leered at her.

Anta pivoted and headed to the gate with the growling dog stalking her.

Anta waited for the junk woman to unfasten the latch.

"When will you bring me the rest? I'll have money waiting for you and more clothes. You're rich now. You can dress like me," Nura said, smiling like she was Anta's friend.

"Later more dollars," Anta lied.

Nura held the umbrella over her head and opened the gate.

"Bring me more dollars. You won't get a better deal," Nura called.

Anta ran onto the street with the book bag, *centavos,* and loot.

"And go to the baths," Nura said as Anta rounded the corner.

As soon as Anta was sure the junk woman was not following her, she stepped into an alley, looked around to make sure nobody was watching. She stuffed as many *centavos* that would fit into the woven bag she wore around her neck, put the box and the rest in the pack. She tore holes in the top and sides of the large plastic bag to make a rain poncho and pulled it over herself and the backpack.

Beyond the alley, she heard the sound of many engines. She moved to the avenue and saw, in the first light of dawn, cars with big guns driving past. Behind the gun cars came tanks nearly as wide as the street. Helicopters buzzed overhead. Trucks carried soldiers in a long parade of death going to Us'me.

She didn't have to be told what was happening. Rosas had come for her. She had to save the family.

Anta took all the shortcuts. Day came with dismal gray clouds heavy with rain. The chaotic sound of multiple gunshots came from Us'me. Anta ran faster, her chest heaving, her stomach crying from hunger. She was too late. Fires arose from the hills. The flames spread together until they lit the mountainside. Rosas was burning Us'me.

Anta pushed through a crowd fleeing in the opposite direction, and came to lines of back-to-back soldiers. One line faced Us'me, the other, the city. Nobody could get in and nobody could get out. Inside the barrier, soldiers shot dogs, people, anything that was alive.

Rosas and a thousand soldiers could not keep Anta from her family. She hurried across the dump past a *gamín* who was pulling trash over himself, digging in like a dirt beetle.

A hand reached out from the frame of a burnt car and seized her. She wrenched away, but the grip was too strong. Her attacker pulled her to him.

It was Gypsy, Karla's son, their neighbor. The fires reflected in the scared eyes. Rain and sweat reflected off his shiny forehead.

"Hide, Anta, they want you."

"I-family?" Anta cried and tried to pull away, but Gypsy held her tight.

"All family dead, all dead." Tears rolled down his checks into the black stubble of his beard.

"No!" Anta dragged him from the protection of the old car.

A quick "put-put-put," and insect-sounds whipped by Anta.

Gypsy pressed her to his body, sighed and fell forward atop her, crushing her into the yielding pile of trash.

Anta pushed up with her hands to get out from under him. She felt him shiver and then he was a still dead weight on her.

Anta squirmed to get out.

"Cruuuuu."

The box gave her the strength to lift him off her.

"Shraaaaa."

The sound of the red-eyes stopped Anta. She let Gypsy's corpse fall on her and hid beneath him in the bed of old food and discarded paper. From under his arm she looked out to see a skeleton in a dark robe sifting through the dump. Fire in empty eye sockets floated toward her. The dark shape of a skull rotated to where Anta hid. She did not breathe–silently praying the spirits in the box would not make a sound.

"Shraaaa."

The red-eyes lifted the body of an *indio* lying atop a pile of garbage and tossed him aside like a cornhusk. Nothing she'd seen or heard that night compared to the fear that now gripped her heart.

"Shraaaa."

The red-eyes roved past her.

The sounds of terror were all around her as people were dragged from their hiding places and shot by the soldiers. More bullets rocked the dead Gypsy's body atop Anta. His leaking blood grew cold and then sticky on her.

Anta lay beneath Gypsy for the rest of the day. Her burrow filled with water; she became so hungry that she ate the core and seeds of an old apple from the garbage in which she hid.

At dark, the shots and explosions stopped, replaced by the sounds of misery–crying children, moaning, pleas for help and doctors.

When Anta could stand it no more, she pushed out from the garbage grave and stood in the warm rain. By the light of the burning fires she saw black, crusty bullet holes pockmarked Gypsy's corpse. He'd been killed trying to protect her. One more weight was added to the sorrow crushing her heart.

Us'me was still there. It would take a year of soldiers to kill the slum. The dead were being buried or eaten. Those who had survived were taking what the dead had owned. Those who lived would go on until it was their time to die.

Anta knew better than to go closer to her hut. In addition to the red-eyes and Rosas, all of Us'me would be hunting for her, hoping for a chance to earn a reward. Nobody had a friend in Us'me when ten *centavos* were on the table. Still, she had to know, she had to be sure.

Anta darted from shadow to shadow, avoiding light and the soldiers prowling through the remains of Us'me. She came to the slop of mud and burned cinders where the hut had stood, stooped and picked up a small corncob doll Koya had made for Ati.

Gypsy was right. All the family was dead. Anta's eyes filled with tears. Pain in her throat made it hard to swallow. Everything that she had loved in this ugly world was gone.

The rain fell and hissed on the embers and splattered against her plastic poncho. Anta swore to *Tatya-Masi* and the *Christo* that she'd never go back to this smelly dump, and crept down the mountain for the last time.

CHAPTER THREE
THE RAINS RETURN

The private jet cut through the storm on a direct path into Rosas International Airport. A light on the tail illuminated the flaming winged-serpent logo of New Granada Petroleum. In the cabin, Theodore Moss, the lone passenger, stared through the oval window down at the dark jungle where stone pyramids and hieroglyphics stood in silent witness to forgotten gods and previous worlds. A modern mind had trouble comprehending that dead hands could reach into the present from the grave of an ancient civilization. Harder to believe that the fate of humanity would be decided in the next six days–if they had six days.

Rain or snow was falling on every continent. That the rains had returned so close to the predicted date of the winter solstice was causing the kind of worldwide panic that could only be brought on by the widespread belief that this was the end of days. Was it Du? Was he back?

Two years ago, Moss' sixteen-year-old son Du had opened the box and revealed himself to be *Tatya-Masi*. Precipitation had fallen everywhere. Deserts had coursed with water. Dams had burst. Only when Moss had helped retrieve the *tunjo* from Du had the clouds cleared. But five days of rain with no scientific answer or solution to the global cloud cover, with escape routes flooded, mass panic had been the response to the inexplicable. Millions had drowned or died from diseases and the economic ruin that had followed. Now, it was starting again.

The power to bring destruction to the Age of Man was in four jewels, remnants of a comet that had first brought life to the primordial oceans of the world. Called the Jewels of Life, two were embedded in the eyes of the *tunjo* and two more in a scepter controlled by the *Xucha* witches. If Du ever held all four Jewels at once, nothing could save the modern world.

Was it up to him to again find the *tunjo?* Moss didn't think of himself as someone who could save the human race. By appearances, he was a successful businessman in his early forties whose hair had started to gray on the sides in a distinguished manner—a thoughtful and quiet man who had everything he could want. But he was a slave to a master whose unblinking eyes never stopped watching him. His servitude was difficult to explain to anyone who'd never experienced the command a spirit could exert over a human life. Where some served for love and piety, Moss obeyed from fear. He liked to think of himself as a good man, someone who would never have married his wife's sister while still married to his wife unless he'd been obeying *Quetzal.* Moss believed that he was strong and resourceful enough to attempt an escape from a physical confinement, but these shackles were inside—wrapped around his heart and mind.

The day Moss had married Lilia Morales, nearly nineteen years ago, *Quetzal* had not only possessed Moss' soul, but also his body. *Quetzal* was the father of Du as much as he was.

For Moss to be free, *Quetzal* had to be freed and only Du could free *Quetzal* from *Inika* the Lordess of Water's spell.

* * *

Moss' limousine and military escort sped up a highway that had been emptied for his passage. Trucks, cars, and buses lined the side of the highway cleared by army troops for his rapid passage.

Quetzal the Plumed Serpent met Moss in a hallway of the Presidential Palace. Despite his many encounters with Gabriel Ayala, Moss paled and his breathing became labored at the sight of his master, a skeleton draped with loose fitting skin, red eyes burning in his skull. The half-life that animated the skeletal remains of the conquistador Gabriel Ayala, dead nearly 500 years, was purely malignant without a trace of human warmth or compassion.

Du had been clever to only partially release *Quetzal* and the other eleven conquistadors. That was why *Quetzal* had continued to protect him. But with the winter solstice only days away, and the *chacs* loose, Moss wondered how long the Plumed Serpent could protect Du from the other Fire spirits.

The question was barely formed in Moss' mind before Ayala's low and muffled voice came from someplace other than lungs and a throat. "We leave after this meeting to find the Water god."

"The Assassins of Fire will follow us to him," Moss thought.

"I can no longer protect him. Come, we must deal with this puppet that *Mitnal* the Smoking Mirror has possessed."

Moss followed Ayala into a study where Hernando Rosas sat behind an ornately carved wooden desk. Rosas wore a military uniform that resembled something from an Italian opera with padded shoulders hung with gold braid, high red collar, epaulettes, cords, studs, tassels, and a chest covered with medals. Even in this ridiculous uniform he was a strikingly handsome man, someone you wanted to like and trust. Moss knew his charisma was due to his possession by *Mitnal* the Smoking Mirror who had possessed a human innately without scruples, a ruthless hand to control the site of the battlefield where the fate of the next and final age of Earth would be decided.

Beside Rosas, *Kinchel* the Avenger, a Fire spirit who could assume many bodies and forms, appeared as *comandante* Ochoa, commander of the New Granadian Armed Forces. Two revolvers in white holsters hung on either hip of his military uniform.

The Fire spirits spoke to each other at a rate far too fast for the human ear to decipher, in a blur of squeezes, chirps, and high-pitched whines. Moss heard them as you would your own thoughts: a combination of images, feelings, and words.

Mitnal would not show outright disrespect for *Quetzal*, who was a son of *Xiulu* Lord of Fire, while he was only a spirit who served *Xiulu*. "Greetings, Prince *Quetzal*. It is always a pleasure to see you looking so well."

The comment of how he looked angered Ayala, whose ungainly body lurched as if to reach with a skeletal hand to seize Rosas around the neck.

"Careful, Prince. We don't want to damage this handsome body I possess." *Kinchel* continued to torment *Quetzal*. "Have you spoken to your father? Oh no, of course not. I forgot, your powers are limited. Shall I tell you what the Lord of Fire says?"

"Speak, you simpering dog."

"Your father, Lord *Xiulu*, says we cannot risk the Water god reuniting the four Jewels of Life. He does not want to lose this World."

"And who lost possession of the two Jewels in his possession?"

"This is a regrettable but easily rectified situation. I am here to say to you, tell you, that you can no longer protect the Water god. We must find *Tatya-Masi* and destroy him."

"And I tell you this. I will be free of this curse and the Water god will free me."

"We all hope and pray this unnatural miracle to be, but you will understand if your Lord father doubts a Water god will ever free a Fire spirit. *Kinchel* sends his Assassins to where we know the god to be."

"And where is he?" *Quetzal* demanded.

"Why, I thought you knew. I am sure you know, so I won't be repetitive."

Kinchel the Avenger said, "Prince *Quetzal*, we have found the witch mother. The *Xucha* magic that hid her from us has weakened. If the Water god is going to free you, he must do it now, because we have found them and they must die."

A vestige of the love Moss felt for his first wife, Lilia Morales, gave him a momentary pang of pity that these zombies would soon be hunting her. He doubted that either his son or ex-wife would be alive by December 21.

When Rosas spoke, the conversation between the spirits had been completed. Rosas raised his eyes to Ayala and said, "I want that girl who stole the *tunjo* brought to me. She is an Indian, a *gamina*, a street urchin. I already have her brother. They are common thieves. They broke into my palace and were able…"

Ayala interrupted Rosas, "You can see from the rain that she's already opened the box. The *chacs* have been released. We almost had her in the sewers, but when she closed the box she got away. My men are following her now. We will have the *tunjo* back soon."

Few would dare argue with the ruthless dictator. Rosas glowered at Ayala with such fury that Moss wondered if a man who spent hours inventing new titles for himself–one more grandiose and preposterous than the last–would be able to contain his arrogance or submit to the will of anyone, even a Fire spirit. "I want the girl for myself." Red serpent-eyes glinted in the despot's brown irises.

"I care only about the *tunjo*," Ayala said and lurched toward the door in his ungainly, rattling walk.

* * *

Two hundred miles to the east of Quesada, the jungle was as thick as it had been nine hundred years before when the La'ku had marked the date of the winter solstice as the beginning of the Sixth World. Rain dripped through twenty layers of leaves before it fell on a camp of resistance fighters hiding from Rosas' army. They could not even build a fire for its smoke, a dubious remedy to ward off the bloodsucking insects that sought any exposed skin.

A lone figure leaned on the rotting remains of a fallen tree. Eduardo Morales' fifty-one-year-old muscular body filled out the jungle fatigues. His full dark beard was graying on the edges. Brown eyes expressed a mix of sorrow and intelligence.

Eduardo examined his hands, red and wrinkled by rain. Am I being digested, he wondered? The overarching trees might as well be the jaws of an anaconda closing around him. The digestive process starts with rain that falls until you can't remember what dry is. Then heat steams you into a soft corpse that attracts swarms of flies to suck your blood and leave your skin exposed to rashes and parasites.

He found little encouragement in the twenty men and women—all that were left of the Army of Liberation.

Pacho **Núñez**, a squat actor from *Teatro Pancarta*, was practicing his role as the god *Tatya-Masi*. Eduardo had to admit that if nothing else, his troops were talented thespians. The getup made of padding and plastic had been created by—according to **Núñez**—a renowned costume designer.

Dress-rehearsing in the costume, Núñez did look like Eduardo's nephew Du Moss. The masquerade had proved effective in getting *indios* to give them food and protection from Rosas.

In a stage voice, Núñez chanted the refrain every *indio* for a hundred miles around seemed to be repeating:

"Move, move to *Tatya-Masi*,

Twelfth month, twenty-first day,

Water washes the Fires away.

Move, move to *Tatya-Masi*.

The twelfth quarter moon,

Move, move to *Tatya-Masi*.

To the Temple-By-The-Sea,

Move, move to *Tatya-Masi*."

The real frog god was a curse on Eduardo's family. What would the lunatics who believed *Tatya-Masi* was coming back in six days think if he told them that he was the monster's uncle? Eduardo wished that he'd never seen Du's ugly face. Let the *indios* think the beast was a god. Eduardo knew he was the weak and stupid son of his sister Lilia.

What am I doing here, he thought? This is hopeless. No, I must not give up, Eduardo thought. The landowners, his class, the ones dispossessed and wronged by Rosas, were depending on him. They called themselves *los Trece*, the Thirteen. They had money but no fight.

With funding from *los Trece*, Eduardo had outfitted and loaded a boat with arms. The *Bestante* was due to sail from Florida and arrive here in six days when the La'ku believed their god, *Tatya-Masi*, would return and drive the Spanish from their land.

Eduardo's plan was to have **Núñez** appear in the costume of *Tatya-Masi* and inspire the peasants to take up some of the weapons being delivered by the boat. That would create enough chaos to distract Rosas so a true revolution could take place to restore the rightful rulers.

A terrifying sight interrupted Eduardo's lament. A specter emerged from the jungle. Norane, a man Eduardo had shot dead nineteen years ago, walked past his guards.

Savages accompanied the ghost. They appeared to be from ancient time, like they'd stepped from one of his father's anthropological drawings. Some wore animal skins tailored so tightly that they clung to every bodily curve. Others sported feathered robes and grotesque wooden masks with leering, sharp toothed, devil-tongued monsters. Their skin was tattooed and painted; their noses and ears pierced, hair thick with red-mud ocher. They were armed with long, straight bamboo blowguns. Darts carried in quivers fashioned from monkey skin hung from their waist.

Eduardo jumped to his feet and met Norane's stare, as they once had as boys, to see if one would back down—neither ever had.

Norane's voice was hollow, speaking from a deeper space. "Lilia's soul is leaving her body. Bring her the Waters of Life. Carry her to Manoa."

The ghost of Norane held out a small vial laced with gold filigree. The contents shined with a beryl pulsing light that radiated around Eduardo's hand.

Eduardo closed his eyes, overwhelmed by the mystical forces commanding his attention. His hesitation cost him any chance to question the message or the messenger. The vision of Norane and the ancients faded into the surrounding jungle.

Eduardo spun and demanded, "Hey, did you see that? Did you hear them?"

"What's that in your hand?" **Núñez** asked.

They'd not seen the spirits. But Eduardo had. His sister needed him.

Eduardo confirmed that he really was holding the radiating vial in his hand, picked up his rifle, and without another word ran into the jungle.

CHAPTER FOUR
RETURN OF THE GOD

Steady rain had fallen for days. Du Moss didn't need to listen to the news reports to know the rains were falling everywhere. He saw the fanged monkey faces of *chacs* in the laden clouds over the Lake of the Frogs in the Sierra Nevada Mountains of California. In five days when the Earth reached the equiplane equinox, the celestial and temporal planes would be the closest. Already spirits were crossing the bridge created by the Jewels of Life into the physical dimensions to fight for the Sixth and Final World of Earth. Whoever held the four Jewels of Life–two in the *tunjo* that Rosas had taken from him in the Cave of the *Xucha* and two in *Cocatamia* the Staff of Life that he'd left in Manoa–would be able to control the bridge from the celestial realm. Either the forces of Water or Fire would rush in to claim the Sixth and Final World.

His uncle Eduardo was on his way to fly them home to Omagua. Du's chance to live as a man was over–time to become the god of Water, to either save or destroy the Earth.

MG, his closest friend, bass player and singer in the band *Apokaful*, drove him into the Sierra Nevada Mountains of California. The last of day's light faded through the branches of the pines. Du observed the slate-gray surface of the Lake of the Frogs. The Water god in him loved the rains, longed for an Earth mostly of water. As MG had once said, wash the planet clean. Start over again.

MG stopped the truck before a red metal gate barring the entrance to the property they shared. She was beautiful and strong in a classic frontier America way, the kind of woman who had settled the West.

Du, in a pair of bib overalls, no shirt or shoes, got out to open the padlock. The metal barrier swung unimpeded. The chain had been cut. Somebody or something wanted him to know that they were waiting for him.

Du hopped to the side of the truck and spoke to MG through the rolled-down window. "Someone's been here," he said. "I'll get my mother and meet you at the southern edge of the property."

He bounded up the dirt driveway in leaps of twenty yards, his webbed hands held out before him for balance. His large head with a monk's tonsure of short hair around a high bald cranium was thrust forward for balance. The rain rolled naturally off his mottled olive-colored skin. What made him swift underwater–the powerful thighs, low center of gravity, flapped ears, webbed feet, and protruding eyes–appeared ponderous and out of proportion on land. Over six feet tall, his two hundred pounds were concentrated in his lower body. What made him a man caused him to dread what made him a god. What made him a god gave him powers to save mankind, if he could.

At the rear of the darkened house, he found a key inside a tool shed and unlocked the kitchen door. Inside was quiet, too quiet. *Kinchel* the Avenger had spent the last two years questing the Earth to kill him.

In his physical form, *Kinchel* was a nine-headed dragon. Eight of the heads, the Assassins of Fire, could detach from *Kinchel* and take on their own animal and human forms to hunt *Kinchel's* prey.

A lightning bolt flashed outside a three-windowed turret illuminating the sparsely furnished room. She was not there.

A faint, familiar presence was near, a memory or a premonition. Down the hall, the door to his room was open. He peered into the shadows, seeing only his musical instruments and computer desk.

His feeling of foreboding came into focus. The barest movement, the hint of a shape, was all he needed to know. Amid the rushing energy of Du's fear was the confirmation of his dread. If Kare was here then the Lord of Fire had found him. Kare would never have gotten this close if his mother, Lilia, had her full powers.

Du remained in the frame of the door ready to leap away. "I'm glad to see you again," he said, conflicted but happy to be reunited with the man who had raised him on the shores of this lake.

Kare stepped into the faint light by the window. Six foot two, strong in the shoulders and arms, long black hair, parted in the middle, and held off his forehead by a colorful woven bandana; he held a pistol in his hand. In an urgent tone Kare demanded, "Have you the power to stop the rains?"

Du hopped into the room. "Where is my mother?"

"I cannot protect the witch."

"But I can."

Kare's expression softened. "Save the Age of Man, Du."

Du sensed the trap closing. The Assassins of Fire had used Kare as bait.

Du closed his eyes and cast a spell his mother had taught him. "*Xichii, Mana-panapi, Coaixl.*"

Six misty, shimmering water-women appeared before him and created a rainbow by holding hands over their heads. Du stepped through the water passage and disappeared just as a man in a plaid hunting jacket and a redheaded woman sprang into the room firing their rifles.

"Where has he gone?" The red-mustached Hunter Assassin pointed his shotgun at a small sheen of moisture on the now bullet-scarred floor.

"To the witch-mother." Kare stepped by the Assassins and left the room.

Outside the house, a multi-hued wall of fog appeared in the garden. Du hopped out and the cloud dissipated.

Where was his mother? Had the Assassins taken or killed her? He closed his eyes and concentrated. She was alive, near; somewhere she knew he would know, the first place he had wanted to go when he'd come home. Du hurried toward the lake and stopped outside the gazebo he'd built to memorialize Edgar Weinmann, his tutor and mentor who along with Kare had been his only companions as a youth.

Du knew that he was doing what the Assassins expected, but entered the rounded structure anyway.

Lilia was crumpled on the wet floor, her straight black hair framing her pale face.

Two eyes burned in the dark behind her.

"Hello Father," Du said as he knelt beside Lilia and touched her cheek. Her skin was cold, her breath and pulse nearly undetectable. The vial around her neck radiated with only a trace of the Waters of Life. She had nearly left the physical plane. He had to bring her to Manoa, to the Fountain of Life.

Du stood and faced Theodore Moss and the skeleton body of Gabriel Ayala.

Moss held a revolver pointed at the ground. Ayala's eyes glowed red in the hollow ovals of his eye sockets. Between the folds of a loose robe, a swirl of light spun from a serpent-wrapped cross on Ayala's bony chest. The light shimmered and expanded into *Quetzal* the Plumed Serpent in his most beguiling form, a beautiful mystical bird with a golden beak, silver breast, and iridescent feathers spread around him.

"Am I not also your father?" *Quetzal* spoke with a Castilian accent.

Du did not waste time with reminiscences or respond to *Quetzal's* irony. "We know I am of both Water and Fire," Du said. "I would free you if I could, as I would save this world if I could. I would save myself. I would save us all if I had the power."

"Where will you find this power?" *Quetzal* demanded.

"I must hold all four Jewels of Life and I must find…." Du hesitated. "Certainty."

"Your weakness will doom us both," *Quetzal* said.

"You want to leave this world while I want to stay," Du said. "Nothing can be done until I possess the Jewels of Life."

"Two of the Jewels remain in Manoa and the other two are in the *tunjo*. The Lord of Fire has lost control of the *tunjo*. The necklace may yet find you. And you may yet reach Manoa."

"The Lord of Fire knows that I do not seek to be a god of Water. Why do the Fire spirits keep hunting me?" Du asked.

"Because they know if you ever possess all four Jewels of Life, you will rule the next Age."

"And if I possess all four Jewels, how do you know I will free you and stop the rains?"

The *Plumed Serpent* spread his fire-tipped wings as if to embrace Du. "Because you love this world and only you can stop *Inika's* flood." The radiant head of *Quetzal* dipped. "Only you may release me."

Their encounter was punctuated by the hunting howl of Wolf Assassin approaching the gazebo.

"Go with him," *Quetzal* said to Moss. "Stay close and protect him. I will do what I can."

Moss started to protest what was surely his death sentence but nodded in obedience to his master's command.

"Shraaaa!" The cry of the red-eyes echoed across the lakeside estate.

One of Du's eyes focused on his mother, the other his father, both human in form, and wondered how he could be so different. A cross between a man and a frog, able to live in the air and water, he had powers that were no easier to explain than his appearance. He would need all those resources to save himself and his parents now.

In a low crouch, his tapered back taut over his oversized thighs; he lifted his mother's emaciated body, ready to flee. His eyes, the size of apples, protruding from sockets on each side of his head, tracked in opposite directions looking for the Assassins of Fire.

"The conquistadors are bound to kill you, as I am now. When we meet again, I will be forced to sacrifice us both to save the Age of Man," *Quetzal* said and in a pinwheel of light withdrew into the cross on the dark shape of Gabriel Ayala.

Du led Moss from the gazebo. He lacked the skill to cast a visibility spell that would cover them both. Only the strongest *Xucha* magic would hide them from the Lord of Fire. His mother was too weak to help. Even if he knew the words, alone he lacked the inner strength, the absolute conviction and trust in the power of Water to hide them from the Lord of Fire.

Figures flitted across the lawn in the dark. Red laser eyes passed over the outside walls of the gazebo.

Crack! A lightning bolt slammed into the water. The bright flash illuminated a muscular teen with short-cropped hair moving to intercept them. Blond Assassin held an automatic rifle in an arm tattooed with a black cross wrapped by a winged serpent.

Lightning flickered and his yellow hair appeared to be electrically charged.

"Shraaaa!"

Blond Assassin's eyes burned red.

Du concentrated on the power of twelve, the fundamentals of

Xucha learning–the power of flow, the inextricable persistence of water.

"*Xipe Tótec, Xipe Tótec Tlacaxipehualiztli!*" he called on *Xipe* the goddess of skin to hide them.

A bizarre manifestation of a creature with knives in eight hands misted out an aquamarine fog. The hellish demon seized the howling Assassin, flayed him alive and threw the skin on Du.

Du strode toward the woods within the fiery confines of the Assassin. The hide, an illusion of Fire, burned him as it covered him, causing his own skin to instantly dry and itch.

"Moss!" Hunter Assassin called to Theodore Moss who appeared to him to be running beside Blond Assassin.

"The witch is in the gazebo," Moss said. "We're going after *Tatya-Masi*."

Hunter Assassin angled toward the gazebo, but Wolf Assassin, hair bristling on his arched back, sniffed the air and stared at Blond Assassin with feral eyes.

If Wolf Assassin came closer, no amount of magic could hide Du from *Kinchel* the Avenger. All he needed was a couple more steps to give him a chance of escape.

The skin burned hotter on Du; so much that steam rose from him. "Water hides and protects me," Du repeated to himself.

"Shraaaa!"

Wolf Assassin caught his scent and leaped toward him.

Du threw off the skin of Fire with all the relief of escaping a burning room and bounded across the meadow, Moss running behind him.

Hunter Assassin discharged his shotgun.

Holding his mother across his arms, Du cut into the nearby woods as pellets dug into a tree by his head.

Blond Assassin reformed within the skin Du had discarded and ran after them.

The forest would not protect Du from the Assassins as well as the lake would. Underwater, he could move faster and with more stealth. Water was his realm, as the Assassins of Fire preferred the woods. But Du would not abandon his mother and even the chance of an alliance with his father was worth the risk.

The skeletal wraiths of the reborn conquistadors joined the chase. "Santiago," their ancient battle cry echoed in the night.

"Shraaaa!"

The inter-dimensional disturbances of the Fire spirits moving in the physical world added to the unworldly sounds. Multiple bolts of lightning struck the trees in front of Du, setting them ablaze, forming a wall of flames that blocked his path. The fire melded into the terrifying form of *Kinchel* the Avenger. Flames glinted off the silver scales of *Kinchel's* arched torso. Fiery wings spread over the forest, inflaming everything they touched. The eight heads of the Assassins of Fire, arrayed around the central snake head of *Kinchel,* reached for Du with flaming serpent-forked tongues flicking between the fangs of their open mouths.

Moss cowered, certain that he'd been revealed as a traitor to the Lord of Fire.

The inferno consumed the woods around them. The conquistadors waited behind in case they tried to retreat. They were trapped.

Burning ash singed Du. Heat made it impossible to breathe. A flaming cedar crashed down, causing him to fall against Moss.

His father started about. "Save us," he said.

"*Inika* Lordess of Water, grant me the power of wind and water. *Papuja, K'ana, Laa, Haka 'ua, Falaa!*" Du called.

The wind shifted and a slanting downpour fell against the inferno, but it only gave them a momentary reprieve. Heat burned Du's skin.

Moss fell to his knees, cowering before the flames raging toward them from all sides.

Believe, Du told himself. He had to believe, to lose himself in the flow.

Du looked to the lake, closed his eyes, and called the waters of the Lake of the Frogs to him. "*M-ah Nas Ta Saba Na!*"

The flaming form of *Kinchel* bent his serpent head and struck at Du, fire roaring from his mouth. Searing pain broke through Du's concentration. He fell to his knees beside his father and bowed his head beneath the flames.

"*Cra! Lor!*" He chanted with his eyes closed.

A circle of dark clouds spun over the lake, faster and faster until a white, dancing spout of water rose into the sky and skipped across the shore to where Du knelt, pulling the flames into its centrifugal core.

Kinchel darted his human and animal heads and struck at the cyclone. The tearing wind and rain sucked the Fire spirit into its powerful vortex.

Bent forward, carrying his mother across his arms, Du led Moss from the steaming battle.

"Shraaa!"

The Assassins were not defeated, only delayed.

Du emerged from the burn zone into the realm of tall pines, their boughs dripping with rain. With his ability to make long jumps, he could have moved much faster in the woods than having to wait for Moss who followed as best he could.

"Hurry, Father. We don't have far." He led Moss over a hill toward the front gate.

Automatic weapons fire cracked. Bullets thumped into tree trunks around them. Wolf Assassin bayed, beaming red eyes moving rapidly at them.

"Follow me." Du led his father through the forest and down a hill to where MG's truck was facing the road.

Du waited for Moss to climb in the rear seat and followed him with Lilia across his arms.

With no lights on, MG drove onto the narrow dirt road leading toward the highway. "There are bad guys the other way," she said.

"Bad guys this way, too," Du said as the lights of a car could be seen moving through the forest toward them

MG grit her teeth and, with only the dim light of the cloud-shielded moon to light her way, accelerated toward the approaching car. Her truck bounced violently on the rutted dirt road. Du was lifted out of his seat. The vehicles entered the same long curve from opposite directions.

The other car would not yield and neither would MG. Halfway through the bend, MG spun the wheel and cut across the path of the oncoming car. The two vehicles skidded sideways into each other with a jarring crash. At the moment of impact Du recognized the other driver. MG had her truck in reverse and was trying to turn around.

"It's Eduardo," Du said.

His uncle emerged from the dented white sedan with a pistol in his hand.

Du opened his door and stepped into the headlights of the other car. "Eduardo, it's me and your sister," he shouted.

Wolf Assassin howled. His red eyes shined in the gloomy forest. Eduardo spun and aimed his revolver.

Du held open the passenger door to MG's truck. "Get in," he called to Eduardo.

MG smiled at Eduardo as he entered the truck. Du bounced back into the rear seat and closed the door.

"*Señorita*." Eduardo bowed his head slightly at MG.

"Well, well, thought I might see you again some day." Her cheek flushed and her eyes sparkled as she pulled onto the narrow dirt road leading farther into the dark wilderness.

Eduardo turned and focused on Moss. Eduardo's .357 Magnum rested on top of the seat. His skin flushed beneath his beard as he stared down Moss. "Now you will answer for what you've done," he said.

"I will tell you only this, that I watched over Lilia the best I could."

"But why did you marry her sister when you knew Lilia was alive? Why do you serve Rosas when he keeps my father a chained idiot at the house he stole from my family?" Eduardo demanded.

"To protect you and him." Moss said, nodding at me. "To save the human race."

"You are insane," Eduardo studied his sister sitting limply between Du and Moss. "How many lives does she have?" he whispered. "Give her this."

Du did not have to ask what it was. He opened the small vial and placed a drop the glowing Waters of Life on his mother's lips.

The revitalization was instantaneous. Lilia sat up from where she'd been leaning against him.

Moss stared at her. "Lilia," he whispered.

She blinked. "Theodore." Her voice was tender, her expression lit with a smile of joy. Then, the *Xucha* witch reasserted control. Lilia's irises were split, natural brown on the top and deep jade on top. She pointed a finger at Moss and in a hollow, cold voice said, "Cast out this servant of Fire, *Tatya-Masi*. He brings only treachery."

Moss looked forward hiding his emotions.

Du silently cursed the spiritual forces that had commandeered their lives and wondered if he'd glimpsed love between his parents when Lilia had first awoken.

MG turned on the headlights. The truck smashed through the

limb of a Jeffrey pine and launched over a sharp peak before bouncing hard on the dirt road.

Eduardo frowned. "Where does this emerge?"

"Where we're going. Leave the driving to me, Eduardo," MG said as the truck skidded around a bend.

CHAPTER FIVE
THE COUNTRY

Anta waited in line behind four *indios* merchants carrying their goods in suitcases and boxes. The open bed of a six-wheel truck had lime and pink painted slats around the bed where passengers rode with the cargo.

"Where to?" the driver asked her.

Anta hesitated. People behind her waited.

She gave the name of the village where she'd been born, "Omagua."

"Fifty *centavos*."

Anta paid the driver with some bills Nura had given her.

"Should be there by morning if the cops and soldiers don't stop us too much," the driver said.

Anta resisted the urge to run. She had family in Omagua; an uncle, cousins, people who knew her. Better to go to Omagua than be a rat hiding in a city of cats.

Rain continued to fall hard as the truck drove through the city and onto the highway leading to the country. The other passengers crowded near the cab where a small area was sheltered by a tarp. Anta stood alone in the rear and faced the rain-heavy wind. Her trash bag poncho flapped as the truck picked up speed.

Tears mingled with the rain on her cheeks. She said good-bye to her little brother and sister, her mother and Koya. She tried to throw her sadness away, but memories filled her mind. Her family did not have much. Everyday they fought to put something in their bellies that wouldn't make them sick. What right did these soldiers have to crush them with no mercy? Did they deserve this because she and Koya had stolen Rosas' money and jewels? Was it their fault that Rosas' men had killed so many in Us'me? Had the gods punished her family for her crimes?

The magic box Koya had stolen beat with its own heart in the backpack. Sometimes the *tunjo* nearly burned her with a heat that spread through her body. She could hear things and see things that she never had before. The necklace moaned for her to wear it, to show her new powers to the world.

She was not going to be stupid. Rosas had killed her family to get the *tunjo*. The red-eyes would not stop hunting her. It wouldn't be long after she put on the necklace that she'd be dead. She wasn't strong enough to hold the *tunjo*.

The truck slowed. Ahead, at the edge of the city, bright lights lit the highway where police and soldiers blocked their way. There was no use in running. Where could she go anyway? Anta squatted where she could see through the slats on the side of the truck.

Beside her a woman sitting on a plastic-wrapped pile observed her. "Where are you going now, sweet potato?"

Anta pretended she hadn't heard the question.

"You're the girl they're looking for, I bet." The woman had a leathery face and hands with thick skin. She spoke with a slow voice as if trying to remember something that speaking too fast would make her forget.

The woman winked like she and Anta had just made a deal. There was no escaping. If the soldiers didn't recognize her, this hick would turn her in. Anta wished that she'd taken one of Rosas' guns.

They rolled to a stop where two tanks blocked the road.

"Everyone out. Open all packages and bags," a soldier ordered. He wore a red beret with the emblem of the fire snake on the front. They were *Fierros*, the worst of Rosas' soldiers.

Anta kept her head down as she climbed off the truck with the other passengers.

Fierros surrounded her immediately. "What's your name? Where you going?" a soldier demanded.

Anta did not look at him. Another *Fierro* pointed a gun at her.

She couldn't think about running away. She wouldn't get one step before being shot.

"Tell us your name!"

Anta started when she felt a hand on her shoulder. It was the woman from the truck.

The country woman stepped between Anta and the soldiers and said, "Please don't scare my daughter, sirs. She is simple and doesn't understand much."

"Who are you?" a *Fierro* asked.

"Why I am Aunt Bu from Palapi. And this is my daughter Lali. I brought her into the city to see a doctor, but…" the old leather face wrinkled, "there's nothing to be done for my little sweet potato."

"Open your stuff."

Aunt Bu unwrapped the plastic around her pile of ponchos. The soldiers threw the weavings to the ground.

"Careful, please sirs, careful of my fine ponchos. I'm an old woman. Think of your mothers."

Anta leaned into the soft belly of Aunt Bu.

The *Fierros* ignored Aunt Bu's pleas. "What does she have under there? Take that bag off." A *Fierro* pointed at Anta.

Anta played along, acting like she didn't understand. Aunt Bu motioned with her hands for Anta to take off her clothes. Anta peeled off the plastic bag she wore.

"Why is she dressed like a *gamina*? She smells like a latrine. Tell her to take off that backpack."

"But sirs, it is wet and she will come down with the grippe."

A *Fierro* aimed his rifle at Aunt Bu.

Another *Fierro* shouted. "Come on, keep it moving. We have a load of *gringos* here."

"I can't stand the smell of her anyway. Go on. Get going," the *Fierro* ordered.

Anta helped Bu throw her ponchos and plastic wrap on the truck. They hardly had time to climb aboard before the driver had the truck in gear. They passed through the blockade and sped eastward.

Anta watched Bu fold her ponchos and place in the plastic. Anta handed a poncho to Bu.

"Where going, now?" Bu asked.

"Omagua," Anta said.

"Live by there?"

Anta did not answer.

Bu's face wrinkled. "*Mucho Fierros* there, bad place. Alone?"

The blanket lady was asking too many questions. When was she going to ask for her reward for protecting her? "I-family there," Anta said.

"Come with me. I teach you to weave, make ponchos and blankets."

How long would it be before the country *india* tried to steal Koya's loot?

Anta pulled her plastic bag poncho over her head, and didn't help Bu fold any more ponchos.

As the *colectivo* drove through the night, Anta could not stay awake and fell asleep leaning against Bu.

At first light, Anta awoke with a cry and sat up, feeling a sense of danger. She moved away from Aunt Bu and stood holding onto the side of the truck. Ahead in the faint light, she thought she saw Mount Susuprina through the clouds.

A farmer said mostly to himself, "Hasn't rained like this since *Tatya-Masi* came."

"Move, move to *Tatya-Masi*," a woman passenger softly sang.

Anta remembered toothless Karla singing to the children. Could that have been two days ago? Before time stopped and a life of pain began.

Maybe *Tatya-Masi* was coming again and everything would start over. No, sad Anta, she told herself; nobody is coming to save you or anyone else.

The road dropped more steeply. Trees entwined with vines crowded each other. In the dawn air, the wind smelled like boiling weeds when they had nothing else to eat in Us'me. An hour more and the truck reached the top of a hill.

"Cruuuu."

Anta listened to the faint calling in the wind, thinking it might be one of her family's spirits. The sound seemed to be coming from the volcano Susuprina.

For an instant, Anta's eyes tricked her. She saw an old woman in the clouds over the mountains. Frog lips carved an ancient face from ear to ear. Big dome-shaped eyes drew Anta into their cores. Anta recognized the vision from the stories her father had told about the supreme witch of the *Xucha*. "Curratta," she whispered. The phantom did not respond. Anta reached behind to touch the gold box on her back. A feeling like the first step into the hot springs came over her, making her feel warm, clean. She did not have the filth of the sewer and dump on her skin. She was strong and healthy. She did not need food or sleep.

"Wear me. Hold me." The *tunjo* had a voice now that blew in the wind.

Anta carefully studied the other passengers to see if they had seen or heard the spirits. They were as expressionless as the cows they passed in the field. Only Bu displayed friendship with a twinkle in her eyes.

Ahead, Anta could see nothing but trees spreading to the east–the jungle.

The truck stopped in the central square of Palapi, the last town before Omagua. Anta stayed in the truck while the others walked away or waited beneath the balcony roofs around the plaza.

Aunt Bu peered into the truck. "Come out of the rain. People will wonder why stay in rain."

Was Bu going to demand her reward now? Anta stood still.

"Come with Aunt Bu? Have nice warm house not far."

Anta did not answer or look at the woman.

"Just ask for Aunt Bu. Everyone knows me." The blanket seller lifted her ponchos onto her head and shuffled away.

Anta raised her arm, but said nothing.

A local cop in a cowboy hat rounded the rear of the truck. "Get down from there," he ordered.

Caught again, Anta obeyed.

"Come with me," the cop said.

One country cop in the middle of nowhere, she could run from, but to where? Damn little town. If she was in Quesada, she'd know the places to hide. Here, she couldn't tell a trap from a hiding hole. There were other ways to deal with cops.

Anta followed him under a balcony. Rain fell in a curtain from the overhang. The cop leaned over her. "You a city girl?"

"No, *Señor* policeman, bring *centavos* by mama for auntie."

"*Centavos?* How many *centavos?*"

What would a country cop want for a bribe?

"Eighty *centavos, Señor* policeman, for medicine."

The passengers and the local sellers in the plaza looked at them.

"Come over here."

She followed him to the edge of the plaza.

"I should arrest you. My captain says to bring in every young girl from Quesada. Everyone is looking for her. Better give me some *centavos* if you want to bring your auntie any money."

Anta started a schoolgirl cry. "Please," she begged "Auntie very sick."

"Give me sixty."

"Please only thirty."

It would have taken a hundred to buy off a Quesada cop.

The local policeman made sure no one could see them. "Give me that."

Anta wished she had kept some money outside her pouch. She had to lift the plastic and unbuttoned the top of her shirt to reach for a bill.

An olive cloud with sparkling light flared from the backpack.

The cop leaned over her. "What kind of trick is that?" he demanded.

Anta pulled out a fifty.

The cop snatched it and put it in his pocket.

"Shraaaa."

Anta looked past the cop across the street to where unblinking ruby eyes burned behind a rain-streaked window in a pickup truck the color of a fire engine.

"Take your gypsy tricks and leave Palapi," the cop said.

Anta ran past the cop, hoping for a place to hide. She'd been stupid to go to her home village. Every cop in the country was on the lookout for a girl from Quesada. Rosas would know that her family had come from Omagua. The *Fierros* would be waiting for her there.

She ran toward the *colectivo*. Stop, she told herself. Never be the first to run, Koya had said.

"Next stop Omagua," the driver said to her as she walked by. Over her shoulder, she saw the red-eye still watching her. She climbed into the *colectivo* and kept her head lowered.

The red pickup followed when they drove out on the highway. The evil spirits would not lose sight of her now. What were they waiting for? She should be scared beyond thinking, but was not. Maybe she was like a cup filled with water that could hold no more. Warmth spread through her body from the box. The *tunjo* made her feel like she was not a young girl, but someone else with big powers. Fear no longer burned in her belly. She could hear conversations from inside houses they passed. She could see the hair on a dog walking in front of a farm a mile away. Maybe she'd just gone *loca*.

The red-eyes' truck followed the *colectivo* into the central square of Omagua, the town where she'd been born. The *La'ku* used to live in the nice little houses that lined the street. Now, there were soldiers everywhere.

Anta boldly met the stare of the beaming eyes behind the streaked window in the truck.

When the *colectivo* stopped, Anta jumped off and hurried into the market. She couldn't help looking over her shoulder to see a priest with fire eyes get out of the truck and follow her.

Anta hurried past an old woman sitting in the rain behind a blanket on which jade *tunjos* lay among piles of roots and healing powders.

"I am *Xucha*," the old woman said. "I serve *Tatya-Masi*. Bring me your troubles. I will cure them."

Short pig-hair whiskers grew from moles on the witch's face. White film covered her eyes. The rain didn't seem to bother her. The *Xucha* was crazy to say the name *Tatya-Masi* in public with red-eyes near.

The pack grew heavy on Anta's back. She could hardly carry the weight.

"*Xucha*. I serve *Tatya-Masi*. Bring me your troubles. I will cure them."

Anta stepped past the witch.

A cold, strong hand reached out and dragged Anta down. Her life in Quesada had made Anta quick, but she could not free herself. The witch's face was next to hers so she could smell a spice on her breath. "Fire is close. Move to the fifth fall by the school."

The *Xucha* released her. Anta's arm stung where she'd been held. Now was the time to run and Anta did.

What school had the *Xucha* been talking about? What waterfall? In dry seasons there was one waterfall that fell into the jungle. A second waterfall formed when it rained. The fifth fall came only when it had rained hard for days, and was near the school *el patrón* Don Carlos Morales had built for the La'ku. Anta knew the way but wasn't going to run into the countryside because some *bruja loca* had told her about fire.

"Shraaaa."

A red-eye dressed in a bishop's robe moved toward her. Three skeletons were one step from her. She ran to her right.

"Crack!" A thunderclap broke over her head.

The sky darkened. Windblown straw and twigs whipped her face. The *tunjo* flared on her back and surrounded her with a flickering light. Evil hands reached for her. The violent gusts blew around her and formed a protecting wall.

Where she was running was calm. All around her a thousand cats howled in a hurricane wind. Trees were bent nearly to the ground.

Roofs of houses, tables, sheets of metal blew past her.

The red-eyes were slowed by the nightmare storm that pushed her forward just out of their grasp. She felt as if she'd been picked up and was flying.

The mad wind blew Anta to the side of the *Xucha* who'd tried to grab her in the market. The hag held herself up with a crooked walking stick, bent over so far her free hand hung to her foot. Yet as fast as the wind carried Anta, the *Xucha* always stayed beside her.

Rosas could not keep up with them.

"If you want to save your brother, come with me," the old voice said. "Koya lives in *Tskwal-utenai*."

Anta couldn't have imagined that. Where or what was *Tskwal-utenai*?

The wind pushed them out of the town, past the banana fields, the school, and off the road onto a muddy path to the edge of the cliff. Trees were thick overhead. Ruby eyes shined through the black clouds behind.

The wind suddenly stopped and left Anta standing at the edge of a frothing brown river that flew into space.

The *Xucha* had disappeared.

"Shraaaa."

The deadly sound of the red-eyes came from all sides.

Rosas and a pack of six red-eyes nearly had her. Where was the *Xucha*? There was only one answer, into the dark pit that opened up beyond the cliff, the jungle.

Anta saw the witch jumping between rocks beside the waterfall.

"Shraaaa."

Anta leaned against a strong blast of warm wind that pushed her over the cliff. The red-eyes nearly had her. Anta lowered her foot to the first step.

The wet air forced her down a vine-bordered trail past where rock spires rose up from the spray. The pushing wind didn't give her time to decide where to put her foot on the steep slope. Always moving down, she teetered at the edge of a slippery shelf with nowhere to step and slid until she caught a vine and came to rest where water crashed around her, blinding her with spray. Hanging from both arms, she lowered her foot only to feel air, stretched until she could reach no farther.

Bats, dark creatures, flew from a hole in the side of the rock and screeched around her. Anta hissed as her hands slipped from the rough bark. She flailed to find another hold. The gnarled rocks passed beyond her reach as she fell through the mist and landed on her back in water.

The swirling current closed over her, spun her onto her face, pushed her under. She frantically kicked and paddled with her hands, trying to find the surface. Her feet touched bottom. She forced herself to the surface and passed through the swirling water to the air. Gasping, she reached out for the shore. Her hands slipped off whatever they touched. Her fingers clawed for a hold, pushing through wet leaves, until she was on land.

She lay panting on her back, felt her body and found that the pack was still on her back. She'd not lost Koya's loot.

Water pounded against rock and water. What was not rain was waterfall. Put anywhere in the city, even in the palace of Rosas, she would have an idea of how to get out. Nothing she knew would work here.

Koya had said never to be afraid because fear made it harder to think. She forced herself to feel the strength of the *tunjo*, to find her bravery. Her sight was pulled to the jungle. Her breath stopped again.

The wind whistled. Twigs snapped. Monkeys yelped. Ruby eyes stared at her from the jungle wall of plants. A jaguar as big as a dog was in attack position staring at her.

Anta ran toward a shape that pushed from the jungle. A lightning bolt blasted a tree into flames. Thunder shook the air. Ahead in a flash of lightning she saw the god, *Tatya-Masi*, half-man, half-frog, as big as the trees. It took a moment for her to realize that the god was made of stone.

Anta ran up steps to where the kneeling statue of the god formed a flat area.

The cat loped in smooth strides after her.

Anta retreated. There was no place left to climb. The jaguar streaked up the stairs faster than Koya running through cars.

Anta ran to the edge of the terrace. The cat growled behind her, and then she was falling through a hole in the platform. She landed hard, her wind gone from her again.

Lights danced behind her eyes. Her breaths came in gasps and moans.

Burning eyes glowered at her as the cat lowered its head to jump. Anta reached to push herself up. Her hand fell on a cold, moving pile. Snakes! She gasped and rolled to her feet.

Thousands of snakes hissed. The moving weight of the reptiles crawled over her feet. Dripping water echoed with a *plop, plop*. The cat yowled as it flew through the black air. Fiery pain ripped her shoulder. A heavy weight crushed her cries and threw her into the slithering pile of snakes.

The box on her back flashed with a brilliant light.

Xucha witches came out of the center of the light crying, *"Chan koxol teol! Chan koxol teol!"*

Curratta, with a bald head and raised shoulder, supreme shaman of the *Xucha*, a thousand years old, the one who had first brought the Jewels of Life from the peaks of Susuprina, shook a silver stick at the cat.

The strongest *indio* Anta had ever seen leaped on the jaguar. The howls and grunts of their fight were unlike anything she'd ever heard.

Anta pushed herself away from the undulating nest of reptiles.

A pulsing aura surrounded the clash between the *indio* and the jaguar.

The cat pinned the strong *indio* beneath him and thrust his long white teeth at the *indio's* neck.

The *indio* raised a knife and stuck at the tawny hide. With a final wail of defeat the jaguar staggered and died. The *indio* pushed it off and sheathed his bloody knife.

Anta did not know if she'd gone into the afterworld. She rocked on her feet, waiting to see what would happen next. Blood dripped from her shoulder where the cat had clawed her.

The witches and the magnificent *indio* gathered around her. The *indio's* chest was marked with bloody cuts from the jaguar's claws.

They spoke in a dialect Anta recognized from the old La'ku songs her father used to sing.

"The cat was *Balaam*," Curratta said.

"*Balaam?*" another witch asked.

Curratta said with an ominous tone, "The Lord of Fire make new alliances. See the serpents. *Ekchuah* and *Hunab K'u* have joined. The battle will be fierce and hard fought. We must do our part. Norane." She called the warrior to her side. "Take the *tunjo*. It is time for you to leave."

The *indio* reached for the glowing box on Anta's back.

Nobody was taking her brother's loot without a fight. Anta pressed against the rock wall and protected Koya's treasure with her body.

Curratta hovered before her. "There are not many who can resist the urge to possess the *tunjo*. Will you give up the necklace to save your brother Koya?"

There were not many Anta trusted—not these spooks. She looked for a place to run.

"I cannot help you if you don't give me the necklace," Curratta said.

"No need one-help," Anta said.

"Should I take it from her?" Norane asked.

Curratta observed Anta with cavernous, unblinking eyes. "She is strong, Norane. She has the making of *Xucha*. Our clan needs new life. Daughter," Curratta said to Anta, "I am going to take the *tunjo* from you, but I am going to leave you with a promise. When the battle is over, I will bring you to Manoa and teach you the ways of the *Xucha*."

Anta crouched and snarled at the witch, "Come by and I teach one Us'me way."

The witch cackled a breaking-glass laugh, pointed a bony finger at Anta, and whispered, "*Azki xzaluoh nopliki ka!*"

Anta felt helpless as her hands involuntarily dropped to her side. The backpack lifted over her head. The beautiful box fell to the ground. The lid opened.

The *tunjo* floated in a luminous haze and fell around Norane's neck.

Despair at the sight, pain from her wound, weakness and hunger overwhelmed Anta. She collapsed to her knees amongst the snakes.

Anta bowed her head, too weak to resist.

Curratta said, "She cannot stay here, Norane. She has suffered much to bring us the *tunjo*. Bring her to her people. *Inika* may have another plan for her."

Norane lifted Anta. She tried to free herself but hardly moved.

"*Balaam* has left his mark on her. She needs to be tended by her own kind if she is ever to live in her world again," Curratta said.

Maybe it was being near the *tunjo* or in Norane's strong arms, but Anta felt safe and could not keep from falling into a deep sleep.

CHAPTER SIX
HERDED

Eduardo twisted from the passenger seat and glared at Moss, sitting in the rear beside Du and Lilia. Revolver in hand, he confronted Moss. "I should kill you for what you've done to my family, to my country."

Moss held his gun ready on his lap and met Eduardo's challenge with an impassive stare.

MG reached over and touched Eduardo on the wet fabric of his pants. "Easy," she said.

"He's here to help us," Du again defended Moss.

Eduardo's lip curled beneath his upper teeth in a cold expression of disdain. "There is no *us* here."

The jade in Lilia's eyes flashed. "Believe in *Tatya-Masi.*"

"I am only here for you, Lilia, or what's left of you," he muttered, lifting his gun from the top of the seat and facing forward.

"Have you ever opened yourself to Du, felt his power?" MG asked.

"I will happily open him up with my machete."

"He is our only hope," MG said.

Eduardo's voice rose. "You ask me to accept the helplessness of us all before these so-called gods, these ancient spirits that have risen up from their graves to bedevil us. What I accept is that they drive people mad. I accept that they exist and *he,*" Eduardo jerked his head toward

Du, "…is their manifestation on Earth. But I refuse to believe that we are their hapless servants. We are the living. We make our own fate."

Du felt great sympathy for his uncle. Eduardo had been with Norane and Kare as boys when they'd found the totems that had allowed the Lord of Fire and Lordess of Water to enter the physical world. While the others had helplessly submitted to domination by the gods, Eduardo had never allowed the celestial influence to override his great will. His uncle was a man who confronted obstacles. His rage was fed by not knowing how to fight these ephemeral foes who had swept him and his family into this battle. But then neither did Du.

His large eyes focused past the occupants of the truck and glinted as he contemplated the sheets of rain. A simple way to understand their predicament was as a game that under certain conditions could be manipulated by the powerful unseen hands of gods. In one sense Eduardo was right. They were not completely helpless, but it would take more power than Du now possessed to end the rains this time.

Two years ago, he'd been able to use his primitive influence to stop the Lordess of Water's first attack. Perhaps *Inika* had been trying to give him a taste for might. Since then, he'd learned to better perceive these tilts of the game board, but at the same time he'd also come to understand how little he could do to alter the flow of destiny or counter the deities trying to assert their will over him and the nature of the coming World.

Just as they all had their fates, so did the Earth. The planet would reach the center of the Milky Way in five days. At this point of cosmic balance either the Lord of Fire or the Lordess of Water would prevail; either men and women would continue to live in a World of Fire or the Age of Man would be swept away by a new Age of Water.

The Fire spirits were desperate to stop him from reaching Manoa. After all, he was a creation of Water. No matter how much he said he wanted to live in this world, they would not take the chance. They knew that once in possession of all four Jewels of Life, Du would act as a magnifying lens that would focus the power of Water. If he held all four Jewels again, he'd be able to see every ploy, gain every advantage and best the other gods in their contest for the Earth.

Two of the Jewels were already in Manoa with the witches. If the *Xucha* had recouped the *tunjo* and now possessed the four Jewels of Life, then the old prophecy would come true and the rains would fall until all the fires of man had been extinguished.

As MG drove through the storm, Du accepted that to stop the rains, he would have to gain every bit of strength and knowledge he could, however he could. But he also knew that the closer he drew to the source of his omnipotence, the harder it would be to conserve his humanity. He hunched his back and held his hands between his legs, despairing that his and the fate of the planet were increasingly one of Water.

* * *

MG sped past the entrance to the Placerville airport.

"Think it's clear?" she asked Du.

Du closed his eyes and concentrated, seeking signs of the Lord of Fire. "I think so." He looked at his mother.

Lilia showed no concern on her face.

MG parked on the tarmac beside a swept-wing twin-prop plane.

"Do you need anything? Money?" Eduardo reached into his jacket pocket.

"No." She touched his arm. "Money is not a problem now."

"That is good." Eduardo raised his eyes to meet hers. "Some day when this is over, I'd like to have some quiet time with you."

"That would be a switch." She laughed.

"Good-bye for now then," Eduardo said and stepped out of the truck.

When everyone was on the plane and the right prop spinning, Du emerged from the cabin and hopped to where MG stood at the foot of the stairs. Rain dripped off her black motorcycle jacket and baseball cap. He pulled her close. "Good-bye." His voice caught. Both knew there was no telling when or if they would see each other again.

MG pushed him away. "Why don't I go with you as far as Florida? Those creeps will probably be looking for me here anyway," she said.

"No." Du shook his large head. "You've been the best…friend. I can't be responsible for your safety."

"Who said you're responsible for me?" Anger tinged MG's voice and her broad shoulders expanded.

"I didn't mean…"

"If anybody needs help, it's you," she said.

Du stared into the rainy night. "Kare's here. Get behind me."

MG hurried up the steps of the plane.

A dark figure carrying an assault rifle strode across the tarmac.

With a puff of black smoke the left propeller started to spin. Du warily waited to see if Kare had brought the Assassins with him.

Eduardo appeared in the door of the plane, his pistol in his hand.

Kare, his long black hair pasted to his face by rain, stopped beside Du. "I've come to protect you," he said and stepped past Du onto the stairs of the plane.

"You gonna fight for us or Rosas?" Eduardo blocked his way into the cabin.

The two men stared at each other.

"Let him come, please," Du said.

"Why not, we can always use another gun." Eduardo walked, head lowered, to the cockpit.

MG was seated in the copilot's seat. Moss and Lilia were in two rear-facing seats, leaving two forward-facing seats open for Du and Kare.

Eduardo started to close the door.

"Wait," Du said, "MG has to get off."

"She's going with us," Eduardo said and shut the latch sealing the cabin.

Du followed his uncle to the cockpit. Eduardo slipped into the pilot's seat and put on a pair of headphones.

"MG, I wish you wouldn't come. It's too dangerous," Du said.

"Sit down, Du," she said.

He knew the futility of arguing with her.

Eduardo flipped an overhead switch and the plane began to roll.

They climbed at a steep angle for ten minutes over the dark, rainy Sierra Nevada forest before they broke through the clouds and leveled off.

In the cabin, Du looked at MG and Eduardo lean their heads to hear each other over the sound of the engines. Had MG come to be with him or Eduardo? Du was embarrassed by his immature jealousy of his uncle. What difference did it make what MG did? He would not be part of her temporal life for long. His bargain with the *Xucha* and *Inika* had given him two years to be a teenager. Now he had to pay. The whole world had to pay.

He closed his eyes and spoke to the goddess. "Lordess of Water stop the rains," he repeated the prayer that had ended the worldwide deluge two years before.

Lightning flashed. The plane dropped as it hit a pocket of turbulence.

If he made it to Manoa and regained control over the four Jewels, would he have the strength to defy *Inika* and end the rains this time? The Earth had orbited too close to its cosmic rendezvous with the equatorial plane of the galaxy for him to be able to assert his will as he had when he'd first held the *tunjo* and had released the Water spirits. Too many other forces were now in play. Even if he were to completely renounce his role as *Tatya-Masi* Bringer of the Sixth World of Water and abandon *Inika's* quest for control of the next Age, the forces of Fire would never cease their efforts to destroy him.

His mother was sitting bolt upright with the strength of the Waters of Life. The *Xucha* had made sure he would not surrender and would go to Manoa. He must go back for her and for his grandfather whose spirit waited in the golden throne of El Dorado to be reunited with his body. The journey to the Cave of the *Xucha* would not be easy. The Fire spirits would pursue him everywhere. If he was not willing to fight, too many would die.

He longed to be of this world, to be a normal man–to dream of a future with someone he loved. When the moment came, would he sacrifice his life for all the other lovers of the world, to save all the mothers and fathers from seeing their children drown?

* * *

A police car slowly drove past where MG had left her truck.

An officer with an auburn mustache and an eerie, fiery mote in the center of his eyes entered the flight services office. He wore a patch with an emblem of a serpent wrapped around a cross and a name tag that read Titus Creation.

"What do you know about that plane that just took off?" Creation asked the woman behind the counter.

"It's a charter out of Florida. Came in earlier, around noon."

"You have the flight plan on it?"

"Why? What's the matter?"

"Might be carrying something on board they shouldn't."

"Here's what I've got." She lifted a sheet of paper. "It's on an IFR, heading to Port Everglades."

"That's what I need." The police officer took the sheet from her and pivoted toward the door.

"Hey, I need that."

Titus Creation ignored her and strode to his cruiser.

* * *

Above the rain over the Gulf of Mexico, the dawn cast coral shades of pink in the cumulous clouds that billowed from horizon to horizon. The plane bucked on waves of turbulence.

Kare made his way to the cockpit and spoke to Eduardo.

"They know about your boat, about the weapons. Rosas has sent Major Bruto to eliminate you. We can get another plane at Marathon. Here are the coordinates." Kare held out a slip of paper.

"Why should I believe you?"

"What choice do you have? This plane has a transponder. They know exactly where we are."

Eduardo did not take the paper from Kare's outstretched hand. He flexed his jaw muscles. "I have spent the last eighteen months fighting Rosas," Eduardo said. "I will fight him again, and again."

Loud repeated bleeps could be heard throughout the cabin. A light blinked beneath the fuel gauges on the computer screen in the console. Eduardo reached overhead to a fuse panel and twisted a knob that stopped the warning.

Kare sat and held his rifle beside his leg.

After another hour of flight, the plane descended until Du could see flocks of white birds sailing over mangrove trees in the unmistakable mixture of land, water and trees of the Everglades.

* * *

A steady precipitation fell on Marathon Airport as it did around the world. A group of men sat in two crimson utility vehicles. The front passenger studied a computer screen.

"He's going south."

The driver spoke into his cell phone. "Major Bruto, they're heading for the boat."

* * *

They flew so close to the tops of the trees that Du saw individual branches and rain-pockmarked puddles between the trunks of pines and banyan trees.

With the fuel gauges dead on empty, Eduardo made his final approach to a muddy field cut into a forest of pine trees. He cursed under his breath.

"What's the matter?" MG asked.

"Perhaps Kare speaks the truth," Eduardo muttered and banked away from the field. "Behind your seat in that bag is a gun."

MG reached into a leather sack and pulled out a black Glock 19.

"You know how to use this?" Eduardo asked MG.

"Yeah."

Eduardo's tone was clipped. "I'm asking if you will use this?"

"I'll use it." MG took an extra clip of bullets from the bag.

"If something happens to me, I want you to kill Moss and Kare."

"I'll use it to defend us." She grimly looked out the window as if the danger might come at them at any moment.

Eduardo circled the field, and flipped the plane so the left wing was facing earthward. Hidden in the shadows of the trees were a car and two open trucks loaded with men carrying weapons.

"The La'ku bastard's right. It's a trap," Eduardo said and started to climb.

Then the engines quit.

The plane trembled as the propellers slowed so that the blades moved only by the pressure of the wind, pointing their nose to the ground. In the sudden silence, the wind passed loud and whining. They were already diving in a crash.

Eduardo flipped a switch and gently adjusted the flaps. The whirring of the wheels dropping into place lasted too long as they fell rapidly into the pines.

Du thought Eduardo was going to attempt a landing in the bay, then realized he was coming down on a dirt dike running through the swamp.

The levy was too narrow. The base of the plane seemed wider than the pointed pile of dirt and rock.

Eduardo gently pulled the yoke to gain another few feet.

With a scraping sound of wood against metal, a treetop snapped off beneath them. The plane tipped forward.

Du put his arm out to brace his mother for a nose-first crash.

They dropped onto the embankment with a jarring crash, bounced, fell and landed with an impact that violently shook the plane. The end of the causeway, a final barrier of wood and water, was in front of them. The wing tip scraped a bald cypress, pulling the plane sideways at a speed still over ninety miles an hour. Somehow Eduardo managed to keep the wheels on the dirt and straightened their path along the levy.

Firmly and steadily, he pressed on the brakes. But the end of the dike was too close. There was no way to stop in time. Eduardo jammed the brakes in desperation. The right wheel collapsed, causing the airplane to tilt radically and slip off the embankment. The airplane wrenched around and slammed to a stop, nose pointed into the water.

Du was on the low side of the wreck.

Kare pushed open the plane door. The stairway extended upward five feet over the ground. Kare braced himself against the side of the fuselage and helped Moss to the exit.

"Go ahead," Moss said.

Kare maneuvered to the end of the stairs and, holding his rifle in one arm, jumped to the ground.

Moss stepped back inside the plane.

"Let me help you, Lilia." He reached for her.

She ignored him, and appeared to float past him to the door.

Du and Moss glanced at each other. Du moved around Moss, held his mother around the waist and jumped clear of the plane.

Inside the plane, Eduardo aimed his pistol at Moss. "You go first," he said.

Moss frowned and exited. Eduardo waited for MG to pull herself through the door and onto the steps. He remained in the doorway and aimed his gun at Moss.

Trucks and cars raced along the top of the dirt dike toward them.

A barrage of bullets punctured the fuselage and drove Eduardo back into the plane.

On the ground, Kare shot his rifle at the trucks.

Eduardo emerged from the door, shooting his pistol as he ran along the steps. He jumped and landed in a crouch on the levy.

Men in the rear of two pickup trucks were standing, aiming their weapons at them. The "brattt" of automatic weapons fire cut into the air. Bullets plunked into the plane. Du and the rest were exposed, with nowhere to hide.

A blood-colored car followed the trucks. The seven-foot frame of a man filled the rear seat, so big he leaned over to accommodate his head. A protruding supraorbital ridge rose above narrow-set eyes. Filed metal-tipped teeth glinted from the loose-lipped leer of Rosas' enforcer, Major Bruto.

Du shielded his mother behind the plane while trying to keep an eye on MG. She was beside Eduardo, firing a pistol at their attackers. Where could they go? He could escape to the water, but what about the others?

A muscular black man in a Hawaiian shirt climbed up the dirt-and-stone side of the levy between them and the approaching assailants. Standing in the path of the trucks, he discharged both barrels of a shotgun. The windshield shattered. The lead truck skidded. The vehicle behind crashed into it, forcing the truck off the edge of the levy.

Bruto's car skidded to a stop behind the crash. Led by the giant, the three occupants piled out.

The man with the shotgun pointed toward the swamp. "*Venga! Venga!*"

"Go with Cramee!" Eduardo pushed MG. "He's the captain of my boat."

Eduardo and Kare continued to battle Bruto and his men as Du led his mother and father after MG over the edge of the embankment into the swamp. Du jumped onto a narrow beach overhung with curtains of Spanish moss where he helped his parents over the gnarled knees of bald cypresses, onto a small island. Gunfire reverberated behind them. Bullets kicked up water at Du's feet and blasted bark off a tree in front of MG. A water moccasin sidled from beneath the bank. They ran to a board serving as a gangplank onto a rickety, overloaded trawler. *Bestante* was painted on her square stern.

Du helped his mother onto the deck of the boat. Cramee, the man with the shotgun, stared at Du and whispered in Caribbean-accented Spanish, "The La'ku frog god!"

Just as the stern drifted from the bank, Eduardo ran down the shore and jumped aboard. With a long stride, Kare landed atop a solid, three-foot-high wood railing that surrounded the deck.

Eduardo swept a tarpaulin off a machine gun mounted on a tripod in the stern and began to fire a deadly fusillade toward the levee.

The rapid concussions of Eduardo's gun punctuated the sound

of the rumbling engine beneath the deck. Black diesel smoke swirled with the white cordite discharge of the guns in the humid air. Du wanted to be anywhere but here. Lilia stood exposed on deck, as if nothing could possibly harm her. Du guided her to the shelter of the wheelhouse. MG knelt behind the port side railing with her gun aimed at the shore.

Kare pulled the rope to gain enough slack to remove the line from the cleat, but the moving boat had stretched the line too taunt.

Cramee had to put the boat into reverse to relax the tension. Kare slipped the final mooring line off and let it fall into the water.

Slowly the boat began to churn through the swamp. A flurry of bullets dug into the hull and the boxes piled high on the deck. Eduardo let go with the machine gun toward the top of the dike where Major Bruto and his men were trying to find a clear shot at them.

Cramee spun the wheel and the boat glided behind the trees on the island, laboriously gaining speed through a narrow channel.

In the moment of their peril, Du had a vivid sensation of the vibrant nature of the swamp. Clouds hung low over the trees. Giant herons flapped their wings and lifted from the rain-disturbed surface of the water. A kingfisher dove and emerged with a wiggling fish in its bill. The bleached carcasses of storm-damaged bald cypresses protruded from black-bottom pools.

Eduardo removed a tubular weapon from an oblong box set beside the machine gun. "Everywhere we turn, Rosas is waiting for us," Eduardo said. "I tell you this, Kare Kuwaru'wa, you will either fight with me or die with me."

The trawler lurched to a stop.

The high whine of an engine carried across the water. An airboat driven by a large propeller sliced around a bend and flew toward them.

A rocket-propelled grenade flashed across the lagoon. A tree on the shore beside the *Bestante* exploded with a shower of splinters.

Kare aimed a salvo at the airboat. Eduardo swept up the weapon he'd just assembled, aimed, and released a rocket at the speeding craft.

Du blinked and the airboat came apart with a blast of smoke and fire.

Cramee put the props into reverse and gunned the engines, but the boat remained stuck.

In the wheelhouse, Moss said, "Everybody and his mother's going to be responding to that plane crash. Get her off. We can't be here to answer their questions."

Cramee cursed in Spanish. "We're aground. I'm not familiar with these waters."

Du dropped his overalls and jumped into the water in his underwear. He dove to find the keel jammed in the crook of a submerged limb. By standing on the tip he was able to lower the tree branch and free the boat.

Du rose out of the water beside the trawler. "Follow me," he called and swam just below the surface, leaving a faint wake.

At full speed, the *Bestante* trailed Du on a twisting course around the sandbars and sunken trees waiting to snag the heavily laden hull.

Du's overriding sensation was relief as his dry skin absorbed the moisture he craved. He felt safer, more useful, surrounded by the briny water.

A dark shape hovered below him. Du pulled up, and then realized he was passing over a manatee–a gentle, harmless lolling swamp leviathan. Du's pupils expanded to their greatest width. In the murky light, he saw other ghostly round shapes lying on the silt bottom.

As he swam toward the ocean, he fantasized ways he could fake his death to convince the Lord of Fire that he was dead. He could swim away. He had money. He could appear like anyone he wanted. No, he could never escape. He could no longer hide from the Lord of Fire.

While, at this moment, the Fire spirits were the ones trying to kill them, he felt no safer trusting the Lordess of Water. On one side was his mother, the medium of the *Xucha*, and on the other his father and Kare, the servants of Fire. *Quetzal* the Plumed Serpent knew his thoughts. Du felt like the sparrow that God sees fall—a comforting assurance if you believe in a benevolent deity, but a paranoid nightmare if you are trying to hide from vengeful, manipulative spirits.

His musing was yanked into the present by a primordial instinct that he was being hunted.

There were many shades in the mixture of salt and fresh water. From this gloom he saw a whipping motion propelling a creature toward him. An alligator! He could swim fast but not as fast as a full-grown Florida gator.

Du's feet fluttered with fear as he sped to the boat. He rotated an eye to see the creature nearly on him. Du rose to the surface and reached for the side of the boat. The alligator's tapered head parted a wake aimed directly at Du.

MG shot her pistol over the side. The gator's eye exploded just as it opened its teeth-lined jaw to seize Du.

The creature grunted in agony and rolled away.

Du reached for a line hanging over the side and pulled himself aboard.

"Thanks," he said to MG.

"Glad I came now?" She was shaking, soaked with rain.

He put his arm around her shoulder. "Yes."

His close encounter with a natural death somehow reinvigorated Du. The Lord of Fire and Lordess of Water might have their plans, but there was also the full force of life flowing with its own strength and inexorable will. If Du could keep his mind and body in the physical world, he might yet find a way to escape the machinations of the spiritual realm.

The trawler was nearing the edge of the swamp. Eduardo stood behind the machine gun and continued his confrontation with Kare. "How did they know about the boat?"

"Rosas knows everything about your revolution. If we escape Major Bruto here, Rosas' jets will be waiting for us as soon as we are within the territorial waters of New Granada."

"Then why are you here?"

Kare scanned the shore before looking Eduardo in the eye.

"Because I have accepted what you won't. We're here because the gods want us to be here."

"Baaah," Eduardo spat out his derision. "I fight in this world *for* this world."

Du was heartened to hear his uncle echo his own thoughts.

"You fight to restore the elites," Kare said. "If there is to be a revolution, it will be an *indio* revolution."

"And who will lead the peasants?" Eduardo demanded.

Kare looked to the door of the wheelhouse where Du stood listening to them. "They are men and women, not peasants, and they will fight for their god," Kare said.

"*Los indios* will be slaughtered," Eduardo said.

"And so will we unless the gods protect us."

"I'll protect myself," Eduardo said and pushed past Du into the wheelhouse. "Hold it here, Cramee," he said, lifted a pair of binoculars from a chart table and studied the open bay that stretched a quarter of a mile to the white line of a reef.

"They are waiting for us again," Eduardo said. "Well, I have a little something they might not have been expecting."

"Let me check before you do anything," Du said.

"Oh no you don't." MG reached to stop him, but Du was already over the side.

The thought of more alligators made him swim faster and keep his focus. He sped over a coral reef into the open ocean until he was beneath the dark shape of a fiberglass hull. He pressed his ear to the side to get an idea of the intentions of those on the boat.

He heard a man's voice. "We're at station three . . .No way they can escape. Roger, over and out."

Hoping to avoid more violence, Du rose to see if he could find any evidence that the boat was not there to harm them.

Someone flicked a cigarette into the sea where Du's head was bobbing. Du ducked under the water, leaving only a slight ripple, but the smoker had seen him.

"Damn!" Du heard the man say.

"What is it?" his companion asked.

"I don't know, a fish or something."

"Was it a frogman?"

"Yeah a frogman . . . a real big . . . real . . . yeah, a frogman," he said.

"They should be coming out of the bay any time now. Get ready."

Du had to tell Eduardo what he'd found but was afraid of what his uncle would do.

The *Bestante* waited behind the final barrier of trees. Du hoisted himself over the side with one pull on an overhanging line.

Eduardo was on the roof of the wheelhouse kneeling beside a mortar, a box of shells beside him.

"They're not fishermen." Du avoided Eduardo's stare.

"They're Rosas' men," Kare said to Eduardo.

Du looked from Kare to Eduardo. "I might be able to find a way around them."

Eduardo ignored Du and dropped a round into the short, angled tube.

"Whoomp!"

A geyser erupted beside the cabin cruiser beyond the reef.

Eduardo pressed the binoculars to his eyes, then made adjustments to the angle of the tube.

The cabin cruiser's engines gunned as they tried to escape. The next shell exploded to their port side. Water blew into the air rocking the cruiser.

Eduardo calmly made more corrections.

The other boat didn't have a chance. The shell traveled on a perfect arc that ended in the middle of its roof. The boat exploded in a ball of fire that roiled into the rainy sky. The bow pitched upward as the stern plunged into the bay.

A deep sadness filled Du. Who was he to be the agent of so much destruction? He stood by the wheelhouse with his head lowered. He'd killed those men. The brief contact he'd had with them had been enough for him to establish an empathetic connection, to garner a sense of their hopes and dreams, their families and friends. Those trying to kill him might be right. Better that he was dead.

MG came out of the cabin and stood beside him in the rain. "We have to survive." She put her hand on his upper arm.

"Why?" He spun to face her. "So that more can die? So that a dead Indian religion can be vindicated?"

She shook her head. "No. So that they will leave us alone."

"It's all a mistake. Me. Everything! Somebody up there has got something crazily wrong. Can't you see that?" His voice rose in pitch, filled with self-pity. "These gods are just using us, playing with us. They'll never leave us alone."

His mother flew out of the cabin and seized him by the arm. He tried to pull away, but could not free himself from her painful grip.

The voice of the Supreme Witch Curratta spoke through Lilia. His mother's split eyes glowed. "The Lord of Fire wants you to surrender. Do not give into the weakness. When they have stolen your powers, they will cast you aside. Do not listen to their lies."

The energy of the Waters of Life burned through her. "Nothing will ever make sense to you unless you accept who you are," Lilia continued. "Only then will you be able to control or resist. Until then you can only lament. Remember the lessons I have taught you. *Ometecuhtli, Calaari, Xibalt, Ekahau, Chamahez, Puc, Xipe, Kisin Chac, Hapikern, Tlaloc, P'tecatl, M'uilxochitl*–the power of twelve, the wisdom of the ancients–they are all there to help you. Call them! Use them!"

With no comfort or understanding from his mother, no sympathy for what he'd told her so many times, he turned away. He wasn't a god, never could be a god. He was a man who wanted to live in peace.

Lilia's strength faltered. The energy of the Waters of Life was being consumed faster by her anger. She lost her grip on his arm, appearing frail and wet on the deck of the trawler. "Mother, let's go into the cabin. You shouldn't be out in the rain."

In the distance was the sound of a helicopter.

Eduardo pushed past them and threw open a box in the wheelhouse.

The blades of an approaching helicopter beat over the water. A man hung out of the side aiming a gun at them.

Eduardo hefted a bulky weapon from the box and used its barrel to shatter the glass in the side window.

A high-pitched whine rose from the launcher on his shoulder.

Du raised his arm in helpless protest and mouthed the word, "No."

The rocket streaked from the *Bestante*, picked up the heat of the copter's exhaust, and blew the aircraft apart just as the first bullets splintered the side of the boat. Burning jet fuel-scented air was carried by the blast over them.

Reason and order disappeared into the mayhem. Du looked from MG to his mother, then at the flames on the ocean where the helicopter had crashed.

Two powerboats were closing fast, engines roaring. Kare's machine gun fusillade assailed Du's senses.

He would be part of no more death. Du cupped his webbed hand over the ocean and cast the spell of *Hapikern*. Wordlessly, Lilia stood by his side in the prow of the boat. With eyes closed, in synchronization they slowly lifted their arms in an arc, and drew the surface of the ocean over them. And like air inside a bubble, they were invisible to the radar and men in planes and boats pursuing them.

CHAPTER SEVEN
THE WHEEL OF HISTORY

Du and Lilia sat beside each other in lotus positions. The spell required them to constantly imagine their invisibility while seeing each point of light reflecting off the boat. No rain fell within the bubble they cast over the *Bestante.* Theirs was the only dry deck on the oceans of the world. The magical film of water encasing the moving trawler even awed Eduardo, who joined the others in not disturbing Du and Lilia.

After five hours of complete focus, Lilia fell over from exhaustion. It took Du a minute to rise through the levels of consciousness. First a few drops, then the full force of the rain washed over the boat as the bubble collapsed around them. They were again visible.

Eduardo lifted Lilia and carried her across his arms to the wheelhouse.

Du rose unsteadily to his feet and held the railing for support. The trawler rose and fell as it plowed through three-foot seas. Black diesel smoke blew back from a pipe rising at the corner of the wheelhouse. Clouds hung low over the sea, and there was little possibility of being spotted from the air. Still, Kare stood beside the machine gun, ready for an attack. His long black hair dripped from the steady rain. He and Du looked at each without speaking. He'd known Kare his whole life, knew him as well as anyone. They didn't need words to express their joint sense of impending doom. They'd escaped one calamity only to wait for the next.

Du followed Eduardo and closed the door to the wheelhouse against the blustery, wet wind. MG was taping a garbage bag over the port window Eduardo had broken when he'd shot down the helicopter.

Eduardo placed Lilia on a short bunk behind the wheel. The cabin smelled of mold and diesel fumes. Boxes filled and blocked the entrance to a hold beneath the deck.

Du took out the tube Norane had sent. The Waters of Life radiated from the intricately designed holder. Even by touching the container, Du's hunger and exhaustion disappeared. Drink the Waters and he'd ascend from the temporal bounds of his body. Yes, and then what? Du placed a drop of the Waters on Lilia's lower lip. Again, the effect was immediate. She sat up, vibrant with the power of the *Xucha,* the bottom of her irises radiant green.

MG stood beside him, observing Lilia's rejuvenation. "Man, I could use a hit of that myself," she said.

He put the tube back in the pocket of his bib overalls. "You don't want it. You really don't."

"Why's that?"

"You'd never be the same. You'd give up everything."

"Yeah, I've got a lot to give up now. I'm wet, starving, and wouldn't mind knowing where we're going."

"I'm sorry. You shouldn't be here."

She put her hands on her hips. "But I am." She pointed at the short stairwell packed tight with crates. "If we're gonna be cruising, we need to move these boxes out on the deck and make some room in here."

Whatever affection and false gallantry Eduardo had showed MG, it disappeared beneath his scowl. "I wasn't expecting company."

"Great, just leave me off somewhere where nobody's shooting at me. In the meanwhile I'm not gonna sit in the rain or stand all the way. Help me, Du."

MG strained to lift an oblong box.

Du went to help her, and bumped into Cramee at the wheel.

The black man moved aside. "Pardon me, *Tatya-Masi.*"

"Sorry, it was my fault. And please, call me Du."

"*Sí, señor* Du."

"Steer the boat," Eduardo said to Du. "Cramee, help with this, you, too," he said to Moss. "Do some work. You can do that, can't you?"

Moss didn't react to Eduardo's scorn. Whatever he was doing here did not depend on the approval of his brother-in-law.

Du took Cramee's place behind the wooden wheel.

"Keep it on the same heading," Eduardo said as he carried a box onto the deck.

Du vigilantly kept one eye on the compass floating in a black sphere atop the control panel and the other on the hazy horizon. Windward squalls blew across the bow, making constant corrections necessary to maintain their heading.

When the steps were cleared, MG insisted that they also make room in the lower cabin where there were bunks, a head, and galley.

Moss helped at first, but came back to the cabin alone while Eduardo, Cramee and Kare arranged and tied down the cargo now higher than the cabin roof. The scent of bacon cooking arose from the galley where MG was fixing a meal for everyone. Du turned an eye to his parents. Lilia sat on the stained cushion. Moss stood by the taped window, his face pale, looking wet and miserable.

"You can't imagine how many times I thought of being with both of you, being a family," Du said. "When I was young, I mean." He looked at each parent with a separate eye to see if either recognized the sincerity in his voice.

Moss stared through the rain-streaked window at the rolling gray sea. Lilia didn't react. Du might as well have been speaking to himself. "Nothing like this, of course."

Moss pursed his lips, took a quick look at Du and said, "You think we had a choice?"

"I guess that's the whole point–do we have a choice?"

Moss clenched his right fist. "Release *Quetzal,* save the Age of Man."

"How? Do you think I'm hiding some great powers?"

"You must find a way."

Lilia flew off the bunk to the other side of the wheel from Moss and gripped Du's forearm with a powerful hold. The jade in her eyes shined and the ancient voice of Curratta spoke through her. "Do not scorn *Inika*. Should the Lordess of Water abandon you, this life you long for will be short and painful."

And if *Inika* didn't get him, *Quetzal* would. With his parents glaring at him and each other, Du gave up turning to them for understanding or sympathy.

Was his destiny unavoidable? Were the gods so strong they could overpower free will? Did they have a choice? Everything was playing out as these meddling gods had ordained. They'd arrive in New Granada in three days, on the twenty-first day of the twelfth month of the twelfth year. He'd come from the ocean, and then what? Could he stop the worldwide rains again?

Youth called upon to overcome divine challenges–and also to overcome evil fathers–were common in heroic sagas. But what had been the motivations of these stalwart young men? Had Rama, Beowulf, Mwindo felt as unsure as Du that his sacrifice would lead to a greater good? Did they also want to escape as fate crushed their selfish dreams? Was the role he seemed to be unavoidably forced to play more worthy than his desire to live freely as a man?

A religion buried a half a millennium before was to rise, while the heirs of the Spanish were to descend on the great wheel of history. Cortes and Pizarro, the Spanish conquerors of Mexico and Peru, hadn't been gods, but they were willing, unquestioning servants of their God in whose name they'd succeeded. Modern historians might say the Spaniards had the more advanced weapons and had met a people ready to be conquered. Du had seen pictures of the Inca fortresses, the high snowy passes and stone redoubts carved into the sides of Andean mountains. Some historians argued that the Incas could have held off an attack on the Andes by the combined armies of Europe. Yet a hundred and sixty-nine Spanish conquistadors had climbed the steep trails with their few horses and cannons, and defeated a well-organized and experienced army of over 100,000. "Santiago! Santiago!" the conquistadors had cried as they slaughtered the Inca court and conquered one of the world's great empires in a single afternoon. The only Spaniard wounded had been Pizarro who had been cut on the hand while saving the Inca king, Atahualpa, so he could be ransomed later for a room full of gold.

Du lacked faith that *Inika* would deliver such a miraculous and harmless victory. He was terrified and felt a lone sacrifice to a dead cult.

The sight of a slender line of a naked mast on the horizon interrupted Du's pondering. He remained on the same heading until the bobbing object on the horizon came into view. A flimsy boat with people packed on a deck smaller than the *Bestante* was adrift. Du turned toward the distressed craft.

Eduardo, dripping rain, rushed into the wheelhouse and took the wheel.

"Look at them. They need help," Du said.

Kare lifted a pair of binoculars from the chart table and studied the other boat. "Haitians," he said.

"It is not our concern," Eduardo said. "We don't have supplies to spare. They'll swarm over this boat like rats."

"Give me the wheel." Cramee pushed Eduardo.

The two powerful men wrestled, knocking Du into Moss. Without a hand on the wheel the bow swung aimlessly off course until Cramee seized control. Eduardo stepped back toward the door and pulled a pistol from his pocket.

Cramee smiled at him. "You ain't gonna get this boat to anywhere you want to go without me, so put your gun away."

Eduardo snarled a curse, swept up a rifle, and climbed the boxes outside the cabin to the roof.

Du stood beside MG and looked out the window as Cramee steered toward the refugees.

Over fifty men, women, and children were on a weathered wooden sailboat with a broken mast.

Cramee cut the engines and the *Bestante* glided toward the other boat.

Du took over the wheel while Cramee and MG carried two plastic water containers and boxes of crackers onto the deck.

At the sight of the provisions, the refugees' begging changed to applause and broad white smiles on their dark, haggard faces.

"We've been on this boat for five days without food," an old woman shouted in poorly spoken Spanish. A thin man in a ripped white shirt threw a line onto the *Bestante*. Cramee set down the water bottle and reached for the rope before it could slip into the ocean.

As soon as Cramee held the line, the Haitians pulled to close the distance. Their boat began to capsize. They shouted in Kriol and pushed each other to redistribute themselves on the rickety boat.

MG leaned over and held out a box of food. Too many hands reached for it. Their boat tipped and passed a point of seaworthiness from which it could not recover. The hull came apart. Seawater rushed over the sides and rose up from beneath the deck, first as a thin sheet, then up to their legs. The wailing mass of despair vainly tried to find the highest points of their sinking deck, accelerating the floundering.

A man frantically pulled the rope to draw the *Bestante* closer. Cramee strained against the weight.

"Let it go!" Eduardo shouted. "Push away!"

The refugees' voices raised up in vain commands and hysterical cries. Some scrambled to the still dry portions of their deck, while others tried to reach the *Bestante*.

"Brat-Brat-Brat." Eduardo fired his weapon from the roof, not appearing to hit anyone, but it didn't stop their efforts to reach the *Bestante*.

Cramee leaned back as his feet were pulled to the edge.

The first man was nearly aboard. Two thin teenagers pulled themselves over the rope after him.

"Brat-Brat-Brat." Eduardo gun's spoke with deadly intent. A red stain of blood spread across the first man's filthy white tee shirt. He appeared to be surprised that all his suffering had been for this. His hands slipped and he fell into the ocean.

"Let it go!" Eduardo yelled at Cramee and jumped to the deck.

Cramee's hands relaxed, dumping one of the teenagers into the ocean and the other onto the sinking side of the Haitian boat.

The other refugees hesitated, their fearful eyes on Eduardo, and then rushed in mass toward the *Bestante* as they abandoned their lost boat.

Eduardo, red-faced, the muscles in his arms bulging, entered the wheelhouse and took the wheel.

"*¡Vámonos!*" He pushed the throttle forward.

They pulled away as Haitians swam to reach them.

"*Non tek'e foot een 'e han.*" Don't leave us, they cried in a combination of English and Creole.

A woman holding a dead or unconscious baby slipped from the sinking boat into the water. A shark fin, a slick gray triangle, knifed through the waving arms and bobbing black heads. A wail arose from the pack, and they reversed their direction and tried to retreat to the diminishing portion of their boat that was above water.

Eduardo shouted at Cramee that the next time he tried something like that he'd shoot him; that he could find his way on his own. Cramee scowled at him, lowered his eyes and muttered something Du couldn't understand.

Long after the others had lost sight and could not hear the death cries of the drowning refugees, Du stood at the railing, wanting to be below the surface anywhere but here. Tears streamed on his long sloping cheek, tasting bitter as they dripped over the semi-circle of his cartilage-rimmed lips.

Nothing suffered like humans. The gods were cruel to give empathy, guilt that he'd not done more. Help was dispensed as a jailer gives a starving prisoner stale bread, a meager sustenance to continue to live and suffer. A god of man! He would never admit to such a flaw. Any part of him that was animal was far nobler and more forthright than a supposed deification could ever raise him. Man was created in the image of these malevolent gods, killing and torturing each other in their names. The big pushed down the little, the weak rose up to conquer the strong, and only the suffering continued.

Du wanted to be absorbed into the air, rearranged and reborn with a cosmic consciousness that saw no good or evil, only the laws of nature.

Fall. Fall into the ocean, under the bow, into the deep until he was no more. The same flaw that kept him from jumping, kept him from dying. He lacked the courage to resist the powers that controlled his life. He could have done something, reached into the minds of those on the refugee's craft, calmed them, taken control. "No. Stop!" he berated himself. "I'm not a god. I can't say who lives and dies. I can't control the destiny of those around me. But oh God, Lord, Buddha, Jesus, Mohammed, the Spirit of All, how can you tolerate such suffering? Is that your plan? Is there a plan?"

CHAPTER EIGHT
LA'KUANA

Norane carried the unconscious Anta across his arms from the temple through the jungle. He wore the traditional knee-length pants of the La'ku. A black leather vest hung open over his powerful body. A band with colorful jungle feathers held his long hair. Another leather strap was wrapped around his biceps. A woven belt held two throwing knives. The gold *tunjo* Anta had carried from Quesada hung from his thick neck. Its emerald eyes beamed in the dim light with an angry vengeance. Rain dripped in torrents from the staggered levels of the canopy: treetop branches to broadleaf palms to the creeping vines of the dark understory. Norane didn't break his long stride on the slippery path until he'd carried Anta to La'kuana, the center of the jungle.

La'kuana, by tradition and choice, adhered to another time. The village, built around an ancient stone pyramid, was little changed from the time of Norane's ancestors. The La'ku resisted the influences of the missionaries and international development agencies that offered metal churches, cement houses and schools, fishponds and modern agriculture. They spurned the wealth promised by the oil and lumber companies.

Since the Sixteenth Century, the land had been under the domain of the Morales family. While other Spanish conquerors sought to lead the natives to the enlightenment of the church and the whip of servitude in the mines, fields, and estates of their masters, the Morales had protected the La'ku and honored their culture.

This arrangement had gone uninterrupted for 500 years until Hernando Rosas seized the Morales estate. The General took what he wanted from the jungle as he did from New Granada, the country he'd created.

Rosas left La'kuana alone because of his mother, Naj, a shaman. She practiced the old arts of healing and communication with the spirit world. Late in life, she'd given birth to a son she'd called Makia. By the time he was six, Makia had insisted that he be addressed by the Spanish name his absent soldier father had given him, Hernando Rosas.

When her sister died, Naj had taken in the young orphans Norane and Kare. She'd observed with understanding as different spirit masters possessed her son and nephews. Naj did not have the magic to cast out *Mitnal* the Smoking Mirror from Rosas anymore than she could expel the spirits of *Quetzal* the Plumed Serpent from Kare, or *Inika* Lordess of Water from Norane.

But the magic she knew and the vestigial love of her son was enough for him to banish her to La'kuana where her old La'ku ways would not embarrass him. Roads and modern commerce pierced the rest of the jungle, but Rosas did not tamper with the deep jungle preserve to which he had sent Naj.

Norane carried Anta to a palm-thatched hut built on stilts above insects, animals, and flood.

"Auntie, do not be afraid, it is Norane."

He carried Anta up a narrow ladder leading to a woven curtain of grass that served as a door.

The old woman sat on a narrow leaf-mattress bed. Tools and

gourds hung from a single rafter. By the light of a candle set inside a human skull to guide the spirits of the dead home, the man appeared to fill the room.

Naj wasn't as tall as Norane's chest. She pushed her white hair from her wrinkled forehead. "Why does the ghost of Norane come to old Naj?"

"I bring the daughter of Uma. Will you care for her, Auntie?"

Naj approached the figure, squinting, not sure what she was seeing. "Uma, the daughter of Mesa, gone so many years? But why does Norane bring the daughter of Uma here?"

"Makia," he used Rosas' La'ku name, "seeks her because she serves the *Xucha*. He will not look here in the home of his mother."

Naj's cataract-filmed eyes rolled upwards. "Yes, my son seeks nothing of his mother."

"You will take her?"

"Set her down on the bed. I will prepare a healing tea." Naj bent to pick up a leaf-wrapped packet of herbs. When she rose, the girl was on the bed and Norane gone. Naj stuck her head out the doorway and examined the darkness. She smiled and mumbled, "So, I have lived to see the coming of *Tatya-Masi*."

* * *

Through the window of the only cement building in La'kuana, Major Romeo García saw the girl emerge from the *bruja's* hut. The child wore ragged city clothes, not the dyed cloths and weavings of a native. At last something new and unusual in this god-forsaken hellhole. When he'd been sent here two years before to guard Rosas' mother, he'd told himself it was a great honor, a stepping-stone to a big command. Perhaps the General would express his gratitude for García's dutiful attention to his mama with the awards of some land and business licenses. The years had gone by and all he'd gotten was a taste for monkey meat and maddening itches from the rashes that devoured his skin. A steady rain for five days had not left García in a good mood.

He thought she looked like an Indian, but you could not tell. Maybe she was the girl everyone was supposed to be on the look out for. Of all places to catch her, this would get him out of here–get him his reward! Had she hurt the General's mother? That would be bad for him.

But no, there was the old hag with the girl, introducing her to the other Indians. What the hell was going on?

García powdered himself with more antifungal medicine, buttoned his army shirt, pulled on his boots, donned his plastic poncho and rain hat, picked up his rifle, and went to investigate. The Indians disappeared when they saw him coming. They had a way of being hard to see even when they were standing in plain sight.

* * *

Anta smelled a cop as soon as she saw the man in a cowboy hat walking toward her through the rain. Her instinct was to run, but to where? She limped away from him. Her body ached from the jaguar attack. She was in no shape to run anywhere even if she knew where she was.

He easily caught her. "You're new here, hmm?" the cop asked.

Old Naj stepped forward. "Do not bother us *bobo*." She used the slang for idiot, showing no respect.

The cop scowled. "Show me your papers."

"Away, away…" Naj waved her hand, "Or I'll tell my son you're bothering me. We La'ku have no papers."

García's lips trembled, but whatever he was trying to say did not come out. He slapped an insect on his neck, and appeared ready to weep. He slunk away, jumping over puddles and kicking a chicken that got in his way.

"He won't bother you here," old *india* Naj said.

Where was here? She'd gone to another time where there were no cars. *Indios* walked about barefooted, wearing nothing but towels around their waists and feathers on their heads. They lived in houses made from branches and leaves. While she'd lost the *tunjo*, amazingly nobody had stolen her pack with the money. Was there a market, a restaurant? She was as hungry as the worst day in Us'me.

Anta's wide brown eyes looked into the trees pushing and falling against one another, so thick she could not see ten feet into the jungle. The air was close and hot like the public baths in Quesada. The witch who'd led her down the cliff had told her that Koya lives in *Tskwal-utenai*.

Anta had to get to *Tskwal-utenai*, wherever that was.

Indios came from their huts and out of the jungle to watch her with expressions that were both respectful and fearful. They spoke softly in the old tongue. Anta understood a few words, *Xucha*, *Tatya-Masi*.

Naj took Anta's hand and led her to an open fire where food was cooking. Soon Anta was eating with a wooden spoon, porridge with meat, good, spicy with the taste of smoke.

The women and girls took her to the river and, laughing like she was the *bobo*, pantomimed that they wanted to clean and put a paste on her wounds. Anta didn't want to take off the rain poncho to reveal the backpack or her secret pouch.

Naj said to her, "We are your family, do not fear us."

Anta remembered her real family and the feeling was like a sharp stick poked into her heart. She grimaced, bent over and pulled off the plastic, then her shirt and pouch at the same time. Her eyes never left the pink backpack and pile of clothes on the riverbank. Nobody tried to go for the loot.

When she was done with the bath, she smelled like the forest, not the sewer. Naj patted Anta's wounds with crushed plants and bark, and covered them with leaves tied around her body. The energy from the tea Naj had given her was nearly gone. Anta's arms felt weak and sore. She had trouble putting on her wet clothes and pack.

"Come sleep now." Naj took her hand to lead her to her hut.

Anta pulled away and said in her most polite voice. "Tell-I where be *Tskwal-utenai?*"

The old woman bent over, her head raised at an angle from her stooped shoulder, focused a milky, unblinking eye on Anta. "That is the old name for Omagua."

"I go by there, right way."

"I cannot help you go there. It's a bad place now, a place of pain. We used to have solid houses before the soldiers took them. I knew your mother, father, all your people there. Now the people live where they can."

"Find I-way." Anta left the old woman by the pyramid and followed a narrow pathway into the jungle.

Indios followed her. "Show I-way by Omagua?" Anta asked them, but they only stared at her. "Road, where road?" Nobody acted like they understood her.

She carried her shoes through the rain and mud. Her vision blurred from the fever. Her breath came in gasps. She was glad the village *indios* stayed with her. The memory of the weight of the jaguar and its teeth reaching for her neck made her flinch at every sound. All around, the jungle sang its scary song of insects and quick movements in the plants. Once she saw a snake as long as a car with a big bulge in its neck. An *indio* shot a monkey out of a tree by blowing a dart through a tube.

Anta's misery and fear increased until she could not stop a whimper that bubbled up her throat. She swallowed hard and kept moving toward the smell of smoke. The jungle opened and she saw the pyramid. The realization that she had walked so far in a circle took the last of her strength. Anta climbed the ladder to Naj's hut where the old woman was waiting to help her to the bed.

* * *

For twenty hours, Anta slept. She dreamt of snakes, big jungle cats, and witches. Koya called to her. "Be alive. Come Anta, come." Jungle sounds were loud in her ears. Anta cried and sat up. Naj was by the bed. "Drink, drink little *Xucha*, drink."

Anta swallowed the bitter liquid down her raw, dry throat. The room was spinning and she fell into the thin mattress.

When she awoke again, the weakness was gone. The sounds of the jungle were loud. The air was still and hot. She heard children playing outside in the rain. It was time to go save Koya.

She found the cop's house and knocked on his door.

He came out with his shirt unbuttoned and his big belly pressing against a dirty white undershirt. Rain slapped the dirt beneath the overhang of his roof.

"¿*Sí?*"

"Please General, I-mama give me hundred *centavos*." Anta held up a fistful of bills for the soldier to see.

He eyed the money. "What do you want me to do about it?"

"Be there letter store, I-mama send more money?"

He frowned and scratched the stubble of his beard. "You mean a post office? No post office here, little sister."

"You bring money from I-momma?"

"I can't understand what you're saying."

"I-mama have money for I."

"How much money?"

"Many hundred *centavos*."

"You're not making any sense to me."

"I-mama Bu in Palapi. Bu makes blankets and ponchos."

"Yeah, OK. So what do you want?"

"Go to I-mama in Palapi."

"You want to go to Palapi and pick up some money from your mama?"

"*Sí*." Anta nodded her head.

"What are you going to do with so many *centavos* here?"

"Buy clothes for I-family."

García studied her. "You could use some clothes."

"*Sí. Sí*. Buy clothes for all I-family."

"Well what do you want me to do about it?"

"Give hundred *centavos* go by Palapi."

"You're going to give me a hundred *centavos* to take you to Palapi, is that it?"

"Yes, go by Palapi."

"How did you get here?"

"By jungle."

"Then go back by the jungle."

"How come by here?"

"Me?"

Anta nodded her head and gazed up at the man like he was the most interesting person she'd ever met.

"You can get a ride from the oil camp to the highway, catch a bus there."

"Take I oil camp. Give hundred *centavos*."

García scratched the side of his head. "I do have to pick up some supplies." He took the money from Anta's hand. "You have more?" He straightened out the wrinkled bills

"Mama Bu have more."

Anta could tell by the way García leaned closer to her that he thought he was going to get more than a hundred *centavos*. The soldier smiled and talked to her like she was his favorite niece. He would take her to Palapi to rob her, but once she was out of this wild place she'd know how to escape this *puerco*.

Naj was at the beginning of the trail as Anta followed the soldier and a La'ku man into the jungle.

"Stay safe until I get back," García said to Naj.

The old lady didn't say anything.

Anta kept her head lowered as she walked past Naj.

"Move, move to *Tatya-Masi*," Anta heard Naj say.

She glanced at the *bruja*, saw a faint smile, and followed García into the jungle.

The *indio* led them for two hours to the edge of the preserve. Anta would never have been able to find her way. Everything was the same wet tangle of growth until, ahead, the trees broke into a space that had been cleared of jungle for a place full of machines and men.

García waved down a red and yellow bus with padded seats. The bus blew black smoke out the back as it carried them from the jungle to where telephone lines crisscrossed the street. Signs in Spanish for drinks, liquor, cigarettes, hung from storefronts and in windows. Posters of Hernando Rosas stared out at her from a wall. She couldn't read the writing, but quaked to remember her brief contacts with him. He still had Koya. She didn't let herself think that Koya was dead, or what Rosas was doing to him to get his *tunjo*. Naj had said Omagua was a place of pain. What could she do now that Norane had the necklace? She still had most of the dollars. Maybe Rosas would take them for Koya. No, she knew he wanted the necklace.

When she got off the bus, Anta looked around the square expecting to see the blood-red pickup and to hear the sounds of the evil spirits who'd chased her three days before. García was as easy to lose as she had thought. Anta led him through the market in the plaza, walked faster until the fat man was almost running to keep up with her, waited and ran in front of a passing truck, into an alley, and out the other side. From the recess of a church door, she saw him hustle past, then ducked behind him the way he'd come.

The tea Naj had given her that morning had made Anta feel better until now. Her body hurt. She was hungry but didn't stop in the market she passed. A woman bent low, and holding her skirt against the blasting wind, called to some children. A lightning bolt split greenish-blue clouds and raised the hair on Anta's neck. Hard rain fell. The rumble of thunder shook the air, followed by the banging of a door and scratching of branches. The wind howled, carrying the scents of the jungle, flowers and mud, rain and decay. Thunder cracked and lightning lit the clouds around Mount Susuprina. Anta could easily believe that the world was ending. What if *Tatya-Masi* was coming in two days to bring a new world? What did the frog god care about Koya? Nobody but her would help Koya.

She walked faster and kept her head lowered. She had to reach Omagua. She didn't have time to wait for a *colectivo* and went to a taxi parked in front of a bar.

The driver cracked his rain-streaked window.

"Take-I Omagua?" Anta asked.

He shook his head and rolled up the window.

She pulled out a hundred centavo bill from the pouch hanging beneath her shirt and showed it to the driver.

He rolled down the window. "Seventy *centavos* to Omagua," he said.

"Seventy *centavos*," Anta repeated.

The driver shrugged. "Get in," he said.

Anta opened the rear door and sat on the seat.

"And twenty more to clean my car."

"Twenty more," Anta said.

The driver started the taxi and drove out of Palapi.

The volcano Susuprina was covered with clouds that got darker near the top. Verdant shoots grew from fence posts. Tangles of wild vines and trees pushed up from the black soil. Wooden and rock fences marked small fields planted with banana trees or corn. Farmers lay beneath dark plastic to protect them against the lightning and rain. A swayback sorrel horse, its tail to the wind, was tethered to a tree before a shanty. Chickens hid beneath a broken car. An old tractor was covered with grass and weeds.

The taxi came to where three trucks and two cars were stopped at the gate to the Morales estancia. Soldiers in helmets, boots, and plastic ponchos guarded the road with the kind of guns that had killed so many in Us'me. They would shoot her as they had her family.

When the taxi drove past the cars and trucks, she kept her posture rigid, watching the soldiers from the corner of her eye, expecting to hear a command to stop.

The road passed a high knit-metal fence that ran across the land as far as she could see. On the other side, herds of cattle with wide sharp horns and humped necks gathered together under lonely trees in lush pastures.

Damn country, she thought, no alleys, crowds, or sewers, only trees and plants. She couldn't go back to Palapi. The village of Omagua, small compared to Palapi, was where she'd been born. She knew most of the people there and they knew her. Rosas would be looking for her in Omagua.

She asked the driver to let her out before driving into the town, gave him the hundred-centavo bill and leaned forward in the seat waiting for the change.

"You want a ride back, it's another 100 *centavos*," he said.

She knew it was no use to ask for her change and stepped into the rain. The taxi turned around and headed back to Palapi, leaving her alone.

Across the road, a group of men and women were working in an open-walled shed filled with burlap bags and metal drums. The damp air carried a chemical smell. At one end of a long trough, women were dumping leaves from heavy woven baskets into the *pozos,* while men with rolled-up pants legs walked to crush the leaves.

A man who might have been the *jefe* watched her with an expectant expression, as if she were coming to work.

Her heart pounded with fear at the sight of a red truck driving toward her. Koya said that if you are afraid, your brain stops working. Think, she told herself. Watch. Don't dream about what is ahead. Do what Koya would do before he stole. Watch, wait, and strike fast. The truck drove past her without a sign of a red-eye. She moved on to find a way into the estancia where the witches had told her she'd find Koya.

An old wall made up of stones piled on one another, covered with vines and moss, ran across the top of a hill above the lake. Beyond another line of metal fencing lay the beautiful Morales hacienda, big enough to hold a hundred families. Soldiers stood beside a gate at the top of a long black road. If Koya were here, Rosas would be here.

She stepped onto a path leading off the road. The mud was so thick she had to take off her shoes and walk barefoot.

"Squish, squish...", her legs sunk in halfway to her knees. She slogged along the wall until she found a nook in the crevice of the rocks from which she could watch the hacienda. Tanks, trucks, and lots of soldiers were moving around the grounds like they were ready to go burn another barrio. A helicopter flew overhead and a plane landed at an airport beside the lake. Anta began to shiver with the same fever that had come over her in the statue. Her vision began to cross and she saw two of everything. Inside the rain poncho grew so hot she felt cooked in steam. She'd seen death enough times to know when it had you in its sight. She had to go.

She plodded back to the road carrying her Nikes in her hand. Rain poured on her. A shoe slipped from her weak grasp. Anta tried to find it, but her eyes wouldn't work. She staggered and nearly fell, but kept going. She lost the other shoe, but couldn't stop. She had to keep moving. She lifted her foot but couldn't get it on the ground in time to keep from falling over. Her face was pressed against the soft mud and she couldn't breath. She didn't have the strength to rise.

Hands reached under her and picked her up. She tried to squirm away. Her arm lifted and then fell useless.

"Bring her inside," a man said.

She kept losing consciousness. She awoke lying on a pile of burlap bags.

"Move *mata* by her one time."

Anta's head was lifted and a plastic cup was placed to her lips. She weakly swallowed the hot broth.

"Be Anta Raymi. All want her."

"Big reward."

Anta passed out. When she awoke somebody was carrying her in the rain. She lost consciousness again and awoke on a soft mattress in a strange *india's* bedroom. All she could do was mumble a protest as two heavy women stripped off her wet clothes, and took the backpack and secret pouch with the loot. Too weak to fight, she let them towel her. They gave her more *mata* and laid her on a dry blanket. When they left her alone, Anta wanted to get up to find her money, but couldn't rise from the sleep that held her.

* * *

García sat at a café in the plaza at Palapi. The rain was making everyone grouchy or maybe it was just him. He couldn't get the girl with the money out of his mind. What was her story? Why was she with Rosas' mother in the jungle? What had been that cock and bull about her mother and the money? At least he'd gotten a hundred *centavos* out of it. Now he had to quickly make it back to his post before he was reported absent without leave.

García looked up from his beer and rocked back in his chair. Two large men moved to either side of him. They seized him in powerful grips and twisted his arms behind his back.

"What are you doing?" García protested.

A pistol was waved in front of his face. Men with the red berets of the *Fierros* surrounded him. He was taken to a jail cell that also held a taxi driver and an Indian woman named Bu.

Clearly, this was about the young girl. His first suspicions had been right. She was the one General Rosas was looking for. García planned to tell them that he was trying to capture her, bring her to Rosas, but she'd gotten away. García was sure he could explain his innocence and would gladly tell what little he knew. After all, he was a member of the army and had nothing to hide.

His confidence disappeared when the doorway to the holding area opened and the soldier saw who walked in.

A ghoul in a bishop's robe followed a skeleton with hellish red eyes. García's explanation of why he'd been with the girl dissolved into screams that echoed throughout the jail.

* * *

No sickness or coca tea could sedate Anta's sense of danger.

"Shraaaa!"

The demon wail cut through her sleep. She shot up from the bed.

Outside were the same horrendous clatter of helicopters, truck engines and cries of fear as six days before in Us'me. Her uncle was pushing his wife and children into their hut.

Anta was out of the bed and would have escaped, but couldn't find her loot. There it was on the table! She picked it up and headed for the door. Locked! The latch was pulling free, but there was not enough time.

The man with the ruby eyes and the skeleton in the red robe were nearly at the door.

Anta ducked away, but the red-eye caught her by the wrist and pulled her so violently that pain shot through her arm. He ripped the pack from her grasp. She cocked her foot and kicked the way Koya had taught her, a quick, powerful shot. Her foot hit only bone. The red-eye slapped her so hard she flipped. She tried to run, but he was too fast, and she too weak.

Bones clicked as he picked her up and threw her against a wall.

She was choking. His bony fingers were death around her throat. Her cries rang like a bell in her ears. She tried to fight, keep her eyes open, to find a way to escape, but passed into a sleep from which she knew she'd never awake.

CHAPTER NINE
INIKA'S STORM

The afternoon of December 20, Eduardo stood in the wheelhouse scrutinizing the horizon. Rain and spume obscured the wind-vibrating glass. He steadied himself as the bow angle dipped.

MG cursed from the galley where she was trying to heat food.

"Are we near?" Eduardo asked Cramee.

The big Kriol's legs were spread for balance behind the wheel. He'd proven himself a good fighter, but Eduardo was unsure of his seamanship.

"We're near. Should be there tonight."

The plastic garbage bag MG had taped over the broken window snapped as a gust rocked the boat.

"What about the weather?"

"This da storm gonna bring *Tatya-Masi,*" Cramee said.

Eduardo thought of Pacho Núñez, the fat actor dressed up in the costume of *Tatya-Masi,* saying his lines, "Twelfth month, twenty-first day, Water washes the Fires away."

Eduardo knew the myth as well as anyone that the god would arrive on a great storm and appear at the Temple-By-The-Sea on December 21. "That's not what I asked you."

Cramee looked at a barometer on the cabin wall. "Never seen a storm like this." The terror in his voice scared Eduardo.

"Can we make it to shore?"

"I'm trying. We get there when *Tatya-Masi* says we get there," Cramee said.

Eduardo focused on where Du sat like a frog Buddha in the prow of the boat. He'd been that way for the past two days, ever since the Haitian incident, not eating, speaking to no one, lost in his own world. Maybe he was a god. That bubble that had been cast over the boat was unlike anything Eduardo had ever known. Eduardo didn't care. He refused to bow to Du or any other deity. Let the sky rain frogs, he'd decide his own destiny and control his own fate.

"Where is our father's body?" Lilia softly asked.

She sat on the cushion behind him, and spoke in her own weak voice, not the insane channeling of a witch. He hesitated to tell her the truth but decided it was better to keep the conversation in the realm of reality than fabrication. "He hasn't spoken in two years. Rosas keeps him in Tatua's old room."

Lilia looked to the darkening horizon with her weird eyes. "Papa lives in Manoa now. He's happy there." Her voice was barely audible above the wind.

"He lives like you, by magic. Can you bring him back to his body?"

"*Tatya-Masi* will reunite his spirit with his body."

Eduardo frowned. Who was he talking to? Before Norane gave her the box with the *tunjo*, she'd never spoken like this. "I am a man of this world. I've always been a man of this world. I can't understand you, Lilia."

"This world, as you call it, is more than you can see."

"Then let me see our father as he was. I wish to apologize to him."

She placed her hand on his. "He forgives you."

Eduardo scowled.

"He's waiting for you. Join us."

"There are things I have to do in this world before I go into another."

"The place where you think you are and where you want to be are the same. What we believe is not always what we are."

"I have no wish to insult you, Lilia. But what you describe is delusion and madness." Eduardo looked to where Du sat in the prow of the boat. "Even he doesn't believe that there is a better spiritual world working in our favor."

"He is overwhelmed by what is demanded of him. Like his uncle, he wants to stay here in the physical plane."

"Then on that at least we agree." He picked up the binoculars and studied the gray horizon.

* * *

The days Du had spent withdrawing into himself had perversely heightened his awareness. He needed no news bulletins to know the damage the rains were wreaking on modern civilization. He'd foolishly hoped that by removing his consciousness, he absolved himself from blame. Do not believe you can control or stop these things, he repeatedly lectured himself. You have no power, no control of the weather, and if you did, you would stop the rains, surely you would.

His thoughts were brought back into the moment by the smell of the cream of tomato soup MG carried out to him. Hunger overpowered his ascetic urges.

"Thanks MG." He stood, took the cup, and hungrily poured the hot broth into his large mouth. "What happened to your hand?"

She looked at the reddened skin. "Spilled some soup on it." Wind-driven rain soaked her blue denim work shirt and jeans.

"You should go back inside," he said.

"What about you?"

"You know the rain doesn't bother me."

"You gonna be able to stop it, aren't you?"

He frowned and finished the last of the soup.

"Sorry. You'll do what you can."

"You know I'm not a god, don't you?"

She bent her head into the gale. Her words held a challenge as she raised her voice to be heard. "I know you don't want to be, but sometimes you gotta do what you gotta do. Oh, look!" Her red cheeks rose in a smile that brightened her blue eyes as she clapped in delight.

One after another, in pairs and threes, humpback whales breached, rising completely out of the water, twisting their 40-ton bodies in the air and falling back with tremendous splashes. Dolphins, porpoises, flying fish, sharks and rays broke the surface around the boat. Du was aware of a growing cavalcade of fish: schools on schools of squid, marlin, barracudas, groupers, jacks, tuna, swarming in and around each other, lime, silver, yellow flashing through fingers of white coral. The world of Water was rejoicing, marshalling the energies of its combined life forces to join *Tatya-Masi,* to claim the next world for Water.

The cabin door slammed. Lilia pulled her way through the great gusts to Du and MG. She appeared so frail that only the power of the Waters of Life could explain her not being carried away by the bawling wind. The jade in her eyes shined in the dank gloom as she spread her arms and cried in the ancient dialect of the *Xucha,* "Witness the face of *Inika* Lordess of Water."

Du looked to the west over the bow. A four-headed jaguar emerged from the purple clouds. A fit of *mysterium tremendum* struck him and his knees sagged almost to the point of falling back to the deck at the sight of the numinous apparition. He'd never seen *Inika* before. He'd felt her, had heard her, had known her from the moment of his conception, but she'd always been something in another dimension.

Now four breaths blew over him in hot humid blasts from eight black nostrils.

MG took a step back and reflexively reached for him.

"Command me." *Inika's* voice was a quadraphonic whine in the banshee wind.

Was he a god or a fearful mortal? He had a split-second to choose—rule or submit. All his doubts and resolve had settled on this moment. With clenched fists and raised chin he whispered. "Stop the rains."

Quadruple cat maws snarled a hellish screech. The intensity of the storm increased ten-fold. MG was spun around by a blast of hurricane wind. The declaration of his mortality had placed him and everyone on the boat at the pitiless mercy of the Lordess.

"Oh Du, you've chosen Fire," Lilia said. In the moment of the quitting of her unnatural life, her brown eyes rolled into her head as she was lifted by the spray-laden wind. She'd have been carried away had he not dropped the cup and caught her by the arm.

He'd not chosen Fire; he'd chosen weakness. Regret staggered him. *Inika* had asked him to prove he was the Water god. Only *Tatya-Masi* could command *Inika*. The goddess would obey no mortal. She abandoned him as she'd abandoned all restraint on her assault on the Age of Man. Loaded with boxes, top-heavy on the deck; the *Bestante* floundered in the furious sea of Inika's wrath. The bow dropped into the deepening hollow of a wave that grew steeper than the boat could navigate, falling as he was, through space without a hold to right himself, into a watery pit.

"*Nohochayum, Hacha'kyum, Chicchan!*" Du pleaded, but the gods of the ocean, wind, and lightening would not protect them from *Inika's* storm.

He pulled Lilia back to the meager shelter of the cabin. MG extended her hand to pull him through the door into the wheelhouse.

Cramee held the wheel with one hand, the throttles with the other, trying to keep the nose of the trawler pointed into the face of the growing swell. Moss stood aside so Du could lay Lilia on the soaked cushion behind the wheel. The boat rolled to the point of tipping, throwing MG against Eduardo, who held onto a railing on the cabin wall, staring into the face of the hurricane as if the storm was a foe challenging him to mortal combat.

Du called over the wind to Moss. "Will the Plumed Serpent help us?"

Moss gripped the edge of the bunk. His angular face was white in the flickering light of the single bulb that lit the cabin. "*Quetzal* can't help you here. Find your own strength. Become the god. Be the god!"

The *Bestante* complained in her caulking as the violent currents tore at her planking, confirming that no force of Fire would come to their aid.

Du removed the vial holding the Waters of Life from his pocket. Though there was barely a drop left, the dispenser glowed in his hand. Energy and confidence radiated through him. There was only enough for one dose. He could try to take this last, desperate route to the divine, or save his mother.

She lay on the bench, eyes closed, no breath raising the saturated running suit pasted to her chest. Du slipped his hand beneath her head to give her the last of the Waters.

A line broke with a snap unleashing a box that hurtled through the window over the bunk. Glass shattered, knocking the tube from his hand. The Waters spilled, glowed for an instant, and mixed with the storm water sloshing on the cabin floor. The garbage bag ripped free, creating an open conduit for the wind to whip through the cabin. The *Bestante* rolled in a radical tilt as the cargo shifted on the deck.

"I can't control her!" Cramee shouted over the howl of the wind.

"We have to ditch the boxes," Kare said and scrambled down into the galley.

Eduardo moved to the door. "We can tie them down. We must bring them back inside."

Du followed his uncle onto the deck.

"Help me," he said to Du as he pushed a leaning box back atop the stack.

Kare came out of the cabin holding a knife. He reached for a line and started to cut.

"You will not betray me again!" Eduardo screamed in Spanish and drew his gun.

Kare raised his knife and Norane aimed his pistol at his chest.

"No!" Du shouted.

A wave buried the bow and washed over the two men.

Du held onto the railing as the draining water pulled him overboard. When the wave passed, Eduardo was hanging onto a lashing and Kare was not in sight. Du regained his footing and looked for him in the ocean and among the boxes hanging from burst lashings. The man who'd raised him had disappeared into the drowning churn of the storm.

Du dropped his overalls and hopped into the ocean. "Du!" he heard MG's voice as he rode a roller to the top and saw Kare being pulled away by a swirling froth of whitewater. Du dove beneath surface, where the wind could not affect him, and swam using all the leverage he could exert from his webbed feet and hands. He came up where he judged Kare to be, but the storm had taken him another thirty yards. Kare was furiously but futilely paddling, getting no closer, only exhausting himself.

"Swim, Kare. Don't give up!" Du dove and rose beside him.

Kare clung to him with a desperate embrace.

"Easy. I have you. You don't have to hold me so tight," Du spoke to him soothingly. "Trust me. You know I'm good in the water. That's it. Work with me."

The truth was that the ocean terrified Du. His eyes and nose burned with irritation. He could not absorb oxygen through his skin as he could in freshwater. His breaths came in gasps as he exerted himself against the powerful currents that were pulling them away from the boat. Without supernatural assistance, with his strength sapped from two days of fasting, he was in no better shape than Kare to survive in the open ocean. He kicked up the side of a curl and saw the *Bestante* below, like a house in a valley about to be buried in an avalanche. As they fell, the boat rose so that a shifting range of peaks separated them. Du paddled but the distance to the boat was increasing.

"Hold your breath," he said to Kare. "We have to go under."

"I can't."

"We must. Ready?"

Kare filled his lungs, closed his eyes and nodded.

Du pulled him down into the dark calm. A minute passed and Du tried to swim up to the air, but found only more water until he worried that he'd been turned around and was swimming deeper. A lighter shade above indicated he'd been traveling sideways. Kare panicked and kicked free. A wave built over them, adding fifty feet to the surface. Du caught Kare by the back of his shirt, and paddled hard. The pressure in his ears lessened and he pulled Kare into the air.

Du gasped, coughed, and was washed over by another wave. The *Bestante* was close by. "Hold me." He reached for the sputtering man's hand and swam him to the side of the boat.

A line flew from the deck but was caught in the wind and nearly blown back aboard. Kare caught hold of the rope and pulled himself through the draining water onto the deck.

The current pulled Du away. The line sailed out again. The boat rolled toward Du and he swam to where Moss hung over the side extending his arm.

"Thank you, father," Du said when he was aboard and would have hugged him, but he was already following Kare into the wheelhouse. In the riot of the hurricane, had Moss heard him call him father? A burst of joy that Moss had risked his life to save him caused Du to smile and his large eyes to gleam for a moment. Then, the storm reasserted its dominance over his thoughts.

The boat dropped in a stomach-raising free fall. The *Bestante* slid crossways to a wave the size of a locomotive. If they were hit that way they'd roll. Kare entered the cabin ahead of Moss just as the dark wall of water fell on them and they turned turtle.

Du was holding onto the railing, Moss the doorframe, as the boat rolled to the point where they were dangling underwater. The trawler's keel pointed skyward and fell into the water, pulling the superstructure back into the air. Water flushed through the cabin, picked Lilia up and carried her out the door. For an instant Moss caught her by the wrist as she swept by him and then was pulled off the boat with her.

"Water washes the Fires away. Move, move to *Tatya-Masi*," Du heard Curratta's voice come from his mother.

"Mother! Father!" The blasting wind caught his words and threw them back in his face. Whipping spume stung his eyes as he scanned the sea. There! He saw Lilia and Moss, two mites on a rising black sheet, their hands locked in a desperate hold.

How could he go out there again? He was too exhausted to save them. His parents disappeared. He lowered his head, gasped and jumped back into the maelstrom.

The water gurgled as he swam beneath the waves, rising and falling with the root agitation. He swam with his head thrust forward, his arms pulling to his side, his legs spreading and joining in a breaststroke, coaxing as much speed as he could muster from his exhausted body. He knew that rapid currents could separate his parents and pull them to where he'd never be able to find them. His muscles burned. His natural tendency to breathe through his skin worked to his disadvantage as salt irritated and clogged his pores. He was forced to the surface for air and found himself in the depths of a wave. He sucked air and dove. There, forty yards ahead, he saw the faint glow of the vial his mother wore around her neck, shining as a beacon guiding him. Beneath the agitation of the waves, he was able to quickly cover the distance and wrap his hand around Lilia's thin forearm. Limp and unresponsive, he pulled her into the crook of his arm. Moss paddled weakly beside her. Du caught him just as a wave pushed them under and spun them around.

"I have you now," he rasped when he regained the surface and held them in a lifesaver's grip.

Even empathetically he sensed no response from his mother. If Lilia were alive she would not survive long in this tempest. But then neither would they. He couldn't take both of them underwater as he had Kare. He had to stay on the surface where his dwindling strength was little match for the forces of 170-mile-an-hour-winds and roiling sea.

"You can let me go, son," Moss said.

In the midst of his deadly predicament, Du's joy returned at the familial evidence. If they were to die they'd die as a family.

"No." He pulled his father closer. The ocean opened up beneath them and they slid into a deep canyon. Holding his mother in his right arm and his father in his left, Du used his powerful legs to frog his way up the concave face into the turbulent wash of the chasing flood.

He hung in the spindrift at the crest and sought the boat. As they descended into the next bleak chasm, he had to accept that they had been swept too far away–they were alone on the ocean. Even if the *Bestante* was still afloat, there was little chance the boat could find them.

Holding Lilia and Moss above water awkwardly, having only his legs and webbed feet to counter the power of the waves, Du swam on his back to the top of one mountainous comber after another, knowing that if one broke on them, he'd never be able to reach the surface in time to keep his parents from drowning.

Du swam until he thought he could never kick another stroke. Exhaustion and fear settled into a single thought to survive.

As the hours passed and rather than lessening, the storm grew more savage and the waves more threatening, Du accepted his mortality and many times was ready to surrender, but something, a feeling that this was not his time, kept him going. They were doused by three monster waves in succession. When Du arose from the third pummeling, his father was limp in his arms. Du weakly backpedaled up the face of another wave, unsure either of his parents were alive. Sheets of rains rushed over him.

"*Inika*, help me. I am weak and will die if you do not come to my aid."

A wall of lightning swept across the sea, dancing in bolts that charged the water with reverberating choruses of thunder. Du moaned with hopelessness and was ready to give up and drop beneath the surface when the wind stopped. No rain fell. The sea calmed. A curtain of lightning moved ahead of another drapery of fire on the windward side of the hurricane wall.

Tips of glistening white and red coral gleamed in the faint light of a quarter moon. The Atlantic pushed Du against the reef and sharp edges lacerated his salt-inflamed skin.

He could go no farther. The sucking current of a rip tide pulled them into the moat of a breaker rearing over the reef. Death would come by being pummeled against the razor-edged coral. The sea hissed as it was drawn into the implosion of the all-encompassing form. Du planted his feet until they were nearly impaled, gathered his remaining strength, and leaped.

Holding his parents in his arms, he bellowed, "CROAR!"

The urge to survive and save his parents beat a constant tempo in his blood, pushing him on. He had to reach the beach before the eye of the hurricane passed. He turned on his back and counted a hundred kicks of his feet, then started over, hypnotizing himself against the pain of every movement.

When he finally touched bottom, he didn't know who he was, where or why, he knew only to drag himself and his cargo another twenty yards.

As he staggered up the beach, the outer wall hit with an explosion of wind, rain, and lightning. He was thrown forward into the sand. His eyes rolled skyward. In the moment before he lost consciousness, framed in the white electrical discharge, he saw a startling image.

The hurricane had swept clear the tangled jungle growth and exposed a forty-foot-high statue of *Tatya-Masi.*

CHAPTER TEN
AND WE SHALL PERISH

For seven hundred years, the Temple-By-The-Sea had lain in anticipation of the twenty-first day of the twelfth month of the twelfth year. Built into a cliff located a half-mile from the normal shoreline, thirty feet off the ground, stocked with water and food, the ancient retreat had served as a place to survive a bad hurricane. And nobody had seen as bad a hurricane as this one.

A brutal tidal surge had swept a mile inland, washing over all in its path. Condensation rolled off prehistoric paintings and carvings on the rock walls. Torches flickered as the storm ran through scales of fury that climbed, dropped momentarily, and then shot higher to new crescendos of keening wind and sheets of rain.

A mix of the living and ancients, made animate by the power of the Waters of Life, gathered around a stone cistern held aloft with carvings of four jaguar heads, the enduring symbol of the Lordess of Water.

Norane's pulse beat with a greater excitement than he'd ever known. He tried to tell himself that it was purely anticipation of the coming of *Tatya-Masi*, but in his heart he longed for Lilia. Was she alive? Was he? Soon they would be together again, either in this or the spirit world.

The *tunjo* Anta had stolen from Rosas, hung around Norane's neck, throbbing with urgency, as if sensing that the moment and purpose of its existence had arrived.

Ancients, revitalized by the magic of the *Xucha* witches, gathered around Norane awaiting his command. The ancients appeared to have sprung from the petroglyphs on the cave's walls: warriors from the past, fifteen blowgun hunters, Quatzanales, twenty Parquanits, in tight-fitting animal skins and armed with obsidian-tipped clubs; the same battle dress in which their ancestors had once gone to war. Amongst them were people from the modern age: farmers, doctors, holy men, mothers, all longing to see the answer to a promise made before the first Spaniards had arrived. They were drawn together by the frail gossamer threads of a myth, told in many variations and tongues. United even when time, distance and the oppression of a social and political class vastly stronger than theirs had isolated them in pockets of ignorance, dissembling their natural alliances. More pilgrims would have been there, but the land was nearly drowned and the jungle roads had been made impassable by the weeklong rainfall that had preceded the hurricane.

On the other side of the cave a shaman, resurrected by the *Xucha*, wore a fearsome carved mask inlaid with shells. He shook a rattle to chase away Fire spirits and intoned:

"Moon, go to the gods.

Tell them we cannot survive the Fire of the Sun.

We are nearly dead.

Lordess, owner of Water.

Send *Tatya-Masi*."

The ancient warriors responded,

"The great wind blows when *Tatya-Masi* appears,

And we shall perish."

Parquanits, their tattooed chins and cheeks illuminated in the wavering light of torches chanted, "And we shall perish."

Norane walked farther out from the entrance of the cave and let the powerful wind push against his body. Palm branches flew by and leaves pelted him. The wind roared and rain tore at him. His doubts of what he'd done to prepare for the advent of the god and the fears of what would happen if he had failed were as tempestuous as the storm. Norane tried to encourage himself by humming a refrain from a *Xucha* chant, one of the first he'd learned at their ancient hands:

> "Life force, raging river,
> Confusing path, wild torrent,
> May I slow you?
> Mount you, force you to
> Carry me where I will?"

Norane had faith that no matter what obstacle Fire presented, *Tatya-Masi* would appear on the day ordained by the timeless myths of the *Xucha*. Only the fulfillment of this aged prophecy would unite the impoverished and brutalized population he hoped to mold into an army. He also knew his plans depended on Du, the mortal boy who'd fled Manoa and taken Lilia with him.

Nineteen years ago, he'd brought Lilia's spirit to Manoa where he'd been one of the four beings who'd fathered *Tatya-Masi*. The man in him knew the feeling of dread that his son and the woman he loved were out in that storm.

* * *

After six hours of battling the storm, the *Bestante* was a splintered wreck, but miraculously still afloat, as if the sea was too angry to allow this small scrap to sink. The propellers whined as the bow dug into the valley of another house-size wave. Cramee held onto the wheel like an insane rodeo cowboy riding a demonic bull. The cursing fisherman worked the bent rudder against the massive forces of wind and water that sought relentlessly to destroy them. The stern lifted and kept rising until the trawler stood on its nose. By some wizardry of seamanship, Kare again punched through the crest of another wave and sent the boat slipping into a world so dark that you could not see the sky, dropping so far into its depths that they were sheltered from the wind. Then with tons of seawater falling on them, Kare steered up another wave to start the cycle over again.

A comber rolled the boat and banged Eduardo's head against the bulwark. He couldn't find his footing. He'd been hit hard before, been knocked out, but never anything like this. His legs went wobbly, his eyes crossed. He tried to find something he could hold to keep from being pulled from the cabin like his poor sister, but he couldn't focus. There was no static point. Every wave seemed to attack from a different angle, blasting them the side, above and behind with the force of a speeding truck. The hurricane yowled in his ears. He was growing weaker.

MG fought through the draining water to reach his side. Her strong arms protected him. She was all he had to lean against.

Suddenly, a fist of white, glistening coral punched through the hull. With a long wail of defeat, Cramee called, "Reef!"

The ocean sought to claim them, rushing in up over their heads. Cramee tried to pull himself out the window. The victorious sea snatched him and flung him into its dark, churning depths.

Eduardo gasped for air. The boat pitched forward and the water withdrew. The *Bestante* was lifted like a surfboard hurled on the crest of an ungodly wave. When they hit the sand, the crash felt as if he'd jumped off the cliff at Omagua, rattling his teeth inside his jaw and shaking his bones so hard that the joints painfully snapped against each other.

Kare shouted, "We're on a beach."

Eduardo fell forward. Grimacing from the bolts of pain that shot through his brainstem, his head rested against MG's wet shoulder as she steered him from the cabin. She was the biggest, strongest woman he'd ever known.

Wind and rain whipped his face. The tide swirled around the broken boat, which shifted, throwing them forward. He was desperate to get off before they could be sucked out into the sea, but was too weak to climb the angle of the deck.

MG steadied him against her side, waited until the next wave withdrew, climbed over the edge, and helped him through the swirling tide.

The current pulled them back. They fought to maintain their foothold in the sand until the next wave threw them forward. Eduardo clung to MG's arm and fought the retreating surge. The surf tore at them and then they were free.

CHAPTER ELEVEN
THE GOD APPEARS

Dawn, December 21, Du awoke to the hiss of the retreating sea. He lay facedown on the beach. His parents were crumpled where he'd left them last night. Consciousness was painful–a fist of agony that racked his battered body, punishing him for opening his eyes. Each rasping breath felt like two pieces of sandpaper were scrapping the inside of his abraded throat. He was naked, his clothes either torn from his body by the sea or discarded in order to swim better. It was still storming, but the steady rain and gray clouds were mild compared to the forces of weather he'd battled the previous night. A hermit crab scurried across the beach, carrying the shell of a sea snail on its back for protection. Du's first thought was how a creature born so defenseless into the world had managed to survive such an onslaught of nature. But then he pondered–if you could call this torturous flaying of every nerve, life–so had they.

He lifted himself enough to confirm that his mother and father lay a few feet up the beach. He got on his knees and opened his birdbath-size mouth to capture the rain. His eyes rotated, seeking signs of habitation or commerce. Misty clouds clung to cliffs that rose from a flood plain covered with mud, sand, and the detritus deposited by the storm surge.

The moonlit apparition he had seen last night stared at him with stony certainty. The forty-foot-tall carved image–kneeling as he was–mocked him with its glorification of a man-frog, terrified him with what it confirmed. The stone representation resembled the figure he'd seen on the ancient stone wheel in his grandfather's study, and on the box of the *tunjo*–the necklace he'd possessed and lost to Rosas, and the similar statue at the foot of the falls that guarded the cave of the *Xucha*.

But there was something more immediate about the way this anachronism forced itself from the vines, coconut and mangrove trees, into the present to seize and drag his soul into timeless eternity. How long had the monolith stood here? How had those who built the giant idol known that he would arrive at this spot, at this moment on December 21? How many more manifestations of the past lay in the jungle behind the statue, waiting to spring forth into the unsuspecting modern age?

The rock carving was a bridge in time taking him to an earlier age before the origins of man and the cosmogony of the Earth; a signpost pointing the way to a place he dreaded. All the currents of the world–the forces that drew him to this moment–trapped the wind, tide, and rain in his blood.

He groaned as he crawled toward the statue where his parents lay on the steep slope of the beach. His mother's hair was matted with sand and her skin pale. The vial with the Waters of Life had been lost in the storm. He touched her face and lowered his ear to her dried, cracked lips. He could detect no breath or pulse. He closed his eyes and swayed with a deep sadness. Had she lived only to deliver him to this impossible destiny?

His father rolled onto his back. Du's relief at Moss' survival lasted only a moment. Fear seized his heart. A cacophony of separate but syncopated sounds filled his mind. Trees complained as they rubbed against each other. A limb shook loose and crashed to the ground.

Birds and monkeys shrieked. Lizards and snakes slithered across wet rock and mud. Human voices, padding feet, metal scraping against rock. A wave crashed the shore across the salt marsh.

The walls of time collapsed. Animal-skin-clothed ancients rushed from the jungle toward him crying, "*Tatya-Masi*! *Tatya-Masi*!"

Du lost all sense of who or where he was.

"CRROOOOOOAAAARRRR!"

The primordial sound exploded from the depths of his gut. He hopped to the base of the cliff and leaped up twenty feet, landing on the lap of the statue.

"CROAR! CROAR! CROAR! CROAR!"

Naked, jumping in place, his arms outstretched, fists clenched, the convulsive cries rattled out of him, reverberating in the ears and minds of every living creature in a quarter-mile radius. For that second, the intense complexity, the Darwinian race to survive, the perpetual vibrancy of the jungle, went static and then released a positive response; a bolt of a million different life forms coalesced into concentrated energy that pierced him and charged every electron in his body.

Tattooed, ochre-caked warriors wailed and wept, holding their hands up in supplication, falling to their knees, rushing to the base of the statue, ululating ecstatic howls. Some spun in a whirling dance, while others seemed to fly as if held by invisible wires, their arms and legs locked in running positions.

Du could not stop bellowing. "CROAR! CROAR! CROAR!" The explosive outcry he made at times of extreme fear was now the voice of a deity. "CROAR!" The *vox deus* rattled out of him one more time, then stopped when he saw a familiar figure amongst the ancients.

There was no mistaking Norane's broad muscular shoulders, black hair parted in the middle, the leather vest, the feathered band around his biceps. It didn't take much empathy to sense Norane's complete vindication.

Tatya-Masi had arrived at the exact spot, at the exact time as foretold by the *Xucha*.

Norane proclaimed. "*Tatya-Masi! Ña Nati: Añe'êkuaamichimi mante guaraníme, anga! Tatya-Masi* has come! Liberty is ours! Cry for our salvation! Run to your neighbors! Carry the news! *Tatya-Masi* is here! The prophecy is fulfilled!"

Du fixated on the *tunjo*, the totemic representation of himself, hanging from Norane's neck. A longing filled him to again hold what he'd once possessed. The aura around the eyes of the pendent expanded with sympathetic reaction to his desire.

Norane spread his arms and hailed,

> *"Inti K'anchay! Khuyakzk!*
> *Qhapak kay! Willaka chzray.*
> Rain shower! Cloud of Mercy!
> Water God! You are with us.
> Give life to the gardens of the Children of Water.
> We have waited patiently for your restoration.
> The fields have lain fallow for all these years.
> The tools are well maintained.
> Never in the long domain of Fire
> Have we lost our faith.
> Oh, *Tatya-Masi*! Bless us with your presence!
> Lead us to Water."

Behind Norane, amongst the ancients, dozens of moderns stared at him with unmitigated awe, while others bowed their heads as if the sight of him was too stunning to behold.

"Move, move to *Tatya-Masi*!" the chant built.

Two of the ancients–their naked breasts and faces tattooed in swirls–flew toward the statue. Norane stopped them with a brusque command.

The bent legs of the statue formed a terrace that extended twenty feet from the body. Du staggered back from the edge and leaned against the rounded stone belly. For a minute the worshipers were out of his sight, then Norane walked around the side of the statue.

Du eyed him with trepidation and then his sight locked on the *tunjo.*

Norane knelt before him on one knee, and in La'ku appealed, "Accept me as the Warrior-Brother. Command me!"

"Cruuuuuu."

The chant of the *Xucha* vibrated the air between them.

"Wear me. Hold me."

"Cruuuuuu."

Inika Lordess of Water might have forsaken him, but the presence of the *Xucha* was growing stronger, impatient for Du to fulfill their bargain. Curratta, the ancient froglike spirit crone, was near, watching, ready to drive him to his destiny. He'd sold her his soul and deliverance was due.

His physical hunger was nothing compared to the longing for the power of the *tunjo.* Every desire and satisfaction was focused on the fetish and could not be quieted until he'd given himself completely to its allure.

Since his first thoughts of self-awareness, he'd felt himself to be nothing special. In his youth, with only Kare, Edgar, and the occasional hiker or boater on the Lake of the Frogs to compare himself, he told himself he only looked different. Kare's tales that he was a god whose coming heralded the end of the Age of Fire and beginning of the Sixth World of Water, had provided him fanciful notions of superiority when he'd felt lonely and freakish. Even when he'd gone to the cave of the *Xucha* and his mother had taught him to perceive and command the spirits, when he'd commanded the rains to stop, he'd felt that he was an imposter. Now, an epiphany overwhelmed his doubt and forced him to acknowledge that mysterious cosmic forces had delivered him to a place and destiny for which neither science, probability, or sense of self could account. Somehow, seven hundred years ago, people had known that a being with his unique characteristics would appear at the statue they'd carved in his image on December 21.

I am a man named Du. I am Du, he repeated to himself, resisting the lure and the intoxication of the deification. He would not relinquish his freedom to those who would make him *Tatya-Masi*.

"Cruuuu." The *Xucha* chant vibrated the air.

"Wear me. Hold me," the necklace called.

Du extended his hand to the pulsing talisman.

With a hint of a smile, Norane rose from his knee, removed the necklace and held it over Du's outsized head.

Du shied away, but was unable to resist bowing to receive the *tunjo*.

At the touch of the chain, the fabric of Du's consciousness exploded outwards. His consciousness was sucked from his body by a great imbalance of pressure between this plane and a greater void, through a tear in the substance of air, rock and water, into a realm where the limits of dimensional space were multiplied: time, memory, dream, consciousness, manifolds, orbifolds, entropy; the measures of disorder were as meaningful as up and down. The borders between Earth and cosmos, temporal and celestial, blurred and crossed. The lessons his mother had taught him of command of spirits and communication with the divine were his to discharge.

"Cruuuuuu!" The chorus chanted with a thousand voices.

The power of the *tunjo* was more than revitalization. It was regeneration. Du felt his cells multiplying, plasma bubbling through his veins, filling and expanding muscles, evaporating fatigue, removing self-doubt.

Strong, imperious, he stood. His skin no longer itched. He neither thirsted nor hungered. His fatigue and weakness were gone. He saw the flight of the farthest bird on the horizon, heard the soft falling of drops of water from the branches and leaves in the jungle. His empathy was magnified far greater than what he had experienced when he'd first held the *tunjo* two years before. The hopes and longings of his supplicants flowed into him as oxygen feeds a fire.

"Cruuuuuu."

The *Xucha's* rapturous exaltations coincided with the dance of an aura that spread from the necklace and surrounded him in a halo. Comprehension did not equal control; born into a new life, he felt the pressure on untouched nerves of a fantastically more complex existence than he had known and experienced as the present. Then the propelling force lessened and, like a ball on a string, he was pulled through the hole.

Just that brief moment on the other side transformed him. In a flash, all he was, all the pain of his human existence, the limits of his perceptions, disappeared.

He was reborn as *Tatya-Masi*.

"What of the woman and man?" A voice called from the beach.

With the removal of the *tunjo*, Norane appeared weaker, thinner. A line around his body wavered as his presence in the temporal world diminished.

"Bring the woman." Norane's voice quavered and was nearly drowned by the waves and falling rain. Yet, the ancients heard him and brought Lilia to them.

Her black hair draped over the muscular arm of a spirit warrior, his mother was carried up the stairs, and placed at Du's feet.

With a wave of his hand, Norane dismissed the ancient who

backed away and withdrew from the lap of the statue.

The last time Du had seen Norane and his mother together, Norane had been furious with her for taking Du from Manoa. Now, Du detected a flicker of joy soften Norane's stolid expression as he removed a gold-filigreed tube from a woven pouch slung across his shoulders. The top was sealed by a likeness of Du's webbed hands crossed over a representation of his upturned head. Norane pulled the top with his thumb and a single drop of the Waters of Life rose to the pursed mouth of the likeness of *Tatya-Masi*. He lovingly raised her head and placed the elixir on Lilia's lips.

With his enhanced perceptions, Du could see his mother's spirit had traveled too far into the dimensions of dreams and memory. Not even the Waters of Life could reunite her body with her soul.

Norane placed another drop of the Waters on her lips. The seconds passed and still Lilia did not revive. Norane hung his head and held Lilia's lifeless hand.

Oh, the longing, the self-denial. Even as the *tunjo* enthralled Du, a single rational thought pierced his delirium. How could he be a god and be so ambivalent? How could he be so unsure?

Don't give up your life as a man, he told himself. You can still escape. It's not too late! River, ponds, and lakes are nearby for you to hide in. Escape to what? To be a man? A half-man, a half-creature living in the wild?

He trembled as he forced his hands to raise the *tunjo* over his head.

"No, *Tatya-Masi!*" Norane said.

Du released the necklace and it fell to the dirt. He was now too weak to stand and collapsed to his knees. As high as the power of the *tunjo* had taken him, he fell that much lower.

Norane picked up the necklace and held it out to him. At the touch of the *tunjo*, Norane's presence strengthened.

"She needs it." Du's trembling hand reached up in supplication, abjectly begging for Norane to place the necklace around Lilia's neck.

The *tunjo* had been created from the Jewels of Life to give *Tatya-Masi* the spiritual power to secure the next Age for Water. Norane's hard stare was betrayed by a glance at the lifeless body of the woman he'd loved since they were children. He'd led her to the *Xucha* to be the mother of *Tatya-Masi,* knowing that as a Castilian, she might not survive Curratta's test. Norane tilted his head toward the western horizon as if to seek advice from a distant voice.

"I command you to give her the necklace," Du said, knowing that Norane would obey him.

Norane nodded and slipped the necklace over Lilia's head.

She regenerated into youth and beauty. Her eyes opened and focused on Norane. "Love, oh my. . ."

Then, the jewel-colored half of her pupils darkened. The ghostly shape of Curratta, deformed head resting on a raised shoulder, arose from her body. "Be strong, *Tatya-Masi,*" the crone said.

But he was weak, and as his remaining strength ebbed, he slipped to the wet stone to suffer as a man.

CHAPTER TWELVE
QUETZAL'S SERVANT

Eduardo opened his eyes. His bearded face pressed close to MG's soft pink cheek. She gently pushed him away. He rolled onto his back and grimaced against the pain that squeezed his nerves with each new level of wakening through which he arose. The skin on his head felt tight and burned from a wound that he'd received last night. He tried to stand, but collapsed to his knees. His clothes were wet and caked with sand. The driving wind and rain had passed, replaced by a softer squall. They were on a beach, bordered by jungle and split by a river, whose flow was probably little more than a stream in normal times, but was now a gushing torrent carrying a cargo of fallen trees, dead animals, and silt.

He got to his feet, growled at the pain in his head and staggered to where the *Bestante* lay on its side, cast a hundred yards from what was now the shoreline. A few of the boxes of weapons were scattered about the sloping mudflat and on the deck.

Kare repelled down side of the boat with a machine gun and a machete strapped to his back.

"Did you find a weapon for me?" Eduardo asked.

"This is all I found."

"Let me have the gun. You keep the machete."

Kare walked over to one of the boxes. "Plenty of guns in these boxes, aren't they?" he asked.

"Give me the gun, I told you," Eduardo said.

"No. I'll keep it."

Eduardo stepped unsteadily toward him, ready to fight.

Kare contemplated him with a thin smile.

Eduardo cocked his fist.

"Hey, you two," MG said. "Was there any food on board?"

"It's ruined," Kare said. "Everything is soaked." He lifted the machete. Eduardo warily stepped aside. Kare passed him and picked up a coconut.

"You son of a La'ku whore. I'll see you dead," Eduardo cursed and used the line hanging off the side of the wreck to pull himself up to see what he could find. He looked about the destroyed cabin and confirmed what Kare had said. The scraps of food left on the boat were ruined. He doubted Kare's gun would work. He did find a tool kit that contained a hammer and assorted screwdrivers.

Eduardo exited the boat the way he'd gotten on and went to work opening the boxes on the beach. Fortunately, the guns were packed in grease. He broke out an M-16, shoved in a magazine and test-fired a quick staccato in the direction of Kare. The damn La'ku didn't flinch, even when the bullets were chopping the branches over his head.

"What the hell are you doing?" MG asked.

"Just seeing if the gun works."

"Yeah, well watch where you're pointing it."

Perhaps she preferred the Indian to him. This was not the place for romantic games. He ignored her while he opened another box and found some grenades. When he'd armed himself, he used the screwdriver to tear off the hairy husk and punch holes in the eyes of a coconut. The sweet milk gave him energy. He sucked it dry, then pulled away the fibers and broke open the nut to eat the firm, moist meat.

MG stood at the edge of the estuary looking in both directions on the foggy beach. He handed her another coconut he'd prepared.

"Thanks." She drank the milk and scraped the white meat with her lower teeth.

He shook his leg to loosen clotted sand on his pants. He'd been helpless last night. If not for her, he wouldn't have survived. "Thank you for helping me last night," he said as he would to a man and handed her a rifle.

"*De nada.*" She again looked around. "You have any idea where we are?"

He saw nothing familiar. There were hundreds of bays like this in this part of the country. Going north would mean crossing the river and scaling the cliffs on the other side or swimming out to try and get around the outcropping of rock. He'd had enough of the ocean. He figured the nearest town would be to the south. "We'll go that way." He nodded in the direction away from the cliffs.

"The Temple-By-The-Sea that way?"

"There is no such place."

"But that's where Du said he was going."

Eduardo sighed. "MG, he's gone. There is no way they could survive that storm."

"We did."

"Yes, but we had a boat."

"Du said he was going to the Temple-By-The-Sea."

"Yes, just like he was going to Manoa. These places are myths. They don't exist."

Kare had been scavenging on the boat. He climbed off with a coil of rope over his shoulder. "We'd better get going," he said. "They'll be looking for us."

"We're going south," Eduardo said.

"The Temple-By-The-Sea is that way," Kare pointed the opposite way over the river.

"Do you think Du is alive?" MG asked Kare.

"He is alive." Kare walked into the jungle.

MG looked from him to Eduardo. "Let's go with him. We might find the others too."

Eduardo pressed his lips together. "I'm going south."

"We should stick together."

Forget her—if she had so little sense as to follow Kare Kuwaru'wa, there was nothing more he could do for her. He had to find some people to transport the weapons before Rosas' men discovered them. "Safe journey, MG," he said and walked away.

"Come on," she shouted at Eduardo's back. "Du's alive."

Eduardo didn't slow and she didn't follow him. The last he heard of her was a call that they should stick together.

* * *

Kare was secretly pleased the blonde chose to follow him instead of Eduardo. He'd known her for two years, ever since Du had left the cabin by the lake where Kare had raised him, but he knew little about her and she knew nothing about him.

In another time and other circumstances, he might have talked to her about her life, her hopes, or complimented her on her strength and endurance. Because of all she'd seen, she might understand how and why he was who he was.

He'd been there when the Assassins of Fire had burned her house. She probably thought he *was* an Assassin of Fire. The distinction between serving *Quetzal* the Plumed Serpent and *Kinchel* would be difficult to explain. What was the use of trying? He had one purpose—to serve *Quetzal* the Plumed Serpent. *Quetzal* was the reason he'd survived the storm. *Quetzal* gave him his strength, and told him that

Du was still alive. Someday, if he was ever free of this servitude, he would like to show MG that he was a man who had aspirations beyond obedience to a god.

He could lead her to Du and the Temple-By-The-Sea, but first they'd have to cross the river draining from the jungle into the ocean and then climb up the steep face of a cliff on the other side. It was a wonder that she'd not gone with Eduardo the other, easier way.

"There are two ways we can go," he said to her. "We can swim out into the ocean to get around the river or cross it."

MG looked out at the mud, sand, and bogs separating them from the disturbed sea and back at the churning brown waters of the river. It was forty yards to the other side. A thirty-foot tree, roots and all, was carried by on the flood. "Some choice," she said. "What do you think?"

"If we go to the ocean, we'll be exposed."

"Don't we want to be rescued?"

"The same people who attacked us in Florida will be looking for us here. I say let's try the river."

"That's a tough swim. Look what it did to that tree. It's already in the ocean."

"We could swim to that island halfway across, take it in stages."

"I guess," she said and looked back in the direction Eduardo had walked.

He led her up the bank into the jungle. The forest was fitfully trying to find its voice after the hoarse roaring of the past night. Birds chirped tentatively and flew quickly between broken branches stripped of leaves, rediscovering the safe places. Fallen vines lay exposed and dying across muddy puddles.

They reached a point upriver from the island that he figured was the length of the rope he'd salvaged from the boat. He handed MG his rifle and machete, took off his shoes and shirt, and tied one end of the rope around a tree, the other to his waist.

"Are you sure?" she said.

He dove into the water, kicked and pulled with his cupped hands against the current. The river, like a sick intestine spewing out the waste of New Granada, smelled like an open sore–infected and festering. He tried not to think of the runoff of petrochemical plants, oil facilities, the pathogens and human sewage in which he was swimming, keeping his head above water, his mouth tightly closed, breathing through his nose. The force, even stronger than he had anticipated, grudgingly permitted him to swim forward as it pushed him along. He was twenty yards away from the island when he was nearly caught up in the entangling branches of a ficus tree floating by in the flood.

Knowing that he was going to miss his target, he relaxed and concentrated on avoiding other detritus as he was swept past the island. If the rope had not held him, he would have been sucked out to sea by the torrent. Attached to the line, he was pushed by the river up against the bank.

On the third try, he caught hold of an extended root, and pulled himself onto the muddy bank. He untied the rope from his waist, and tied the line above the crook of a sandalwood branch five feet off the ground.

Hanging from the rope by his hands and feet, the current lapping at his back, he pulled himself to MG.

"You're going to have to carry the guns and my boots," he told her.

"What are you going to do?"

"We need the rope to get to the other side. I'll have to swim again."

He tied his laces together and hung the boots around her neck and the two rifles from her shoulders.

She hung from the rope as he had and slowly moved across the water. She was an athletic woman and crossed without getting the rifles wet.

With the machete on his back and rope tied around his waist, he was able to pull himself through the current and reach the island to rejoin MG.

The second half of the crossing was harder than the first. It took four attempts for him to reach the far shore. He almost made it the second time, but a dead, bloated sloth crashed into him, knocking him off course.

Once on the other side, he again tied the rope to a tree. MG carried the rifles and machete over with more confidence than on the first leg of the crossing.

Once they were both across, Kare untied the rope and let it fall into the water. He didn't want to make it easy for anyone to follow them. There would be no retreat now.

The last barrier to the beach was a cliff that descended into a jetty broken by waves crashing against broken rocks. That left them with the option of scaling a cliff as high as a ten-story building. Sharp, cutting edges of obsidian spars protruded from the ancient volcanic flow. They risked being cut up if they took that route to the top.

Kare heard the sound of a helicopter flying in the clouds. He dropped into a crouch to show MG that the copter had not come to save them. No fool, she hid as he did.

The copter, a military Huey, came in over the beach, no doubt hunting for them. He hoped her blonde hair would not make it easier to spot them. Major Bruto would have surely alerted Rosas that they had escaped by boat. Rosas would be scouring the coast for them. The hurricane probably had provided the only cover that could have saved the *Bestante* from being attacked and sunk by Rosas' armed forces as they approached the shore.

The helicopter swung around over the boat and landed gingerly on the packed sand. A squad of soldiers, guns ready, jumped out and examined the wreckage. Had the rain erased enough of their tracks to hide their direction? He motioned for MG to follow him into the denser foliage where they watched two helicopter troop carriers drop out of the clouds.

Squads of soldiers moved along the beach and into the jungle. The pursuit took the troops to the river's edge, where a lieutenant pointed to the rope still tied to the tree on the island. The patrol leader studied the island and the cliff with binoculars. Helicopters buzzed overhead.

The soldier slowly lowered his binoculars and took a long look at where they were hiding. He raised his hand and with a quick order, headed the troops up the riverbank.

"Boom!" The patrol boat shelled the remains of the *Bestante*.

Kare spun toward the beach and saw shells explode in bright flames, blowing apart what remained of the boxes and Eduardo's hopes to salvage the weapons for his revolution. That door was closed. There would be no new guns to fight Rosas.

They remained motionless for an hour, hiding beneath the thick foliage, ravished by biting insects that swarmed in the humid air. The only benefit of the incessant rain was that they were washed clean of the ocean salt.

He'd been born in the jungle but was finding their situation intolerable. He couldn't imagine how MG was standing it. Rainwater streamed from her lowered head. Welts leavened her sunburned skin. They couldn't stay here any longer.

With troops on the beach and patrols in the jungle, he led her along the bottom of the cliff, across soaked soil and slippery plants, to a spot where he thought he could climb to the top.

With the machete hanging from his back, the rifle slung over his shoulder, he scrambled up the hundred-foot igneous wall rising from the river gorge. His feet slipped and blistered inside his boots. His hands were sliced and bleeding from the sharp-edged holds. He watched MG, athletic, moving confidently as she climbed the gnarled black rock face. In her denim shirt and jeans, she might have been a *gringa* backpacker. Rosas would be on the lookout for a blonde. They had to stay out of sight until he could get her a better disguise. Then what?

Today was the winter solstice, the date the La'ku had predicted the Sixth and Final World would begin. Kare had no doubt that rain was falling around the globe and would continue to fall until the Fire spirits had killed Du and regained control of the Jewels of Life. If the rain was still falling, that meant that Du was still alive.

The sound of crumbling rock brought his thoughts back to the present. MG was sliding down the face of the cliff. She caught a thin sapling, and dangled in space. The roots of the small tree started to pull free. With her right arm bloody from a cut above her elbow, she swung upwards, caught hold of an outcropping of rock, regained her footing, and climbed to the top.

Through a break in the trees below, he saw troops moving back toward the beach, while a helicopter flew up the river toward the ocean. They were in plain sight.

Kare pulled MG beneath a tree as the copter flew over their heads. A soldier with a gun was perched in the open bay, surveying the cliff.

MG pressed her body against his. She felt soft and smelled of sweat and the river.

When the copter had passed, they ran along the top of the bluff beneath a cover of tree branches. Bird cries and sudden movements of animals announced their passage. MG had no trouble staying up with him. If anything, he had to keep pace with her. His feet were growing more blistered. He had to have some socks and she needed a hat.

They followed a muddy trail above the beach, slogging through pond-sized puddles to a battered village. Only the walls of some of the houses remained standing. The body of a dead black man hung limply over the branches of a tree. In the middle of the lone street, they walked around a dead horse covered with flies, swollen, lying on its back, feet pointed in the air. They saw no more villagers, dead or alive.

Kare walked through a herd of three goats and a flock of chickens marooned on an island between muddy pools, and went into an abandoned home but found no clothes. The smell of mud and death nauseated him.

They left the village, taking a steep, winding path to the beach. The rain had created another river across the sand, which they were able to cross by a tree someone had laid between the two banks.

The sand blended to mud where the beach met the jungle. Kare kept his rifle ready and stayed close to the tree line, following impressions of many footprints. The path ran a quarter-mile to the broad expanse of a sugar cane field. Most of the thin stalks lay flat, testimony to the power of last night's wind.

To stay off the beach and out of sight, Kare led MG down a road that circled the perimeter of the field.

A fork led to a deserted village where two men were burying bodies. The men frowned as Kare and MG approached. A toothless, tattooed blind woman sat shoeless in the ruins of a house gumming a piece of raw cane.

"I need two hats and some socks," Kare said to the gravediggers.

"*Sí, patrón.*" The villager led them in a stooped posture to his house and brought out two old straw hats and two pairs of soiled socks. "They's all I have *patrón*." The man kept his eyes down and his hand shook as he handed them to Kare.

There was no question about paying him. Kare had nothing to

give him. His money had been lost in the storm.

"What is the name of this village?" Kare asked as he pulled on the socks. MG gingerly handled the straw hat, stained with sweat.

"Chaala," the old woman said in a wavering voice and stared at the rainy sky.

"Isn't this the village that Cramee was from?" MG asked.

Kare wasn't sure.

"Cramee is dead. I know this," the old woman said assuredly.

Kare studied her, and nodded. "He was a brave man, a great sailor. Where has everyone gone?"

The woman pointed north. "To the Temple-By-The-Sea. *Tatya-Masi* has come."

CHAPTER THIRTEEN
THE WALLS OF TIME

Du leaned against the wet belly of the monument, his hands over his lap to cover his nudity. Moss lay unconscious by his feet. Two distinct groups gathered around him. The moderns, their clothes soaked, crowded up the stone stairs carved into the side of the statue to where ancients, their ochre-caked hair impermeable by the rain, guarded Du.

Norane, who'd reconstituted himself with the Waters of Life, easily lifted a heavy mahogany case that he set before Du and Lilia. The wood was carved with fantastic creatures and inlaid with seashells. When Norane lifted the lid, sparkles billowed and covered Lilia. Her wet, black hair, pasted to her skull, was now dry and wrapped around her head with silver thread. A chartreuse gown clung to her. She'd joined Norane and the ancients in an extraphysical plane untouched by the rain.

Norane knelt and offered Du the tube containing the Waters of Life. The same power conducted by the *tunjo* flowed through the Waters. Du raised his eyes to his mother, seeking her interference with the forces demanding his transformation. Du saw only the emerald cold stare of the witch. The jade splits of her pupils were windows into the cave of the Xucha. She'd pledged her life to *Inika* and her heart to Norane. She displayed no sympathy for Du's equivocations.

A drop of the Waters hung on the carved head of the tube, then fell onto Du's lip. His fatigue and hunger disappeared. Whereas the *tunjo* was a portal, the Waters of Life was an elixir that excited his senses and satiated his temporal wants. He stood strong, confident, and uncaring of those on the stairs and beach who gasped at the sight of him.

"Cruuuuuu."

The *Xucha* incantation wafted through the air, encouraging his ascension. Du's eyes settled on the sparkling *tunjo* around Lilia's neck. The Waters of Life was but the scent of the feast of the *tunjo.* The pulsing light within the eyes of the icon pulled him into their depths, leaving him detached from the world in which he struggled to remain.

Norane conducted the liturgy of his dressing with the formality of a sacred investiture. Each piece of the costume was held over his head as Norane turned and called out incantations to which the ancients sang back responses. After a codpiece and gold inlaid breastplate was fastened around Du's trunk, an elaborate cape, iridescent with thousands of feathers, was placed over his shoulders. *Ix Chel,* the rainbow goddess was depicted with serpents in her left hand, and was attended by frog-faced, fanged *chacs*. Norane tied purple, green and red cotton ribbons around Du's arms and thighs, and with a final benediction, crowned him with a heavy headdress. Eagle feathers and gold thread interwoven with turquoise spread in a half-circle from shoulder to shoulder.

Lilia and Norane then steered him to the edge of the statue's lap, as if onto the balcony of a royal palace on coronation day.

The steady rain drenched the ecstatic gathering of over a thousand local villagers and true believers, drawn by the prophecy that *Tatya-Masi* would appear at this spot on the winter solstice. Among the crowd at the foot of the statue were over a hundred ancients–spectral warriors animated by the Waters of Life. Holding spear, bow, or war club, they flew forty feet in the air and looked Du in the eye as they caterwauled their chants, while hosannas of adulation arose from the moderns.

Had the World of Water already begun? What calamities were already befalling modern civilization, and how much was his fault? What could he do to stop it? No, that was crazy. He had no power. He looked out to where only the white froth of waves remained of last night's hurricane. His chest tightened at the thought of MG, Kare, and Eduardo.

Lilia looked up at him and, with her natural empathy exponentially enhanced by the *tunjo,* read his thoughts.

"There are miracles waiting to happen if you but ask for them."

Du stared straight ahead. Yes. Be a god. "Bring MG and Kare to me," he ordered an ancient hovering before him.

The Parquanits chief, clothed in jaguar skin, raised his spear and a band of warrior spirits dissolved into a spiral of steam and flew into the jungle.

Du turned from the tumult and with a single hop landed beside where Moss lay. He knelt and lifted Moss' head. His eyes lolled open. Du held a plastic bottle of water to his lips and fed him pieces of an orange. More elaborate dishes made their way to them: ceviche, pickled fish, cold potato, a cooked grouper, roasted chicken. If hunger and thirst were the lot of mortality, then its gratification was pure joy.

Moss' strength returned until he could sit. His beard was dark on his face. The skin on his forehead and arms was wrinkled by the rain and blistered by the ultraviolet rays of the sun nobody had seen in a week. "I don't know what you are exactly. But what you did last night in the storm was nothing less than heroic."

Du's earnest black eyes cast a wistful gaze at the horizon. "When I was young at the lake, I used to imagine the day you would come and everything would change."

Moss crossed his arms and with a hint of tenderness said, "This was all...I mean... everything, the whole deal was, well...I couldn't come, you know. Yeah, I guess I could've, but what good would it have done? I can't remember what it was like to have free will."

Norane stood over them and looked at Moss as he proclaimed to the crowd, "The Age of Fire has passed with the coming of *Tatya-Masi*. The wheel has turned. Our god is here with us."

"I'd stop all of this if I could," Du said to Moss.

Moss sat more erect. "You stopped the rains once."

Du's large eyes squinted, and the olive skin over his broad forehead constricted beneath the headdress. "I know how to use more of the power than I did two years ago, but no...I can't stop the rains." He hung his great head. "All I can do is stop being me."

"And be their god?"

Du shrugged his shoulders and the cape glimmered around him. "Be dead."

Du and Moss shared the same silent implication of his doom. If Du couldn't save himself, he couldn't save Moss or free *Quetzal*.

As if Norane could take no more of their conversation, he leaned over and lifted Du powerfully by the elbow until Du was standing on tiptoes. Lilia stepped to his other side and held him with an equally powerful grip. "It is time," she said and steered him to a full view of the mob.

* * *

The sight of the god standing in the gray light surrounded by flying apparitions of jungle warriors raised a collective gasp of awe from the 10,000 people who'd gathered around the statue. A high school science teacher stood in the middle of the crowd. He didn't believe that an ancient god had reappeared in the modern age. The teacher was an atheist, a cynic. Through the lens of his education, he'd deduced that the rush to the beach was the product of a massive hysteria incited by the widespread death, ruin and lost property that surrounded him and his neighbors. In a place where so many lives had been destroyed by a killer hurricane, it was no wonder that so many sought an answer in the promise of a new beginning. He observed Du as he would a huckster at a carnival, curious to see how the costumed freak performed his tricks. As the crowd around him poured their devotion upon *Tatya-Masi*, the teacher's sense of separation and individuality was overpowered. He'd come to observe a spectacle and was now stunned at the manifestation of a miracle. The laws of reason and history were no longer in his thoughts as he bowed his head before the god and accepted the impossible, while the doomed pledged their lives to their messiah.

* * *

Norane held up a hand, silencing the congregation. His voice carried over their upturned faces. "*Tatya-Masi* Bringer of the Sixth World of Water has come to us! Behold! He asks that you follow him to battle. *Tatya-Masi* will vanquish the Age of Fire. Do not fear the grave, for it is only a step to heaven for those who serve *Tatya-Masi*! Follow *Tatya-Masi*! Move, move to *Tatya-Masi*!"

"Move, move to *Tatya-Masi*!" the multitude roared back.

Waves of emotion and longing overwhelmed Du.

Yes, he was a god–a god of death and destruction.

He was only able to give Moss a last look of regret as he was hustled to the beach by Norane and Lilia.

The throngs that pressed up the cliff-side steps jostled each other and blocked their path. A woman screamed as she lost her perch and fell twenty feet into the dense gathering below, as the mob backed down the stairs before the advance of ancients who cleared the way for Du.

They reached the bottom of the stairs where five armed moderns blocked Du's progress. Their leader had the appearance of a local crime boss, short and muscular with a threatening expression conveyed with a thin, tight smile. A soiled suit jacket hung open around a flower-printed shirt. "What's this all about?" he demanded.

The crush pressed closer to the confrontation, creating a space that breathed with tension.

"Do you believe?" Norane asked the leader of the bandits.

"I believe you gonna' give us your gold, *indio*."

One of the robbers reached for Lilia's neck and the *tunjo*.

With no more perceptible movement than the shadow of a bird swooping overhead, an ancient blew a dart that struck the throat of the man reaching for the necklace. He fell to his knees and then onto his side as poison paralyzed his lungs. The shocked thugs stared at their fallen comrade whose swollen tongue had pushed through his clenched jaw.

"Believe," Norane said. "Follow *Tatya-Masi*."

The gangsters lowered their guns as Norane led Du past them toward the jungle.

* * *

Down the beach, at the edge of a grove of tilted coconut trees, Kare stopped and examined the clouds.

"It's the statue by the sea. Du's there," MG said, and rushed past him.

"No!" Kare pulled her back.

Two helicopters flew out of the mist up the shoreline.

Kare pivoted and led MG through the palm forest, running from trunk to trunk.

Behind them, the sound of the helicopters grew louder. The

clouds were thin enough over the beach so that the mob could see the approaching instruments of their annihilation. Propellers chattered overhead. With a roar, two helicopters flung grenades and bullets at a rapid rate. A six-barreled cluster rotated on a single axis making a muttering sound. The followers of *Tatya-Masi* tried to escape, but were packed together and exposed. The living trampled the dying. Prayers replaced thoughts of a living god.

Two jets passed over the tops of the trees. Body-slamming explosions followed the sound of the engines. Kare reached for MG's hand. The feathered tops of the trees erupted into flames. Heat and pain wrapped around him. Kare had the sensation of being thrown, then lifted.

Parquanits warriors, straight out of drawings in the library at Omagua, lifted him and ran through the flames, seeming to skim over the mud. His mouth agape, eyes rolling in his head, deaf from the explosions in a zone of silence, his mind processed what was happening. Two other muscular, tattooed ancients in loincloths carried MG between them.

The silence faded and Kare heard the wind rushing by and the panting of those bearing him from the fire and heat. When they reached the deep jungle, the ancient warriors slowed and Kare's feet touched the ground.

* * *

With his hearing and sight heightened by the Waters of Life, Du sensed the jets flying in over the ocean. The spirits of the conquistadors that had been resurrected in the Cave of the *Xucha* by the Cocatamia were alive in the bodies of the pilots, their hatred concentrated on Du like burning beams.

"Shraaaa." The cry of *Kinchel* the Avenger shook the air and froze Du's blood.

In the cockpit of the lead plane, *Quetzal* the Plumed Serpent in the body of the conquistador Gabriel Ayala, led a formation of twelve jets, noses painted like snarling jaguars. Bright flashes and trailing smoke marked the paths of their missiles, launched from beneath the swept-wings straight to Du.

Quetzal had warned him that he was bound to kill him to save the age of Fire. Du had come too close to possessing the four Jewels of Life.

"Ekahau Itzamná!" Du evoked the god of the traveler. Instantly, *Xucha* warriors surrounded them.

The *tunjo* on Lilia's chest pulsed with arcs of white light so bright that it obscured the outer world to the moderns who saw the transformation. They were surrounded by a radiating ball of energy similar to the one that, two years before, had transported them from the Cave of *Xucha* to Manoa. Globes of primary colors trailed behind them, marking their passage from the statue.

Bacaab, a huge creature with exaggerated lips and ears, long, flapping feet and powerful arms, picked up the orb holding Du, Lilia, and Norane. Du heard the missiles and felt their impact, even as he was carried away from their destruction. Smoke and flames rose up from the spot where he'd been standing a moment before. The host of ancients swept after them like bubbles trailing a rock falling through water.

Through the aqua lens of the energy sphere, the outside world wavered and warped with distended boundaries. Du could see both the physical and meta-worlds. The wavering translucent film that surrounded him revealed dimensions and content within trees, stone, air, and water. It was like being able to suddenly see all the parts of an atom. You might know you were looking at water, but now saw the hydrogen, oxygen–each atom at once unique and at the same time part of a greater whole that reacted with unified intelligence.

The sparking body of *Inika* Lordess of Water lay across the top of the jungle and in the reflection of leaves. Long waves flowed from the manes of her four jaguar heads. Flat angles and rods, rings and creatures grew from her necks and foreheads.

Chacs, their frog-faces reflecting in drops and puddles, flew across the sky bringing more rain.

Yum Cimil, the spirit of death, bones and curved spikes along his spine, skin black with decomposition, lay in each piece of dirt and was wholly the jungle floor.

Across the face of the trees, a monstrous red tongue leapt from the mouth of *Yumil Kaxob*, the spirit of the flowers and vines, orchids and ferns. Blades of plants grew from her hair. Her ears were wide and cupping.

Over all, above earth and sky, in one unifying spirit was the *Itzamná* Lord of the Sun. The supreme spirit watched as Water and Fire vied for the next Age of Earth, knowing that he would reign over all no matter who won.

Du sensed the gods watching him. He perceived sensibilities so immense and alien that he could only draw broad impressions. Lilia had told him these deities existed and he could communicate with them. He'd thought she was speaking of a prayerful state, where one would commune with nature, but seeing them and sensing their interest in him was overwhelming.

He felt a hot rush of embarrassment that he couldn't plead his case as *Tatya-Masi*. His mother had told him he must win over the other gods of the Earth. And what if he didn't? Would that mean they'd join with the Lord of Fire and destroy him?

Balaam, the jaguar god, pursued them in long leaps, his eyes slanted and red, teeth sharp and white, his back arched.

Kinchel the Avenger flew over the tops of the trees, his nine human, animal and snake heads probing for a weakness in the defenses of Water. Du had known and battled eight of those Assassins of Fire when they'd detached from *Kinchel* and taken the form of woman, man and beast. Now, in addition to Nurse Assassin, Hunter Assassin and Wolf Assassin, he saw countless other Assassins curled on *Kinchel's* back, ready to spring into action like the teeth of a shark.

"Shraaaa!"

The Assassins' cries pierced the bubble. Flames shot from *Kinchel's* central snake head. *Bacaab* bellowed in anger as *Kinchel's* fire singed his hippopotamus-like body, causing the demi-god to nearly drop them. Du, Lilia, and Norane rocked from side to side as if they were in the *Bestante* during the hurricane.

Ix Chel, the rainbow goddess, flew at *Kinchel*, her long nose like an elephant spraying water. *Chacs* hissed and flowed from a curved staff she carried.

"The *tunjo*. Use the *tunjo!*" Lilia urged Du. "*Tatya-Masi*, find your power. This is the moment for which you were created."

What could he do? He was not sure he could breathe in the spirit world, much less fight. He might as well have been a bug on a battlefield for all the effect he could have on the combat that was being waged around them.

Itzamná Lord of the Sun threw a rolling ball of swirling light from a hand that appeared to be made of stars, driving *Kinchel* away from them with a roar and a crackling protest that sounded like a forest fire.

"*Itzamná* sides with us now," Lilia said. "You must please him or he will permit *Kinchel* to conquer us."

Side with us? Please him? Du wasn't even sure what he'd been witnessing. How could he please or displease what he had difficulty imagining?

"I've told you all I know," Lilia said. "You can see what I cannot. I only sense that the Lord and Lordess are here. Use what I have taught you. Greet them. Do not anger them! You must try!"

What does any god want? What had every deity he'd ever studied asked for? Submission and obedience to his laws.

"*Itzamná* Lord of the Sun," Du prayed. "Accept me as your obedient servant. Show me your will."

Itzamná's face went dark.

Balaam's howl shook the jungle.

Du could not fool the gods. If what they wanted was an apostle, what they saw was a coward, quaking in terror as all went mad around him, in the honest posture of a mortal facing his deity, prostrate in pure terror and remorse.

A ray of sunshine broke through the clouds and the forces of Water retreated.

CHAPTER FOURTEEN
TRANSFORMATION

The ancients released Kare and MG. The sound of the bombing could be heard as dull thumps. Kare sagged to the wet ground. He and MG had lost their guns and the machete.

A Parquanits chief, with the long tube of a blowgun and an animal-skin pouch slung over his shoulder, stood over him. "Vantu, Vantu ó *Tatya-Masi.*" *Move, move to* Tatya-Masi, the warrior said in an ancient version of the same refrain that had been on the lips of every fruit picker and fisherman since the word had spread that *Tatya-Masi* had appeared at the exact spot, at the exact time, as the myths had prophesied.

"Hasa! Hasa!" *Wait, wait,* Kare said in the modern La'ku dialect and held up his hand.

The chief frowned, then tensed as he watched the foliage.

MG's eyes were wide, her mouth agape. "Man, what just happened to us? Check out these dudes. Man, I felt like I was flying. Are we dead?" She pressed her hand against the side of her face.

"My homeland is full of mysteries," was all Kare could think to say. How could he begin to explain the magic of Omagua?

"This is just getting crazier and crazier. Where are we?"

"The Omagua jungle. I was born here."

He stared at the four ancients around them. The tattooed warriors bent their heads, listening and studying the thick wall of trees and vines.

"Who are these dudes?" MG asked.

"They're something from the past, alive but...not."

"Not alive? Brain eaters?" Her voice trailed.

"They're alive here. I don't know if they'd be anywhere else."

MG's eyes narrowed and she looked from ancient to ancient. "They seem kind of alert for zombies."

The chief waved his hand.

"They want us to follow them," Kare said.

The forest seemed to be full of Howler monkeys barking and wailing as loud as sirens. Toucans with beaks the size of bananas glided through the trees. "Look, the sun is coming out." MG pointed at the beams brightening the mist hanging in the interlaced branches.

Had the Lord of Fire won, Kare wondered? Was Du dead?

One of the natives pushed Kare in the back with the edge of an obsidian-tipped club. "Balaam *vanna*," he said. *Balaam is near.*

"Sa!" *Go*, Kare said.

The ancients spread out around them, ten yards on either side, moving through the dense foliage in quick but careful strides, visible only as flickers between the leaves. They appeared to be losing substance, fading into ghosts, as they led them on an animal trail through the dripping forest. Sometimes Kare would blink and an ancient would appear in front of them and correct their direction by motioning with his hand, pushing them through a dense patch of growth to lead them onto another slippery trail.

They were in the preserve his ancestors had lived in for centuries. The hurricane had stripped leaves from branches, engorged some streams and created new ones. Kare could tell the direction they were moving in but couldn't say exactly where they were. Since Rosas had seized Omagua two years ago, the good-looking criminal had sold the rights to lumber, mining, and oil industries to take what he could, but there remained a hundred square miles of wilderness through which they could wander for weeks and not find their way to a road or settlement. They were trespassing in the domain of jungle cats, snakes, reptiles, and insects perfectly adapted to quickly kill them. The chief had spoken of *Balaam* the god of the hunt, who prowled the jungle in the form of a jaguar and served no master. Unarmed, Kare didn't want anything to do with a real or magical jaguar.

Seven hundred years ago, the people who had time-traveled to guide them had foretold the calamity that was now sweeping the world. They had prophesied that when *Tatya-Masi* returned, the La'ku would rise and drive away the Spaniards. Given the massacre Kare had just witnessed on the beach, the living La'ku would not be of much help to fulfill the ancient promise to rule this land again.

A stream coursed through the jungle with a strong current. MG went first, jumping from rock to rock. Reaching the other bank, she held out her strong arm to pull him over. Exhaustion and hunger slowed them until both he and MG were staggering through the rainforest.

"I have to stop," MG said, and sat on a fallen log, her blond hair hanging around her knees. "My feet are starting to bleed." MG reached to take off her shoes.

"You don't want to go barefoot in the jungle," he warned her.

"Why not?"

Before he could tell her about parasites and thorns, the chief materialized from the forest and impatiently motioned with his hand for them to continue.

"Fantula." *Food, we need food*, Kare said, and pantomimed eating. The chief shook his head and pointed at the jungle. "*Balaam.*"

Kare heard the soft thump of something close, but hidden by the foliage.

The Parquanits spun and disappeared into the trees.

"What's going on?" Insects buzzed around MG's red face.

Kare shook his head. "I don't know. Get down." He pulled her off the log.

Through the trees, he saw the cat head of a black jaguar. What could he do without a gun? He trembled and held MG.

The Parquanits swept them up and they were flying again over ferns and fallen trees. The warriors carried them until they left behind the guttural growl of the jaguar.

When the Parquanits released them, MG didn't complain about hunger or sore feet. Both stayed as close to the warriors as they could until finally Kare and MG staggered to a stop. Kare fell to his knees in a clearing. He looked up to see the stone block rise of a pyramid beneath a closed canopy of branches dripping with sucker vines. Across the sandy-colored base, panels in bas-relief displayed hieroglyphics and images of *Tatya-Masi*, Curratta, Dorado, and ancients similar to those who appeared to have come to life and filled the jungle glen.

Kare had stood with his brother and Lilia at the pinnacle of this pyramid as a child. They were a mile from the cliffs of Omagua. Rosas had ordered a road cut into the jungle, a switchback near the vernal waterfall and cave of the *Xucha* where this had all started, where Eduardo and Norane had found the box holding the *tunjo* and Kare the serpent-wrapped cross. A gate in time had opened. Ancients hooted and danced, ablaze with colored feathers, hair caked with mud and ochre. Chanting witch doctors and holy men wore masks depicting beasts and gods. Warriors coated tips of arrows and spears with poison from skewered frogs they held over open flames.

MG regained her breath first and stood at Kare's side. "Are you sure we're not dead? This is the tripiest thing I've ever seen."

"I've never seen anything like it," he agreed and climbed to his feet.

The throngs of natives parted and the hubbub quieted to a murmur that spread from the jungle's edge to the central pyramid.

"It's Du!" MG cried.

Du, Lilia and Norane walked from the jungle through the ancients.

Kare's eyes went first to his brother. He hadn't seen Norane for nineteen years, the day Norane had disrupted Lilia's wedding and Eduardo had shot him atop the falls. A brief movement of Norane's eyes when he passed caused Kare to hope that his brother was happy to see him. But Kare saw nothing in Norane's blank countenance that distinguished him from the other spectral servant of Water.

Lilia appeared as an idealized vision of herself in the manner an artist might portray a saint, surrounded by an aura radiating from the *tunjo* hanging from her neck.

Du, adorned with a feathered crown and cape, hopped with feet together, arms upraised and bent, head thrust forward. The feathered headdress shimmied on his head. The contrast with Du's excitement at seeing them heightened Kare's sense of what separated the living from the metaphysical being populating the glen.

MG broke out in a deep belly laugh. "Look at you!" She hugged him and then stepped back. "What a get up. You look like something from a Mardi Gras parade. Man, I wish I had a camera. I've been to some strange places, but this is off the chart."

A nattering of concern spread among the ancients. They congregated in the shadows of the trees that still dripped with rain, avoiding the rays of sunlight shining through the mist and random openings in the canopy like spotlights.

Had Fire won? Had Du and the forces of Water been defeated? Maybe the rain had stopped all around the world. But Kare knew that as long as Du was alive, he could still gain possession of the four Jewels of Life and free *Quetzal*.

Kare maneuvered for an opportunity to speak to him, but Norane stepped between them, bowed and spoke to Du in La'ku. "*Tatya-Masi*. Your subjects have been brought to you as you commanded. Perhaps you would be more comfortable atop the pyramid."

Du, Lilia and Norane appeared able to move without effort up the crumbling stone steps, but Kare and MG had to sometimes crawl up the steep incline. Norane ushered them inside a stockade built on a balcony that extended wing-like on the side of the pyramid, and closed a door built of tied sticks, imprisoning them.

Through the open roof, Kare could see a flat platform atop the pyramid, where Du stood with Lilia and Norane. Kare understood why Norane didn't want the god to be seen by his followers in the company of a blonde *gringa* and a man he viewed as a soldier of Fire.

They were in the stockade for fifteen minutes, when the door opened and a wooden platter of maize tortillas and tamales were brought to them. After they'd split the small portions, Kare was overtaken by exhaustion. He lay on the wet stone and slept. When he awoke it was night. A riot of insect and animal sounds arose from the dark jungle. MG was asleep, her head resting beside his shoulder. He looked at her for a moment and again admired her strength and endurance. If he'd not been chosen by *Quetzal* at the age of ten, would his heart have trusted enough to love someone like her?

He rose to a sitting position and looked through the wooden poles of the pen. Below, the moderns had found their god again. Hundreds of the devotees milled around the base of the pyramid for a chance to see *Tatya-Masi*.

Kare looked up through the open roof and in the dim light saw Du standing with Lilia and Norane at his side.

Kare stood and called to him. Lilia stepped between Kare's line of vision and spoke to Du.

"What's the matter?" MG asked, getting to her feet.

"I need to ask him something."

"I'd like to ask him some things myself, like how we can get out of here."

"Du!" Kare called again.

"You want him to be the god, don't you?"

Kare put his hands behind his back. "It's something I can't explain, but yes, he must be the god."

"Why?"

"You wouldn't understand."

"Yeah I do. He told me all about it. It's so *you* can be free."

"If you know these things, why do you ask?" He didn't mean his words to sound condescending. He was asking more for sympathy.

"I guess I was hoping something might have changed."

Kare leaned toward her but couldn't find the words. There was rustling outside and he turned away.

The tied sticks that served as a door opened to reveal Norane. He motioned for Kare to come with him. When Kare stepped outside, MG started to follow but Norane closed the barrier in her face.

"What about the woman?" Kare asked.

His brother ignored the question.

"I'll come back for you," Kare said to her.

His brother led him to the opposite wing where a familiar figure bent with age, stood. Naj, their mother's sister, took his hands. "Karesito. You've come home." She looked up at him with clouded eyes. Kare hadn't seen her since she'd gone into the jungle when her son Rosas had created and ruled New Granada.

He kissed her tenderly on the cheek. "Hello, auntie."

She shifted her attention to Norane. "I thank the gods for giving me the life to see the coming of *Tatya-Masi*."

Norane showed no emotion.

She laughed in an insane cackle. "Oh, the gods. These gods have had their fun with us Kuwaru'wa's, haven't they boys? Each told to stand here, do that, serve this god, serve that god." She took Norane's hand so they were all joined in a chain. "And they're not done with us. Oh no, they are not. My boy Makia, he's puffed up like a blowfish, he's so full of his god. And you, Norane, you have one foot in this world and the other in the next, so that the rains you want so badly to cleanse this world doesn't even fall on you. And Kare, my poor Kare, has had an empty life—no love, no woman, no children. All so you can free the feathered serpent *Quetzal*. Oh, we've all been sorely used, haven't we?"

They both stared at her, as they had when they'd been orphans and she'd taken them in. She dropped their hands and looked from one to the other. "Here's what I want to tell you both. Serve your gods. Do what you must, but remember that while you may be their play things, you are of the same blood, and no god may command a man to kill his brother. No god may command a man to harm his own blood. Do you understand?"

Kare nodded and faced Norane. His brother's blank countenance didn't change. His thoughts remained as impenetrable as the night-shrouded jungle. Naj was wrong. Norane had less than a foot in the physical world and existed almost entirely as a figment of the spiritual realm. Still, Kare relished the chance to see him. Their aunt had given him a singular moment he would not waste.

Norane turned away. Kare reached for his shoulder. There was nothing yielding or warm in the body he touched.

Norane hesitated and then climbed to the higher level of the pyramid, where his god was housed.

Naj placed her hand on Kare's chest. "And the gods can never take away the heart of a good man."

But he can take away his freedom, Kare thought as the day's first sunlight fell on the pyramid.

Overhead a formation of twelve jets flew low above the jungle, disturbing the ancient setting with their screaming engines.

At that moment, Du emerged from his royal hut wearing the feathered cape and headdress, heavy with gold ornaments. Lilia, with the *tunjo* around her neck, followed a step behind. Norane fell in at her side.

"*Tatya-Masi!*" Naj shivered and bowed as Du passed.

Kare moved to the other wing and released MG from the stockade to form part of the retinue of Du's regal descent.

The awestruck La'ku parted before Du as he stepped into their midst. Some fell to their knees weeping and covered their eyes and heads.

The mob followed him to the west, as he strode into the jungle. Within an hour they'd reached the base of the Omagua cliffs where Rosas' engineers had cut a road. Du stopped and motioned for Kare to come to him.

Kare stepped around his brother and Lilia. He had an impulse to protect the boy he'd raised. But he must drive *Quetzal's* bargain.

Du understood what he wanted without him having to speak. "I'll do what I can for *Quetzal* if you'll take my mother and MG into the cave. Will you do that for me?"

Kare wanted to say or do something to indicate that he would help Du for some other reason than to serve his master *the Plumed Serpent*. But his expression remained passive and he was silent.

MG pushed past Norane to their side. "What's going on?" she

asked.

Du smiled at her. "Show time."

"But look, the sun's out. You've done it again. You've saved the world."

"You must go with Kare."

She seized him and pulled him into a powerful hug. "You come back to me, OK?"

"You know I will, one way or another."

Du faced Lilia. "It is time, Mother."

Her split-eyes glowed as she stared up at him. "Bring your grandfather back to Manoa to reunite his soul with his body."

"I will, and yours too." Du lifted the necklace from around her neck, joining for the final time with the flow of the *tunjo*. With a crack of thunder and flashes of lightning, rain returned in slanting sheets.

Kare caught Lilia as she dropped lifeless to the ground. He and MG stood aside as Du and Norane led the living and reincarnated La'ku, revolutionaries, mystics, and believers to war.

CHAPTER FIFTEEN
LOSS OF CONTROL

Gabriel Ayala, in whose body *Quetzal* the Plumed Serpent was trapped, banked the A-37 Dragonfly over a formation of tanks and troop carriers lined up for an attack on the jungle, and led the eleven other jets onto the runway adjacent to lake Omagua.

Ayala climbed from the lead plane and removed his helmet. Gray, worn skin hung loosely from his skeletal face highlighted by florid pupils in hollow dark eyes. Even the *Fierros*, Rosas' elite guard, averted their eyes from the gruesome sight of the conquistador pilots.

A *Fierro* drove Ayala in a closed military vehicle to the Morales mansion, past fields planted with the tubular balls of poppies and squat shapes of coca bushes. Here, as in the rest of the world, there was rejoicing because the rain had stopped that morning.

Ayala spider-walked down the wood-paneled foyer, his arms moving ahead as if to break a fall from the jerking movement of his legs. Rosas and *comandante* Ochoa waited for him in the library.

Rosas looked out the window at the sunlight on the gardens of Omagua. He turned to greet Ayala. "Isn't it a beautiful day? And you're still here. I know you will learn to love this world, *Quetzal*. The rains are over. We've won. *Tatya-Masi* has been defeated."

Ayala's bones rattled as he shook with anger. "You pompous ass, we've won nothing. *Itzamná* Lord of the Sun has found *Tatya-Masi* to be false. Look, now he hides. The *chacs* are everywhere…"

It was true: with a crack of thunder, the rains returned. Rosas knew that it would once again be raining everywhere. This had only been a lull in the battle.

Kinchel the Avenger said, "Until we possess the four Jewels of Life we control nothing. Let us concentrate on what we are here to do. We know the Jewels are near. Let us win this battle and we shall find the Jewels."

Rosas snarled at the two spirits, "Then win the battle. Why are you here? The rebels are in the jungle. Destroy them! Destroy them all!"

In the rapid exchange between the gods *Quetzal* said, "I fear you cannot control your host, *Mitnal.*"

"Are you jealous, Prince *Quetzal,* that I possess a body?"

"You have one job, *Mitnal*–find the *tunjo* that you lost," *Quetzal* said.

Kinchel the Avenger raised his hands as if to stop the argument. "The celestial plane is close. Spirits are pouring into the world. When there were only a few of us here, we had a chance of a fair fight. The battlefield grows crowded. I'm fear our private time on this plane is over. We only have a few days to finish what we came for, or we will have little impact on the outcome."

Mitnal the Smoking Mirror said, "He's right. And I'm sure they too will look with great pity on you, *Quetzal.* But, I for one do not wish to be hampered any longer. Let us be done with this adventure and shame ourselves no more."

* * *

After Ochoa and Ayala had left, Rosas sat in the chair and listened to the sound of the rainwater pouring through the gorged drainpipe beside the window flowing onto the flooded lawn and garden. He looked around the room at the display cases of the La'ku artifacts, remembering standing before this desk the day Norane and Eduardo had brought the box with the *tunjo* to Don Carlos Morales.

The old fool was upstairs. Don Carlos hadn't spoken a word since Rosas had seized his house and lands. He'd kept him alive only because of the other elites, the nation's leading families who called themselves *los Trece*. He didn't fear *los Trece*. He was too powerful to worry about *los Trece* or anybody else. And he didn't need Don Carlos alive.

What he needed was the *tunjo*. Nothing compared to how he felt when he held the necklace, the power that flowed through him. The little thieves had stolen all his peace, rest, and comfort. He had to have the *tunjo* back.

"Send in Baudraz," he shouted.

A uniformed man carrying a general's hat against his inner arm hurried into the room.

"*¡Mi general!*" he snapped a salute.

"Are the troops ready?"

"All will be ready in one hour, *mi general.*"

"And the men understand that whoever brings me a gold *tunjo* with emerald eyes will have his every dream answered?"

"*¡Sí, mi general.*"

"There is a woman with the rebels, Lilia Morales. She's to be captured alive and unharmed. Do the men know this?"

"*¡Sí, mi general.*"

"The rest you can slaughter like the pigs they are. Notify me when the troops are ready to begin the operation."

"*¡Sí, mi general!*" Baudraz saluted again, but didn't leave.

"You have something more to say?" Rosas demanded.

Baudraz's left hand twitched. "You asked to be notified when the La'ku girl was captured." A flicker of a smile crossed Baudraz's pockmarked face.

Rosas leaned forward in his chair. "You have her?"

"*Sí, mi General.* We found her in Omagua at her uncle's. The red-eyes were gone. We found the money. We're certain she's the one we've been looking for."

He'd been smart not to tell the ghoul conquistador Ayala, the captain of the red-eyes, who exactly he was looking for. When they didn't find the *tunjo* on her, they'd left her to go fly their jets. But the conquistadors were useful. There wasn't a soul in the country that was not terrified of the red-eyes. If it *was* her, she would join her brother, and together they would tell him what they'd done with the *tunjo*. And if they no longer had the necklace, they would pay with endless pain. "Bring her to me immediately!"

Baudraz opened the door. "Bring her in," he commanded.

Two uniformed soldiers held the *india* by her arms. Her small hands were bound behind her back with plastic handcuffs. She was dressed in a simple white nightgown.

Rosas studied her and his mouth pursed into a pucker. It was *her*. Yes, Anta Raymi, the filth who'd stolen his *tunjo*. What was left of her life would be a symphony of agony conducted by the maestro of pain. But first she would tell him exactly where he could find the *tunjo*.

"Leave her with me. I don't want to be disturbed. Do you understand?"

"Shall I tell you when the operation is ready to commence?"

"The man who disturbs me will join my little friend here in my room of pain. Is that understood?"

Baudraz swayed. "*¡Sí, mi general!*" He saluted, and addressed his men. "Release her. Everybody out."

A soldier used a razor to slice through the plastic band binding the girl's hands behind her back. The La'ku girl rubbed her wrists and looked at him in a way that told him that her spirit had not yet been broken. Good, Rosas thought. The harder they are to break, the more they scream in the end, when it was not only for their hurt they cry but the betrayal of their bodies. Let their eyes harden at the bite of the first lash. Let them stare bravely at the burning embers or the gnawing teeth of rats. Their nerves were his to command, to pull into paths of anguish.

"Would you like to see your brother?"

The young girl eyed him with suspicion.

"He's here, you know. Come, I'll show you."

Rosas lifted the top of a bronze bust of a Morales ancestor sitting on the desk. He pushed a button set inside the cranium and a panel in the library wall opened, revealing a passage that led into his favorite room.

She flinched when he put his hand on her narrow shoulder as he herded her along a hallway paneled with fine wood and hung with paintings and pictures of torture. Indeed, in that darkest corner of art, the Rosas collection was one of the world's finest. Some of the works predated the Greco-Roman era, on through the Medieval epochs–a particularly productive period for horror-art, where man saw himself as the plaything of the devil, and life a cruel hoax to lead him into Satan's grasp. It was Lucifer's companion, fire, that made the most frequent appearances: a bound man tied to a bench, soldiers placing sticks on a roaring pyre that licked the soles of his feet, witches consumed at the stake.

Rosas was particularly proud of a drawing dating to 1620. Spanish conquistadors were depicted chopping off the hands and gouging out the eyes of *indios* who ran holding their blood-spurting, mutilated limbs aloft. In the background, dogs were devouring other natives. Then, there was the flogging section, stoning, drowning, auto-da-fé, where heretics were burned at the stake, and the most prolific theme, religious martyrs: their eyes lifted to heaven as their temporal bodies were being hung, castrated, flogged and dragged behind horses; culminating with the greatest torture subject in history, Christ on the cross.

A proud curator, Rosas led his victim slowly so that she could view each work at leisure. Especially delicious was the girl's reaction when she entered the room and saw her twin brother strapped to an operating table. Rosas stepped on a floor switch, raising him to a forty-five degree angle. The boy was bruised a bit, but still conscious. Rosas was glad he'd kept him in one piece until she was captured. He eagerly anticipated a double, brother/sister, twin torture. This would be magnificent.

Anta ran to the table. "Koya." Her chest heaved with a deep sob.

The boy was more wary than she was. "Why be here?" he asked.

"Come by you, one time," she said.

Rosas wanted to speak to the girl before she was deranged by the torture he had planned for her. "Let us go to where we can be comfortable." He placed his hand on her back and she jumped. The boy cursed at him.

"Don't worry, we'll be back soon," Rosas said as he guided Anta out of the room.

She looked over her shoulder and said, "Come back, one time, Koya."

"Rosas!" the puny terrorist screamed in his girly voice, as if he could do anything about what Rosas had in store for his sister.

They returned through his gallery to the library. He closed the door, poured himself a whiskey, and sat in a red stuffed chair.

"Please, make yourself comfortable. Would you like some cookies, *leche*?"

She looked toward the laboratory, then at him.

"Where is the necklace you stole?" he asked.

"Give I-Koya. Give necklace."

He could barely understand her barrio patois. She was trying to bargain with him. What a family. It was almost a shame to afflict them. But he didn't have much time, and their time was up.

CHAPTER SIXTEEN
THE BATTLE OF OMAGUA

With Norane at his side, Du led the rebels from the jungle up the cliff toward Omagua. Their force was comprised of a thousand moderns armed with hunting rifles and pistols. Five hundred ancients bore poisoned darts, arrows, and obsidian-tipped clubs.

Rain was falling, proof that *Inika* had forgiven him. With the *tunjo* hanging from his neck, Du's powers were greater than ever. At the top of the cliff, he and the rebels came to where two battalions of New Granadian army units were lined up in trucks and tanks awaiting Rosas' order to attack. Du raised his arms over his head and again cast the spell of *Hapikern,* cloaking the rebels in a bubble of invisibility.

They advanced past the main body of Rosas' forces and split into two groups. Norane led the majority of the force to attack from the side, while a hundred ancients followed Du to the main gate.

Ahead, the hacienda sat on a hill above the lake. Du looked across the rain-pocked brown water to where the volcano Susuprina rose into the clouds. Here was Manoa. Here was his final destination. But first he had to find his grandfather, Don Carlos Morales, so he could reunite his body with his soul as he'd promised his mother he would.

The ancients swept ahead of him and attacked the guards. On the jungle side of the estate, Du heard the explosions of Norane's forces blowing holes in the fences, allowing his troops to enter the grounds.

Once the fighting started, Du could no longer hold the spell. Soldiers guarding the hacienda shot at the rebels. Rosas' units on the road dismounted from their trucks, reversed the tanks and joined the battle. The moderns in the rebel force were a poor match for the army's automatic rifles, grenades, and heavy weapons. But the ancients were not so easily killed. They flew in spirals of light, reappearing at the moment their clubs struck or their poison-tipped darts hit their enemies' necks. When a soldier's bullet did strike an ancient, his body would disappear in a burst of water, leaving nothing behind.

The soldiers panicked at the mystical capabilities of their attackers and began shooting indiscriminately in all directions, often hitting their compatriots.

With a protective guard of ancients flying around him, his feathered robe billowing, Du bounded down the quarter-mile driveway to the mansion where his grandfather was being held.

* * *

Rosas' interrogation of Anta was interrupted by a series of explosions from the fence line of the *estancia*. A red light flashed on a console on the desk.

One of Rosas' personal guards entered unsummoned into the library. "General *Supremo*, we are under attack!"

"How many are there?" Rosas demanded.

The soldier peeped over his shoulder like he'd forgotten to count. "We don't know. They keep coming from the *jungla*. We kill fifty, and there are a hundred more."

Rosas hurried to the window looking out the front of the mansion. A brown wave of humanity, a turmoil of painted faces, animal skins, and masks, was moving across the lawn. The jungle had risen and emptied a human cargo onto the lawn.

Mitnal clamored in his thoughts. "*Tatya-Masi* is here. He can be killed. He is still mortal. Kill him and *Inika's* wraiths will be powerless."

Then Rosas saw it, the abomination, the frog creature, done up like an ancient *indio* king, his feathered coif a vision from the past, hopping up the driveway, coming to him.

Despite Rosas fury that the universe and all its celestial forces were conspiring against him, he focused on the green glow on the freak's chest. The *tunjo!* He had his *tunjo*. Perhaps better than anyone else, Rosas realized that there hopping down the driveway of the hacienda was the embodiment of the end of civilization and its sanctimonious worship of science and history. He had to get his *tunjo* back. He was the lone bulwark against the end of progress.

Rosas shouted to his guards. "*¡Rapido!* Fire on that one, *el sapo*, there, the one who looks like a frog!"

The commander of his security detail turned at the sound of breaking wood and glass. "General," he said. "We must move to a more secure location."

"Wait," Rosas ordered. He pulled his gun from the white holster, and aimed at the La'ku girl. It was a shame that he'd have to pass up a proper torture.

The little mouse darted behind a glass case that exploded as Rosas' bullet passed through. A colorfully painted wooden mask of *Tatya-Masi* caught the bullet and appeared to turn in the air and look at him. The girl was still moving with an uncanny instinct, darting in the right direction, causing him to miss three more shots that tore up his office.

By now the mob had reached the house. Rosas couldn't see the frog monster in the swirling, fighting mass outside. He wouldn't waste any more time on the *tunjo* thief. He had more important prey to hunt. "Kill the girl," he ordered over his shoulder as he hurried to the helicopters.

His security detail ran with him through the battle with their guns drawn.

Rosas reached one of the escort helicopters and panting from his intense effort, climbed into its open side. "Take off!" he ordered the lone pilot.

Rosas' elite troops were falling before the onslaught of spirits and peasants. The security chief tried to scramble in after Rosas.

"Stay and fight! *¡Traidores!* Kill the frog!" Rosas raged and pulled the trigger, destroying the man's face.

The helicopter vibrated as it lifted. "Where are the jets?" Rosas shouted at the pilot.

"They've flown back to the base at Quesada," the terrified young man reported. His name was Fonso Gutierrez, a member of *los Trece*.

Not that he cared what the population he ruled thought of him—as long as they feared him—the one aspect of his public image that Rosas took a personal interest was his titles. He oversaw the list of titles and superlatives that preceded his name in all public references. At this moment of supreme challenge, Rosas took comfort and drew confidence from these grandiose appellations.

"Give me the radio." The Decisive Leader put on a headset and shouted into the microphone. "This is Supreme Commander Rosas. *¡Condición roja! ¡Roja!* I repeat, *¡Condición roja!* Patch me through to the General of the Air Force!"

There was a pause. "Sir, he is indisposed," came the reply.

"The traitor. Arrest him!"

A voice interrupted the transmission. "This is Ayala with the jets."

"Ayala. He's here. *Tatya-Masi* is here in the hacienda Morales. Bring the jets. Arm them with the big *bombas*. I want the village of Omagua and the jungle for five miles in every direction leveled, burned, destroyed. Contact me when you're approaching. I will direct the attack myself."

* * *

After Rosas ran from the room, Anta was still in trouble. A soldier raised his rifle to shoot her. She ducked behind the desk, tripped over an electric cord, scrambled to her feet, and saw the soldier aiming at her. He suddenly slumped with a dart protruding from his neck. Two wild-looking *jungla indios* streaked past the broken window. Three soldiers in the room opened fire at them. One soldier angled to shoot her, but then fled with the others, leaving her alone.

She rushed to the head of a man on the desk that Rosas had used to open the wall, and lifted the metal hair. The wall opened just like it had for Rosas.

She ran along the passageway to Koya. He was still strapped to the leaned-up table, looking like a *gamín* who'd fallen off a bus and been run over by a truck. His eyes were like plums in the market, fat and purple.

"Move-I, move-I," Koya gasped.

The sound of a big explosion rocked the house. "Move-I, *boba*," Koya's voice was stronger this time.

She smiled, knowing he wasn't going to die. Thick metal buckles held the leather straps that she had trouble pulling free.

"Fast, fast," Koya urged.

When she unfastened the belt around his chest, he fell forward, cursing both her and Rosas. He pushed her helping hands away as he yanked at the straps that held his feet. Bloody scabs were where his fingernails used to be. Anta knelt to hug him, not caring that he was calling her names. "Koya, lost dollars and necklace." Better to get the bad news over with fast.

He pulled himself up by holding onto the table. "Rosas? Where Rosas?"

"Be here."

The house shook from another explosion. "There be one-big fight. *Tatya-Masi . . .*"

Koya staggered toward a door on the other side of the pain room. "Show-I Rosas. Kill-I Rosas."

She followed him outside to the lawn where country La'ku were running with sharp digging sticks to fight the *Fierros*. People from the fields lay wounded and dead with blood oozing from bullet holes.

A dead *Fierro* lay on a gravel path, a machete in his neck. Three dead La'ku lay around him. In the daylight, Anta could see more of what had been done to Koya. His face was swollen and blue. He wore only a gown, like a *mujer*. He lifted a pistol from the dead *Fierro's* hand and a fat wallet from his pocket. "Turn," he commanded Anta.

She looked away and waited.

When she faced back, he'd put on the *Fierro's* shirt and was hobbling along the garden path to the fight. The shirt was too big for him and was also like a dress with his skinny legs sticking out like a girl. He was so weak that she could easily keep up with him and had to resist taking his hand to help him like he'd become one of the little ones, the ones that Rosas had killed. She understood why he wanted to find Rosas. Koya had never lost a fight. Even if a gang had gotten him on the ground, or a bigger boy or man had beaten him, someday when they weren't waiting, Koya would repay them. He'd told her once that if anybody ever thought they could hurt you and not get hurt back twice, your hurt would never stop. Everyone in the barrio knew that Koya was dangerous, and that he would protect his family . . . but this was different. Rosas had tanks and soldiers with many guns.

A roaring sound came from the sky. The ground shook her off her feet. Koya was lying beside a stone bench. Concussions and fires erupted around the hacienda. Koya stood and, shaking his head, ran from the fighting toward the village. Anta followed him to an open

Fierros car with a big gun mounted in the rear. Koya slipped behind the wheel and Anta climbed in just as another explosion almost flipped the car.

Koya held the steering wheel and stood up to push his foot on the gas. Anta didn't know he could drive, but was not surprised. Koya could do anything.

They swerved and bounced up the hill. The ground beneath the car shook. Where they'd been a minute before was only smoke and flames. The hacienda Morales was burning.

* * *

Rosas ordered the helicopter to hover above the estate. He hauled himself to the machine gun in the open side bay and surveyed the scene below. What force on Earth could pull idiot farmers from their mud huts, spear throwers from the jungle, and lead them into battle? What, except a god? Then he spotted it, the man-frog surrounded by tattooed savages.

What was happening? The voice of *Mitnal* the Smoking Mirror was shouting inside Rosas' head, a sound like the chatter of the blades beating over the helicopter.

"Stop him! He's heading for Manoa."

What did *Mitnal* think he was trying to do? A fury mounted in him, never stopping until it completely distorted what was left of his rationality. What more could he do when *los Trece*, the elite and his own soldiers were conspiring against him. *Mitnal,* the other gods, everybody was against him.

As the helicopter swooped toward Du, Rosas wildly spewed bullets from the machine gun. His face contorted with insanity. He had only one thought: to kill *Tatya-Masi*, and regain the *tunjo*.

Rosas leaned over the gun, his face a maniacal leer of rage as the tracer bullets led to where the atrocity was standing. He had him.

CHAPTER SEVENTEEN
MANOA

On the shore of *lago Itza Uo*, Du stood with his grandfather's body across his arms. Norane and the honor guard of ancients were arrayed around them. In the midst of the battle, Du paused and relished his last mortal moments, the patterns of falling rain on the still surface of the lake and the gentle lapping of small waves.

Behind him, Rosas' army was now fully engaged. Helicopters and jets joined the battle. Mortars exploded around Du. He could no longer hide himself from the seeking eyes of the Lord of Fire. A copter hovered over him.

"Shraaaaa." The sound of *Kinchel* the Avenger rose above the tumult of the battle. The eight Assassins of Fire were rushing toward him. *Comandante* Ochoa drove an Abrams M-1 tank down the hill to the lake. "Boom!"

Fire vented from the barrel of the tank gun as it hurled a shell at him.

"Gurrrrurrll."

Mitnal the Smoking Mirror, in the body of Rosas, was above in a helicopter.

Bullets kicked dirt in a trail and the tank shell flew toward Du's back. He leaped as the helicopter bullets and tank round shot past him.

It was good to be in a lake again. He admired the sweep of a school of bass fry through the waving underwater leaves, the quiet, and sense of being bathed in peace.

Norane and his *Xucha* guards transformed into a membrane of dancing light that surrounded him, keeping him and his costume dry.

Quetzal's jet flew overhead and released a bomb. The explosion ruptured the underwater calm. The concussion vibrated the sphere but could not pierce the protective energy of the ancients. The bubble carried him through the blades of aquatic plants on the bottom into the opening of the underground passage that emerged in the grotto where Norane had found the box containing the *tunjo*.

The bubble rose up and deposited Du on the shore of the subterranean pool. Du climbed out into a light that flared in the darkness.

"Cruuuuuu."

The voices of the witches echoed through the cavern where the white and yellow teeth of stalactites hung and stalagmites rose from the cave floor.

Curratta the Supreme Witch of the *Xucha* floated from the center of the pulsing light. A large misshapen skull, long and flat, rested on a raised, crippled shoulder. Tufts of white hair sprouted from her wrinkled scalp. Her enormous mouth was ridged with long white fish lips. Large eyes, held in folds of skin, bored directly into his soul.

"*Tatya-Masi* brings forth the Sixth and Final World of Water," Curratta proclaimed.

His vestigial doubts were dispersed by the certainty of his fate. Whatever lingering hope he might escape was lost as the coterie of twelve *Xucha* witches, gray, aged flesh stretched tightly over bony skeletons, joined with the warriors to surround him in a globe of energy that carried him through the black cave, sweeping over canyons, and across the rock bridge into Manoa.

They entered the buried city on a path of polished stone that ran through a brightly lit hallway. Jewels and seams of gold were embedded in marble columns. Large, intricately woven tapestries depicted images of *Tatya-Masi* battling Fire spirits.

His coming had been planned and foreseen. His arrival was the fulfillment of centuries of anticipation. He was leaving this life. Yet, his sacrifice could still give life to his mother and grandfather.

Even as he hurtled toward his ascension, *Quetzal* the Plumed Serpent remained with him as he'd been since his creation.

"Free me, Du," the Lord of Fire whispered.

Du blinked and felt the embarrassment of his mortal self, the remaining hope that he could do anything but submit to the will of *Inika* Lordess of Water.

The golden doors into Manoa opened. The chants of the witches rose into a full chorus of exaltation.

"Cruuuuaaaaaaaa…

Cruuuuaaaaaaaa…"

Rainbow-colored, vibrating novas of lives waiting to be reborn swarmed to Du, creating a pathway of shimmering celestial light as he entered the fabled city.

The *Xucha,* Norane and the ancients reconstituted into their corporeal selves and deposited him at the entrance to Manoa.

Don Carlos was waiting for him at the end of a passageway lined with the murals of memory—a multi-dimensional, constantly changing window into the recollection of events past. His grandfather wore a well-cut sports jacket open on a fine linen shirt over his barrel chest. He appeared little changed, perhaps younger than Du remembered. There was no time for a reunion, barely a smile, as the spirit of Don Carlos reunited with the body Du carried.

He set his grandfather on his feet. Don Carlos faced him.

"My mother?" Du asked.

"Her spirit is strong but her body weak. You must hurry."

Hurry to where *the Plumed Serpent* had always wanted him to go, into the consciousness where he would have the power to reunite a soul with its body. Du looked lovingly into the gray eyes of his regenerated grandfather.

"And you too must go, Grandfather. Take him," he ordered his guard of ancients. Two of the warriors stepped to either side of Don Carlos.

His grandfather shook his head and opened his mouth to protest, but then nodded in agreement. "This is no place for the living. Good-bye, my son. I know we will meet again in another place."

Their quick hug reminded Du of why he'd fought so hard to live as a man. What in the realm where he was going could replace the touch of someone you love?

Before him the hidden city was bathed in aquamarine light. In the center was the *Bratay*, a carving of the frog god wrought from solid jade laced with gold. A long red tongue extended from the mouth of the statue to the edge of the *Longo*, the sacred mushroom. The *Longo* had grown since he'd been there two years before. Surrounded in a semi-circle by the sarcophagi of the twelve *Xucha* witches, its kaleidoscope dome was pregnant with agitated colored balls of light.

The city, also restored by the Waters of Life, was in its final moments of rejuvenation. Large-leafed plants from a prehistoric jungle, a previous world of Water, grew in profusion. Reborn souls crowded balconies of the aqua-blue painted structures built into the cliff. On the other side of the *Longo*, in a large plaza, the warrior-king Dorado stood at the head of an army of ancients, dressed for battle, their faces painted and weapons glinting in the preternatural light.

Norane escorted Du to a gold mosaic of the sun sinking into a stormy sea. Du stared up at the *Bratay*. In the stone hand of the frog god was the *Cocatamia*, the Staff of Life, in which the other two Jewels of Life were embedded in the frog head of the wand. The rejuvenating Waters of Life cascaded from the scepter in a fountain of bursting bubbles of rainbow flares. A chorus of reincarnation rose from the souls in the Water.

The four Jewels of Life beamed between the eyes of the *tunjo* hanging from his chest and the *Cocatamia*. Charges arced between the four channels of creation. The protruding, domed eyes of the *tunjo* and *Cocatamia* were poles through which celestial consciousness pulsed into Du. He convulsed as the fundamental essence of life rushed through him with the pure force of conception.

He saw his mother's ghost standing before him, a shimmering presence in an airy gown. Lilia's soul flowed into the *tunjo* at Du's silent command.

The ground shook with a strong earthquake. Steam and magma fumes rose from fissures in the floor. The clouds that always covered Susuprina were sucked into a vacuum as the full forces of the cosmos streamed into the spirit beam pouring into the dome, merging into the currents transmitted by the Jewels of Life. A rain of *chacs*, Water spirits, cascaded over the mushroom's massive domed head, where colors wildly danced in bright spheres within the milky skin of the immense purple and yellow spotted fungus.

Du took off the *tunjo* and handed the necklace to Norane.

The warrior was as eager to join the battle as he was to restore Lilia's life. He stood with his arms at his side awaiting permission to return to the physical plane.

Curratta nodded and Norane placed the *tunjo* over his head. He and his company of ancients dissolved to their plasmatic forms and swept from the grotto leading King Dorado and his army to battle, and leaving Du alone with the *Xucha* for the rite of his transmutation.

Two lines of witches stood on either side of the statue. Tears marked their wrinkled faces. Quivering, skeletal hands reached, unable to resist the urge to touch him.

"Cheeee. . .

Cruuuu . . .

Cuuuurraaaatttaaaa . . ."

Their wail of anticipation of the moment of change from the World of Fire to a World of Water caused a shiver to pass up Du's spine.

The flow of Water spirits through the ceiling dispersed into a rain that spread across Manoa. Broadleaf plants unfolded and Water dripped from flowers unseen in this world for sixty-five million years.

The witches escorted Du to a moss-covered mound midway on the red tongue that extended from the statue of *Tatya-Masi*.

Curratta leaned toward him. Her face was lined like a cracked desert floor; her eyes set so deep in her head that they appeared as dark holes. Her hands and limbs were bones covered with skin stretched so tightly it appeared to deflect the rain. Then, seemingly in an instant, she was at the curled tip of the tongue.

Pea-colored water roiled in the statue's mouth.

Four *Xucha* stood in a square around him. Ra, the massive frog, snapped his tongue and rolled his eyes from his perch in the arms of an attending *Xucha*. A boa curled and hissed around the narrow shoulders of a witch. An eagle flapped on the skeletal arm of a *Xucha* as a leashed jaguar howled.

Curratta's voice rose above the chants, the moans of the reborn, and the animal cries. "This is the sacred vessel of insemination, the Ra, the force by which the Earthly Mother was impregnated when Warrior-Brother brought the true love of his true heart to Manoa."

The beast blinked, but never took its stare off of him. The giant frog's tongue cracked in the air like a whip. Du closed his eyes. Dread caused his chest to clench around his fluttering heart.

"Cheeeeee…

Cruuu."

The singing of the *Xucha* caused a vibration to run up his spine. The moldy scent of the *Longo*, the sacred mushroom, filled his nose.

He opened his eyes. Curratta floated along the tongue of the statue. Fountains erupted on either side of her. The ancient priestess stepped off the upturned tip of the curled red ramp, and hovered in the midst of the fountain of Water. Her withered, frog-like face trembled. Lime-colored light spun in her oversized pupils. Her large hooded eyes covered by drooping, wrinkled eyebrows appeared to roll in their huge sockets.

As Du marked the last moments of his life as a mortal, he contemplated the idea that when you died, your archetypical dreams arose in a bizarre dramatization, which was destroyed as your life ended–an elaborate psychological version of what had been described by many who came close to dying as their life passing before their eyes.

In a last reflexive longing, his thoughts went back to the Lake of the Frogs, to Edgar and Kare before Du had known that he was *Tatya-Masi*. He'd done his best to be a good man and wondered if he would be able to find his tutor in the celestial realm.

Curratta's cackle was a terrifying mockery of a laugh; slow rolling building into a shriek. The fountains formed a Water support that carried her forty feet into the air over the head of the statue. A ball of translucent energy descended and expanded into an aura of crystalline sparks that snapped around her. Each bubble had a voice that combined into a chorus of exaltation. Drums pounded faster. The earth trembled.

The other witches added their voices to the increasingly feverish pitch. Water gushed from the frog-statue's eyes. With a gold knife raised over her head, Curratta leaped from the height of the fountain into the center of the mushroom. She sank into the spongy plant, cut out its heart, and delivered a cantaloupe-size piece of the fungus to Du on a golden plate.

Du recalled his first inadvertent eating of psilocybin mushrooms at the house by the lake with MG. Was he any better prepared now for the chemical agents to open his senses than he'd been then? The forest mushrooms he'd eaten possessed a fraction of the power of what lay before him, and the small opening of his perceptions that had occurred two years before in California were nothing like what lay ahead. He needed this power to rejoin his mother's body with her soul and to stop the rains. This was not a death, but a birth. He was being used to call something forth, to release a power on the Earth he did not know if he would be able to control. He was a lever tilted under the wheel of history.

The sight of the eerie fungus made him feel famished. He reached for the mushroom heart. The core pulsated green and was surrounded by swirling orbs of purple, red, and yellow light, whose speed and intensity increased as he lifted the mushroom meat to his mouth. The colors were now spinning so fast they blurred. His jaws closed over the first tentative bite. The cave was rocked by another, more violent temblor. He chewed quickly on his last meal, his eyes on the tottering statue. The mushroom heart tasted delicious, of butter and garlic, better than anything he had ever eaten. He quickly devoured the offering and would have happily accepted an additional helping, but none was offered.

The old witches continued to dance and sing. Du kept his eyes on Curratta, as if she was the hourglass that marked his demise. She lay beside Du on the moss mound. Her voice became softer. The skin fell from her hands, then from her arms. She mumbled quietly until she was no more than a skeleton. Her jaws snapped shut one final time, and then she was a pile of dust. A stream flowed from the statue's mouth, and washed her away.

There was a moment's silence before Du's attention was seized by a tremendous shock that shattered the roof of the cave. Everything was happening in slow motion. The flow of Water became a rainbow that radiated with every hue in the spectrum. Du wanted desperately to flee but was rooted to the mound. He opened his mouth; nothing came out.

The statue exploded. There was a grunt as one of *Xucha* was struck by falling debris. Nobody pleaded for help. The cave dwellers had known what was going to happen. Du saw a vast section of the roof falling directly toward him.

"CROAR! CRRRRRROOOOOOOOOOOOOAAAAARRRRRR!" He bellowed.

Finally released from his paralysis, his legs contracted beneath him and shot him upwards. He could not alter his trajectory and was on a collision course with the falling rock. He clenched, held up his hand to soften the impact and passed through the stone into a single stream of Water that held him suspended in its center, and shielded him from the falling stone.

The circle of light around him spun, emitting flares the same colors as the mushroom–purple, yellow–that floated until they disappeared into a vast well.

Du was beyond terror. All he could do was croak, "CROAR! CROAR! CROAR! CROAR!"

He was rocketing upwards. Rings of color sped by him. Ahead was a still pond. He could land there. He focused on the Water, but then heard the low dyspeptic gurgle of *Mitnal* the Smoking Mirror and knew it was a false refuge. As he rocketed past, the hydra-like *Kinchel* the Avenger chased after him, shooting balls of fire at him from his many heads.

A stone door surrounded by flames lay directly in his path. He could not alter his course or lessen his speed. Here was the last barrier, the Lord of Fire's final desperate attempt to prevent him from obtaining his godhead. If he hit this wall, he would be destroyed. Du held up his hands. "Croar!" he roared at the moment of the unavoidable impact, and slammed into the wall of Fire.

Heat incinerated his skin, tormenting every nerve. He'd failed. His tongue boiled in his mouth. How could he save his mother now? He was not a god. He was a tormented child, crying in pain. If he had never come to Manoa, he could have hidden on the Earth as he had for two years.

He thought of the Lake of the Frogs, of sitting beneath the surface by Silver Creek in the dawn, watching the trout school. The trout bent their bodies.

He became a trout looking at himself in the water. The blistering heat was gone. He was in the lake. I am here, he thought. I am everywhere and nowhere.

Then he was the lake, stirred by tide and wind, water and air. His breath was the first and the last. His old and new body cast a shadow of light and dark. He was alone, but life was a circle of which he could sense every point.

Then he was on the Circle of Life, seeing where he'd been. He was his mother, *Quetzal*, Norane, Moss, and MG. He was love, hate, fear, and desire. He knew everything and nothing. Time was a moment that was gone and that never ended. He was Fire and Water.

He was a man. He was a god.

CHAPTER EIGHTEEN
MITNAL LOSES CONTROL OF ROSAS

Rosas ordered helicopter pilot Gutierrez to fly low. His paranoia had convinced him Gutierrez was an agent of *los Trece*. He stood over the pilot's shoulder with his pistol trained on the pilot's head. "Who is the mastermind?" he demanded. "Is it Robelo?"

"Excellency, I am loyal." The young man sat rigid. His hand trembled on the cyclic stick between his legs causing the nose of the copter to dip.

"You lie!" Rosas bayed and rapped the gun barrel against the side of Gutierrez's head, knocking the pilot out. When his hand fell from the throttle, the rotor lost power and the helicopter's nose pointed down at a steep angle.

Indian workers, protected from the rain by garbage bags and soggy hats, lifted their heads to see a helicopter diving toward them.

"¡*Traición*! Fly, you idiot." Rosas pushed the unconscious man's back. The angle of descent lessened as the force of the passing air caused the overhead propeller to autorotate. The copter landed upright with a jolt in the field.

* * *

The American owner of the marijuana plantation, Bobby "Bullguts" Boone's thick Teddy Roosevelt mustache bristled across his ruddy, fat face. He drove his truck to where his Indian workers had surrounded a helicopter that had landed in his field. The braver ones were looking inside the bay when he slid to a stop beside them.

A man in a military uniform staggered from the copter and collapsed to his knees.

"Why did you land that thing in my field?" Bullguts shouted in English, and jumped out. "All right, you boogies," he waved his Australian bush hat at the workers. "Show's over. Get back to work!" He bellowed at the foreman, "Jaime! Get their brown selves back to work!"

The pilot stepped from the helicopter, a bloody wound on the side of his head. "Help him! This is General Hernando Rosas, Supreme Commander of *Nueva* Granada!" he said.

Bullguts caught the name, but did not understand Spanish. "What did he say?" he asked Jaime.

The overseer responded in an awestruck voice. "That is General Rosas."

"Rosas? Here?" Bullguts studied the injured man on the ground. He'd met Rosas at a reception for foreign investors, but didn't recognize the General bent over on his knees.

The General snarled in accented English, his features pinched with hate, "Help me up, you fool!"

Bullguts didn't like the interloper's tone of voice, but decided to be diplomatic. "Yeah, yeah, sure, happy to have you, Mr. President." He brought Rosas to his feet with a powerful lift. "Welcome, Mr. President. Glad to have you drop in. Sorry, you had trouble with your copter. I been meaning to show you our operation. As I told you at the party, Thunderweed is thinking of expanding here. We're coming up with a hybrid that'll grow fine in the rain."

"Help me," Rosas said. "Take me away from here."

"Sure, sure. Glad to. How we gonna get that copter out of here?"

"I'll take care of it."

"What we going to do with him?" Bullguts pointed at the pilot. "He looks hurt."

"He comes with me," Rosas said.

Bullguts steered Rosas to the truck and sat him in the passenger seat. The pilot Gutierrez climbed in the truck bed.

"Don't worry, Mr. President," Bullguts said. "The boogies won't mess with your copter. You sure got a beautiful country, Mr. President, like America used to be before the liberal-global warming commies took over. Like I told you at the party–very charming evening, I so enjoyed meeting your lovely wife and son–your country is the way of the future, people not afraid to work." When Rosas didn't reply, Bullguts turned to see he'd fainted.

The General was still unconscious when they arrived at the portico of Bullguts' mansion, reminiscent of the design of antebellum plantation homes in the United States. Bullguts took a satellite phone from the dashboard and put it into a holster on his belt. He walked around the truck, bent over, and reached down to lift the dictator.

* * *

In his dream state, Rosas was secure in his palace with *Mitnal* the Smoking Mirror inside him, providing strength and counsel. His people loved him and the university students held competitions to bestow more colorful and honorable titles on him.

He awoke to see large hands reaching for his neck, and believing he was being attacked, cursed and hit Bullguts in the face with his fist.

The big Texan reeled, and then came back at him, lifted Rosas by his uniform and violently shook him. "Don't try and sneak punch me, you little beaner. I don't care if you're the President of the United States! I'll punch your greasy little head off!"

Rosas peered into Bullguts' florid face and remembered where he was and who he was. He didn't have any guards with him, just the damn traitor pilot who'd tried to kill him. *Mitnal* was screaming in his mind, telling him to obey his commands. Even the gods were after him. He couldn't rely on anyone but himself. He had to use his own guile and strength to survive. *Mitnal* might have been a Fire spirit, but it was the flames of Rosas' rage that burned the god from his soul. He didn't need a god. He didn't need anyone. He was Hernando Rosas, the beloved Leader of *Nueva* Granada, the Principate of Peace.

"Yes, please excuse me, I was having a nightmare," he said, and Bullguts released him.

"Guess I ought to apologize myself," Bullguts said. "Not a very neighborly way to behave. I beg your pardon. We been having a problem all of a sudden with the workers. About a hundred of 'em up and took off on me. Can't figure it out."

Rosas smiled, constricting his eyes. He knew where they'd gone—to join *Tatya-Masi*, to rebel against him. He was alone in a nation of traitors. "It is quite all right," the Ultimate Benefactor reassured Bullguts, all the while thinking of the pain he'd inflict on the big ox once he had him strung up and gored.

"Wait out here," the Master of Sympathy instructed Gutierrez.

The pilot snapped a salute to his bloody forehead.

The Magnificent Paragon of Pulchritude followed Bullguts into a marble-laid foyer, tracking muddy boot prints on the polished stone. A small *india* was seated at a table in an adjoining room with three *indios* brats. She saw *El Potentado* and lowered her head.

"That's my brown family. Don't mind them," Bullguts said.

She'd been listening to a radio that immediately drew Rosas' interest.

An announcer spoke excitedly in Spanish. "General Rosas, after declaring the country under attack, has disappeared. General Robelo has declared a national emergency and placed himself in command until General Rosas can be found. Wait! This late word . . . General Robelo will now address the nation!"

Bullguts walked into the room and carelessly switched off the set.

Rosas followed him and reached for the radio, frantically twisting dials and flipping levers, ordering Bullguts to turn the program on.

"Sure, sure there, little partner, no point in getting yourself all riled up," Bullguts said, and tuned the radio to the program. "You sure are a crazy son of a bitch," he muttered.

A sonorous voice came on, speaking in a deep baritone.

Rosas, rolling the "r" and holding the "e," hissed, "Rrrobeeeelo."

"Our beloved leader, whose fatherly hand birthed and guided our nation to well-being and respect among the family of nations, is missing. Oh, papa!" he began to weep. "Forgive me, that is what I always called him. He was like a father to me."

"What *caca*!" Rosas slurred.

Robelo continued, "Our beloved nation was under attack by a band of subversives flown into our country by the enemies of progress–powers who would make us their slaves. The Great Leader, the Indomitable Warrior, was the first one to the battle. How like him, personally directing the counterattack of our valiant air force and flushing out the traitorous General of the Air Force Ungo, who, I am disappointed to say, fled the country before he could be captured, tried, and shot."

"I'll shoot you, you bastard!" Rosas growled.

"The report of Supreme Commander Rosas' bravery in the battle of Omagua makes us all proud, and will inspire us to take up our weapons, give us the certainty and confidence that no force on Earth can attack the people of *Nueva* Granada, and expect to succeed and escape with their lives. I am proud to report that every one of the invaders was killed. For this we can thank none other than *Ciudadano Número Uno*, Supreme Commander General Hernando Rosas!"

The Great Father paced the room, fully recovered from the helicopter crash. "Get to the point," he said. "Did you ever hear anybody talk so much?" he asked Bullguts.

"Sorry, Mr. President. I don't comprehenday your lingo." Bullguts handed a glass of bourbon to Rosas.

The voice on the radio grew sad again, "We now have the difficult and sorrowful task of mourning the heroes of our nation, who have made the supreme sacrifice that we may live in peace and strength. The valiant victims of this vicious sneak attack will be mourned, but not forgotten. Their names will forever be written in the hearts and minds of those who love *Nueva* Granada. At the top of that list of heroes and martyrs, it is my most grievous duty to report, may well be the name of Hernando Rosas, the Father of Fame, Protector of Dignity, Bravest of the Brave. Oh, how we will miss you if this sad news is true!" With this, Robelo began to blubber loudly.

Rosas' rage continued to grow. When Cortez had conquered the Aztecs, it had been because inferior tribes had assisted the conquistadors. Rosas now saw that the opportunistic weaklings around him were behind the *indios* attack.

Robelo announced. "Tomorrow night, all who love our country will gather in the Cathedral of the Apostles to pray for the rescue of *El Presidente* Hernando Rosas and give thanks to our benevolent Lord for our great victory and the preservation of *Nueva* Granada."

The Brotherly Leader paced the room.

The woman and children eyeballed him from the table.

"I will kill them all, the traitors! Do they think that I cannot see through their ploy? They are so stupid! That is why I picked them. Robelo was nothing when I made him General. A lieutenant, from a good family, but very stupid…hmm, perhaps not so stupid, allying himself with *indios*. Ambition has a way of making a toad a clever cat. It is obvious to me now that this *indios* revolution can never succeed unless they have help from traitors like Robelo."

On the radio, Robelo sobbed and regained enough composure to continue. "Before we give in completely to our grief, let me be the bearer of some hope . . . There is a chance that Supreme Commander Rosas, Heart of our Hearts, managed to escape. He might well be hurt or confused. Army units are now rushing to the scene of the battle to search for his remains. The Honor of Our Lives was last seen in a helicopter. He could be anywhere. All citizens are urged to be vigilant in our search for the Magnificent Leader. Until the time that the Lord, in His infinite wisdom, delivers our Beloved Inspiration back into our hands, it is my duty–though I dread the awesome responsibility and know that I can never replace the Ultimate Benefactor and will always stand in the shadow of he who went before me–to accede to the demands of my countrymen and step forward in this hour of our nation's need and assume the reins of leadership. I will be a fair leader who knows the ways of . . ."

Rosas could stand no more and threw the radio on the floor, cutting off the transmission.

The woman gathered the children and hurried them from the room.

Bullguts came at him again. "Now wait a minute fella. I'm an American! You can't just be coming in here into my house and smashing up my stuff!"

The Captain of the Just retreated from Bullguts. "I will pay you a million dollars for that radio," he said.

The red drained from Bullguts' face. "What did you say?"

"*Señor* Bugazza." Rosas put on his most convincing and unctuous voice. "I must revert to the capital in such a way that the people do not know it is I, the Manifestation of Their Hopes and Dreams."

"Their what? You mean a disguise?"

"Yes, as you say, as if to a mask ball."

"Yeah, so why'd you break my radio? Little sugarplum liked that radio."

"No one must know where I am. You must not tell anyone that I am here. You must destroy or hide the helicopter."

"Yeah, I guess we could put it in the new drying shed. But say, what's this about a million dollars?"

"I am an honest man."

"You mean, all I got to do is keep your being here a secret and I collect a million bucks?"

"Yes, when I get to Quesada I will send you the dollars."

"You're one crazy son of a bitch, but, Mr. President, you have got a deal!" Bullguts thrust out one of his ham-sized hands.

Rosas shook it, smiling and thinking about how he would actually repay the big Yanqui. Images of the *gringo* crawling across a narrow slit of fire, dragging his spilled intestines behind him, filled the Righteous Guardian's mind. "First, I will need to use your phone."

"Yeah, OK." Bullguts lifted the satellite phone from his belt. Rosas took it and crossed to a corner of the room, turned his back to Bullguts, and quickly punched in the number of his fourteen-year-old son.

"Don't say a word," Rosas said when Enrique answered.

"Pa.."

"Don't!"

"We've been so worried."

"Tomorrow night. Do not go with your mother to the cathedral. Do you understand? Make up one of your excuses. She always lets you do what you want."

"But Pa…but why?"

"Tell no one you've talked to me. If you do, we will all die do you understand? Wait for me in my room. Do you understand?"

"Yes, I understand."

"Good. No one, or you're dead."

"But…"

Rosas disconnected and faced Bullguts who was closely watching him. "One more favor, that rifle by the door—may I borrow it for one tiny minute?"

"My Thirty-Ott-Six? I use that for bear hunting. Got one the other day raiding the cornfield. Why you want my gun?" Bullguts squinted, following Rosas to the foyer.

Rosas checked to see that the shotgun was loaded, slipped off the safety. "This will do fine," he said and opened the door, keeping the rifle out of sight.

"Lieutenant Gutierrez!" he called to the helicopter pilot who was standing out of the rain under a carport.

"¡Sí, mi general!" The man saluted, and walked two steps toward the house.

The Indomitable Warrior blew a gaping hole in the traitor's side.

Bullguts rushed out the door and viewed the gory remains. "God Damn! You *are* a crazy son of a bitch!"

Rosas showed no emotion. "Yes, I apologize. It was messy, but you see, nobody must know that I was here. That man was a traitor." The Herald of Virtue handed back the rifle to the stunned Texan. "And *Señor* Bugaazza never call me a son-of-a-beech. *Mi madre* is a weech not a beeech."

Bullguts shook his head in disbelief.

The Omnipotent Hand of Justice was now ready for his disguise. "You will instruct some of your peasants to bring me their clothes. I want nothing special. Something typical. I want . . ." he hesitated, and observed the horizon in a manner he'd found very effective in public speaking, "...to be seen as a common man."

CHAPTER NINETEEN
THE RACE TO QUESADA

Pablo González, driver of the Mohica Lines' ten-hour run from Palapi at the jungle's edge to the capital, kept the accelerator pressed to the worn metal floor. The tassels that lined the inside of the crowded bus swung wildly as the wheels bounced over potholes and rocks. A CD player, set up below a gaudy image of the *Cristo* and a rosary, blared the latest in Latin American popular music: a type of thickly instrumented techno, lush with strings, horns, and heavily echoed voices.

González knew he was late. The hurricane and nine days of rain had left everything in ruins. Only a master driver like him could manage to navigate the washouts, fallen trees and destroyed bridges.

At every stop he had to answer questions about the battle. His tale had grown from the truth, that he'd witnessed nothing, to tales of dodging bombs and busting through roadblocks set up by guerrillas trying to hijack his bus.

What really had happened was soldiers had boarded his bus three times, looking for guns and revolutionaries. They'd found nothing. González thought about mentioning the *indio* boy and girl who'd gotten on in Palapi. One only had to look at the boy's beat-up face to see that he'd gone through an ordeal obviously related to the unrest. But it was not his business. He had a bus to drive.

It was a matter of honor to González that he arrive on time. If the bus broke down or a landslide stopped him, that was fate, but as long as the wheels could roll, the bus was an extension of himself and its failure was his own. Although the Mohica Company owned it, he had chosen the paints that ran in blue and yellow bands around its side. MOHICA TRANSPORTE was painted in brazen red letters.

The bus was his pride. He received only a pittance to drive it. Most of his salary went into extras, like the music player and the tassels. The honor of his name, *Pablo González, Maestro de Transporte* embellished in black script beside the door, was beyond money, representing freedom and power, elevating him above the common peasants. If the truth be known, it was more important to him than his mother, wife, children, or all the *chavas* he had in the taverns and gas stations along the way. He was always rolling. At the most, he was only stationary two days a month. The rest of the time, he was the King of the Road.

González saw a splash of color through the rainy window to his right on the *Camionetas* Highway as he approached the main intersection in the small town of Guarapo. There was a hierarchy on the road—as in everything else associated with New Granadian society. A truck belonging to the plantation would stop for a passenger car carrying the owners of the land. Just as the universe kept its order, a *colectivo*, the open truck used to carry *indios* and their wares, would stop to allow a bus to pass. Of course, *indios* on foot were at the lowest rung of the ladder and had better beware.

González was determined to reach the crossroads first. If it were a military truck or a fine gentleman's car, he'd wait for it to pass, thus displaying his good manners and patriotism. But no tourist bus or *indio* truck was going to beat him.

Across a field, González recognized the cheap red paint of a bus driven by Domingo of the competing company, usually an hour behind him. It was now even more important that he be the first to cross the intersection. His reputation as a driver, his honor as a man, his *machismo* was at stake. Despite his driving prowess and his superior vehicle, the poor condition of the road and crowded street prevented González from gaining on his rival. The narrow road was lined with huts and filled with unexpected obstacles. It was going to be close.

A goat jumped in front of him. González didn't slow, cursing the dent the animal made in his fender. *Indios* children played in the street. He blew his horn, spitting out curses, swerving to avoid a young girl only because if he'd killed her, valuable time would have to be spent filling out a report at the local police station. He smiled as *indios*, donkeys, pigs, and chickens ran in panic. Then there was a thud. He wasn't sure what he'd hit, and would take no time to find out.

He caught sight of Domingo through an alley. The bastard had gained on him! González prayed for a child to find its way beneath his wheels, but it was not to be.

Domingo had the edge as both buses rocketed into the intersection. There was no way González could get there first. He had only a wink to avoid a collision, but could not admit that he'd been beaten, or find the humility to slow, and allow his peer to pass before him. It was better to die.

González's nerves failed him the moment before impact. He slammed on his breaks, spun the wheel, and his bus slid into the side of Domingo's and ricocheted away from the impact, hit the steps of the church, blew both front tires and came to rest inches from a bunch of terrified villagers who immediately fell to their knees, crossing themselves and thanking God that they had been on holy land.

Domingo honked loudly and gleefully, leaving only a splash of mud for González to curse.

González didn't take the time to repay the insulting honk. He threw open the doors of the bus, ignoring the complaints and protests of the disturbed passengers. He channeled his mortification into getting his tires repaired in record time. Once he was back on the road, there would be no more stopping. González was determined to put the gas pedal to the floor and not lift it until he caught and passed that son-of-a-dog Domingo. It was another hour-and-a-half to the city. A lot could happen in so much time and such a distance.

González grunted in surprise as he labored to jack up the bus. There, trying to help him was one of the passengers, the *indio* boy with the bruised face. The girl in the school dress stood behind the boy watching González with an eager expression.

* * *

Koya relived what he had seen five minutes before. When the other bus had skidded into them, while the other passengers were screaming and calling to God, in the other bus, fearful face pressed against the window, his sweat-stained brim of his cap bouncing as he squealed, eyes bulging with terror, had been Rosas. He'd recognize that evil character in any disguise, anywhere. Maybe there were spirits helping them like Anta said. Koya wished they'd help fix this bus faster so he could catch Rosas.

* * *

The Great Shepherd of the Nation lost control of himself. It had been bad enough having to dress in clothes that reeked of animal dung. He felt like a million vermin were crawling over his skin. But then to be crammed in a sardine can full of stinking *indios*, and to be at the mercy of a maniac bus driver, was more than he could bear.

When the buses careened off each other, Rosas, his face twisted in a homicidal rage, bounced off the window, twisted, and punched the fat, hysterical *india* sitting next to him. The beast had spent most of the interminable journey either slumping over on him, snoring, or breast-feeding her squalling brat, who soiled himself every five minutes. His blow caused her no apparent damage, and was lost in the cacophony of her hysteria.

Rosas flung off the straw hat. He climbed over the sow. The aisle was full of passengers, luggage and livestock shaken loose by the collision. A chicken flew by his head. A piglet squealed as he stepped on its spine.

Rosas fought his way past every obstacle, kicking, slugging, spitting, and his voice rising over the protests and curses. "It is I, Hernando Rosas, your ruler! Out of my way, or you will never know the end of pain!" Somehow, he made it to the driver's seat. Rosas threw himself at the man, and wrapped his fingers around the driver's throat.

* * *

Domingo, still chuckling with elation at his victory over that slow-driving González, was taken completely by surprise. As the savage grip threatened to squeeze the life out of him, all thoughts of driving the bus were lost.

The lunatic was trying to drag him from the wheel, yelling in his ear, "¡*Traidor!* You are part of the conspiracy! They are all in on it, *los Trece*, the military! You are their pawn, but I will kill them all and be king! Emperor! God! No one will challenge my authority!"

The bus bounced wildly off the road, skidding and tilting far on its side, righting itself only when the boxes piled high on the roof flew out onto the soggy field.

Domingo's eyes bulged. His fingers clawed at the hands of his assailant. The wild movement of the bus temporarily dislodged the murderer from him.

Domingo's arm flung to the side and landed on a bottle. It was his only hope. He smashed the glass container against his assailant's head. At that moment, the bus skidded to a stop.

Domingo pushed the unconscious murderer off him, pulled himself to his knees, and gasped for air. His neck throbbed. Never had he felt such pain. Every breath was an effort. He felt faint. The cheers of the passengers revived him. He shook his head, flexed his muscles, and swelled with malice. No crazy *indio* was going to attack him. When he felt the strength, he kicked the unconscious lunatic to the applause of his riders.

"Get rid of him! He is *loco*! He tried to kill us!" they shouted angrily.

"Leave him for the vultures," someone called.

Domingo stood over his conquered enemy and sneered, "I should kill him, but . . . " he pointed to the ornate picture of the Virgin Mary above his rear view mirror, "*Soy muy hombre*, a religious man. My name is Domingo, a holy name." He crossed himself.

"Dominion Day," one of the passengers called.

"No, Domingo Day," the bus driver laughed. "My name is Domingo and this is certainly my day."

He dragged his conquered foe by the feet. The driver had to admit that there was something familiar and appealing about the mad peasant whose handsome head hit hard on the final step. Domingo gave his attacker a final kick and left him sixty yards off the side of the road. He hurried to help the passengers collect and reload the luggage. He knew that González, the son of a *guaricha* who'd tried to impugn his superior masculinity, was not far behind. In his heart, Domingo knew that he would prevail. A man of his virility and righteousness could not be bested.

* * *

The Regent of Righteousness fought to stand, vaguely aware of the departing bus. But his waking was buried under multiple layers of pain–his pain. The feeling was all the more horrible because Rosas felt so betrayed. He idolized pain. His loved one had unleashed its wrath on him. There was nothing left in the world for the Choice of the People to like. His hatred for everything and everyone was complete.

He staggered to the road and, standing in the rain, imperiously tried to wave down passing cars, but he appeared so bedraggled and sinister that nobody would stop for him. Rosas cursed every motorist who sped by. The worst was when a chauffeured landowner's limo splashed him. That man, a personal "friend" of his who'd sworn a hundred times that the Man of Humility only had to ask and any service he could provide would be performed. One of the ingrate's children threw a half-eaten orange at Rosas, which because of his condition, he was forced to eat. No doubt they were going to the Dominion Day celebration in the Cathedral of the Apostles. Rosas had to get to the cathedral to deliver a special message to *los Trece*.

A driver hauling a load of pigs saw the poor man kneeling in the rain, gnawing the orange.

Rosas dragged the Good Samaritan behind his pickup, and shielded from the highway, spent the next ten minutes in a frothy eruption of violence, stomping the life out of the pig driver's body until his feet got stuck in the bloody mess. He emerged from behind the truck just as the other bus roared past.

* * *

Koya saw the pretty, movie star face of Rosas, hurried to the rear of the bus and pressed against the window, watching the object of his hunt begin to follow them. Koya's eyes never left the pickup. He felt the *Fierro's* gun pressing against his waist beneath the white shirt. It would have been nice to pick some more pockets of the dead, but they'd escaped Omagua just in time, before bombs destroyed it. They'd made it halfway to Palapi before he'd crashed the car in a ditch.

Anta, in a schoolgirl uniform he'd bought with the dead *Fierro's* money, pressed up next to him. Stupid sister, the last thing he needed was her along with him while he hunted Rosas. But he had to admit that lately she had a way of being in the right place at the right time. After nine days of shame and torture at Rosas' hand, she'd given him the worst news. Their mother, little sister and brother were dead, killed by Rosas because Koya had robbed the bastard. Weak, stupid Rosas should have killed him when he had the chance. Anybody on the street knew that if you get someone down, you finish him. It was his turn. He would not flinch from what he had to do. Be strong.

His mind had room only for one thought–kill Rosas. Every time he thought of his little sister and brother, his mother, every time his face hurt, every bump that made his side feel like Rosas was sticking a knife in him, made him think of pay back. Whether dressed like an *indio* or a general, Rosas couldn't hide from Koya. When he had him, Rosas, the brute, would beg and plead, crying that he was sorry he'd killed the family, beat him, and locked him and Anta in a cage.

By the time they reached *Quesada,* the road was clogged with cars. Drivers were racing to gain a foot, then slamming on their breaks. Near the center of the city, the bus veered off the main highway and Koya lost sight of Rosas.

"No," Koya complained and wanted to shout at the driver but what could he say, *follow that truck?* He rushed to the front of the bus. They were not moving anywhere. The street they were on was even more clogged with cars.

"Open door," Koya said to the driver.

"Be patient, we'll soon be there."

"Open door!" Koya pulled out the *Fierro's* pistol.

A woman screamed.

The bus driver's eyes widened. He pushed a button and the door opened. "Never had a run like this," he muttered as the *indio* boy and girl jumped off the bus into a thick crowd.

Koya hid the pistol beneath his shirt. The streets were extra-crowded for the Dominion Day celebration. Damn luck, half the city and most of the cops were downtown for the fireworks over the Cathedral of the Apostles. Cops blocked most of his shortcuts.

Koya pushed and shoved, causing many angry remarks and more than a few attempts to hit him as he passed. Anta managed to stay with him. He told her to go away, but there was something different about Anta now, stronger. It was no good to tell her what to do. Besides, she had as much right to kill Rosas as he did.

CHAPTER TWENTY
DOMINION DAY

Rosas had a message for *los Trece* and all who conspired against him. Night had fallen by the time he parked the truck full of squealing pigs in the alley behind his secret garage. He opened the new set of locks into the tailor shop and hurried down the tunnel to his bunker.

His doomsday device was a fifty-gallon drum containing a deadly brew of ammonium nitrate, diesel fuel and ultra-fine powdered aluminum. The Swift Sword of Righteousness wheeled the bomb through the catacombs beneath the plaza. The remnants of the departed La'ku culture mutely witnessed his murderous passage. A honeycomb of open graves and elaborately carved sarcophagi rose above him in multiple layers of the dead. Cobwebs covered the crypts and statues. Mummies leered at him with frozen smiles, long curled fingernails and stringy hair on skulls parched with leathery lizard skin.

Mitnal the Smoking Mirror hectored him, "This is not where we'll find the *tunjo*. You must find the Jewels of Life." As if Rosas did not long with every breath to regain his treasure. But first he had to take care of his enemies and they were here, gathered above him in the Cathedral of the Apostles for the Dominion Day celebration.

He placed his deadly concoction in the center of the ancient temple, directly below the most glorious and historic structure in

New Granada. Three hundred years old, baroque in style, ecstatic spirituality expressed in ornate displays of statues, stained glass, and paintings, a glorious shrine to God and the triumph of Christianity over the heathen Indian.

The Protector of Decency could hear the sounds of the archbishop in the basilica above welcoming the governmental, military, business, religious, and social leaders to the celebration of the revolution that had separated New Granada from Spain. In his radio address, Robelo had said they'd be mourning him. He'd give them something to mourn.

He snorted with scorn as he imagined the candles glistening off the gold and silver-framed icons, the stained glass, the polished pews, and balconies stuffed with *los Trece*, the thirteen families who saw themselves at the pinnacle of New Granadian society. His wife would be in the front pew, weeping at the prospect that he'd been killed, and lapping up all the attention she could get. It was her fault that Enrique was confused about what he was, always dressing in her clothes. He'd miss her.

The light on his miner's cap illuminated the detonator attached to the ten pounds of RDX-based plastique explosives atop the metal drum. He set the timer. In a half-hour, *los Trece* would never threaten him again. Without their allies in the elites, the *indios* would be easy to crush, god or no god. Nobody would be left to challenge him. He'd march from the jungle, where he'd "pursued the invaders." It would be like the days when the army had fought the communists. He'd be the hero, the savior. Nobody could possibly suspect him. The carnage would be blamed on the revolutionaries. There was a positive side to everything. He'd father another, more manly son. His lineage would rule this land for a thousand years.

* * *

While Rosas' timer was ticking, Anta and Koya sloshed through flooded streets to the alley. Anta hung back to look for danger, but Koya rushed ahead when he saw Rosas' truck.

"Rat Rosas go by his hole," he said more to himself than to her, took out the pistol he'd stolen from the battlefield and circled the truck.

A pair of foot cops turned the corner into the alley. Anta gave Koya a warning whistle and ducked behind the rear fender. Had the law seen them? Koya motioned with his head and they scampered up the side of the truck, pulled themselves over, and dropped down into the bed. Anta pushed into the slop as the pigs complained and their bristly flesh pressed against her.

A flashlight beamed into the cab. The gravely voice of a cop said, "I guess it's nothing. If it's still here on the next round, we'll have it towed."

"It could be a bomb," the other cop said.

"Yeah, a stink bomb. It can't harm anybody in the cathedral. Come on, if it's still here on the next round, we'll have pork and beans at the station house tonight."

Anta winced as a pig stepped on her leg. No sooner had the cops walked away than the Evil One himself emerged from the tailor shop.

Anta peered through the slats and watched Rosas get into the cab of the truck. He pointed to something that looked like a television channel changer at the alley wall.

Koya rose up on his knees and aimed the pistol through the mud and filth-splattered rear window. Anta wanted him to wait. She didn't want Rosas to get his head blown off right in front of the cops.

There was a loud "pop!" Koya's hand flew back and the barrel of the pistol hit him in the head. The rear and front windows shattered.

When Anta looked up, the cops were back, Koya was unconscious, and Rosas was still alive.

* * *

The Moral Authority of the Nation ran through the rain toward the police. "Shoot them, they're in the truck."

The police grabbed him and roughly threw him against the alley wall.

"*¡Bobos!* It is I, Supreme Commander Rosas! There's been an attempt on my life."

"Shut up!"

"Look at his legs. They're covered with blood."

The Arbitrator of the Just eyed them with complete scorn. "Take a look at me. Can't you see who I am? I warn you, there will be severe repercussions from this action."

With these words, his bomb exploded beneath the cathedral. Blazing light and a repercussion felt across the city disturbed the night as the remains of the elite of New Granadian society rose in a ball of fire. The shock wave knocked both him and the policemen to the ground. Shards of glass and stone rained on them.

"*¡Santo Dios!*" an officer exclaimed and got to his knees.

The Avenging Hand of Justice recovered first, pulled a Glock 25 from beneath his shirt, and shot the uniformed officers in their heads. Assassins were everywhere–in the truck, in the boulevard. He had to get back to his bunker.

A small figure with a gun rose up from the pigs. The assassin! He launched a fury of bullets at the truck.

Mitnal screamed in his ear. "It's her, Anta Raymi. Use her to find the *tunjo.*"

The figure dropped down amongst the screaming pigs.

Rosas aimed his gun through the slats and saw the *india* cowering between two hogs bleeding from multiple gunshot wounds and panting in their death spires. "Get down here. Let me see your hands. Give me that gun."

As the *tunjo* thief climbed down the side of truck, Rosas hit her on the head with the Glock, picked up her army pistol, lifted the unconscious girl and carried her to the tailor shop.

* * *

Koya awoke between two dead hogs in a puddle of blood in the back of the truck. He squirmed to free himself from the heavy animals, and pushed up from the muck to see Anta hanging over Rosas' shoulder. He knew where he was taking her. He'd been there. The thought of his sister strapped to Rosas' torture table drove all fuzziness from his brain.

The pig truck, or maybe it was his head, rocked as Koya climbed down the slats. He felt dizzy, and staggered as he followed them to the tailor shop. The door had been changed. New, impossible-to-pick-locks had been added. Two cops lay dead in the alley. Police cars and ambulance sirens were closing from every direction.

He went to the open door of the pig truck to look for a key. On the cracked seat was the video remote control he'd seen Rosas pointing at the alley wall. What was that for? He aimed it like Rosas had and pressed buttons. The false front of the building wall lifted, revealing Rosas' garage. Now he knew how Rosas got his tank and red car on the street.

Koya stepped into the garage, stood beside the tank and pushed another button. The wall closed.

A steel door blocked the passageway to Rosas' Bat Cave where Rosas had taken his sister. Koya pointed the video controller at the steel door and pushed all the buttons in different combinations. Again the garage door opened and closed, but not the steel barrier. Maybe it was like the elevator up to the palace from the Bat Cave. Koya couldn't find a slot.

He climbed atop the tank, past a metal speaker on the side into an open hatch. A soldier's helmet with a single star in the center hung from what looked like motorcycle handlebars. He turned the key and the tank engine spun and caught with a rumble.

With this tank, he could drive right out of Quesada and nobody could stop him. But not while Rosas had Anta and not while that *chicharrón* was still alive. There had to be some way to open the steel door. He had to break in before Rosas did to Anta what he'd done to him.

The big gun on the tank couldn't be that different from the pistol. Koya lifted one of the heavy shells in both hands, put it into the open end of the barrel, and closed the door. Where was the trigger? How did you aim?

He turned the handlebars and the tank spun into the wall. He pulled and the tank backed up. There had to be a way to turn the barrel. A small television showed the direction the tank was pointed. Beneath the television was a joystick like in the video games in the pool hall. Yes, this was like a video game. He grasped the stick and pushed. The turret spun around the top of the tank. Koya smiled and touched the stick slightly to line it up with the steel door, and squeezed the red trigger.

Machine guns pumped from the front of the tank. "Bub-bub-bub-bub."

Faint light from the street shown through holes the bullets had punched in the metal backings of the secret wall door.

¡Cabrón! He flipped a switch covered by a red flap on the side of the stick and again squeezed the trigger.

"Boom!" The tank lurched. Fire flashed from the barrel. Smoke poured from side vents.

Koya blinked and saw the steel door hanging open. He slid off the tank and went through the hole he'd created.

The tunnel was dark, smelled of diesel and was filled with smoke and dust. He had no light but had to go on. He held his hands before him and used touch to guide his feet. After he'd walked like a blind man for ten minutes, his hands touched steel. He'd come to the end of the tunnel and another closed door. There was no way he was going to get the tank up here to blast his way into the Bat Cave.

He started to weep, hating the way he cried now. Rosas had changed him into a boy again. A man didn't cry, even strapped to a table, the needles under his eyes, the wires into his teeth. The agony he had endured was for one reason—to kill his tormentor.

"Rosas!" His scream echoed down the dark tunnel.

CHAPTER TWENTY-ONE
ENRIQUE GROWS UP

Rosas' pride and joy scrutinized the rescue effort with intense concern. His mama was in there. Lights were set up and shined into a huge hole. Fires burned in the rain. Who would blow up the cathedral on Christmas Eve?

One of the security people knocked on the door, but Enrique didn't open it. His papa had called and warned him not to let anyone in. He'd told him not to go to the cathedral with his mama. Tears glistened on his puffy cheeks as he carried his mama's kimono back to the closet.

Enrique was still nervous about that closet since the Indian boy had jumped out and attacked him. What came out this time was worse, so terrifying that Enrique screeched and ran for the door.

"Enrique, stop! It's your papa!"

Enrique pivoted slowly to confirm the disturbing sight of his father dressed in rags. "Papa?"

"Come."

Enrique followed him into the elevator in the freaky closet. "Papa, what happened? Mama was in the cathedral."

"She's dead. They're all dead. It's just the two of us now. Quit your blubbering!"

The elevator dropped and opened in a room that Enrique never knew existed. He looked around fearfully at all the guns on the walls and then spotted the little Indian girl strapped to an operating table with drills hanging over it. His chest heaved with sobs. He wiped his eyes with the back of his hand.

His papa handed him a pistol. "Shoot her! Shoot her now!"

The heavy gun danced in Enrique's trembling hand.

"She tried to kill your papa. Avenge me! Shoot her or I will find another more worthy son."

Enrique gripped the gun with both hands and swung the aim toward the girl's head. She squirmed beneath the bonds and stared at him with pure terror in her expression. Enrique moaned and closed his eyes.

"Wait." His father stopped him.

Enrique's gun hand dropped to his side.

"Want to see what she looks like without her skin? I'll show you how to skin someone alive."

Enrique's lower lip twitched and he shrank into himself. "She looks nice like this."

"Didn't I tell you she tried to kill me?"

Enrique nodded.

"I have to get these stinking clothes off me. Wait here. When I come back, we'll have some fun."

His papa went into an adjoining room, stripped, and stepped into a shower.

Enrique looked at the Indian girl. "Hello," he said.

"I-go," she begged.

Enrique looked toward the bedroom. "Why did you try to kill my papa?"

"Be one-good friend by I."

"I don't understand what you're saying."

"I-go."

Enrique shook his head. "Papa doesn't like you."

The girl fought against her straps.

Then steel doors in the front and back of the cave opened. A blinding cloud of dust rolled into the bunker from the rear door and from the front. The Indian boy from the closet, covered with filth like the girl, ran at him with a channel changer in one hand and a gun in other.

"Papa!" Enrique cried and dropped the gun.

The Indian boy leaped as fast as a wild animal and kicked Enrique's legs out from under him, sending him to the floor blubbering, begging for his life.

The boy ran past him and unhooked the straps holding the girl.

* * *

Anta slipped off the table. "This way." She led Koya to the door she'd escaped from the last time. They ran past the bedroom and shower just as Rosas, wearing nothing but a towel and holding a rifle, came out of the dust toward them. Bullets cut the air as she led Koya into the darkness behind the rear door. A searing pain above her ankle dropped her.

* * *

Rosas thought he might have hit the girl, but the boy had gotten away. He couldn't understand how these two ragamuffins kept getting into what was supposed to be a secure bunker. The *indiesitos* must have come in from the garage and left through the rear door, letting in the dust from the explosion.

He couldn't risk it anymore. You couldn't hold one without the other showing up. This time these fleas were going to die.

"Come on boy. I'll teach you how to hunt." Rosas armed Enrique with an M16 and handed him a helmet equipped with night vision goggles. Darkness would be their ally. The vermin were heading toward ground zero.

Mitnal the Smoking Mirror screamed at the Mighty Piety.

"Stop wasting your time with children. The *tunjo.* Find the four Jewels!"

Ignoring the god, Rosas pulled the night scope over his eyes, and led Enrique into the rubble-clogged passage. The La'ku rats couldn't have gotten far.

He saw their pathetic efforts to crawl through the dead bodies and remnants of the destruction of the cathedral, crept up until he was right behind them, and hit the tactical light on the housing of his automatic.

* * *

Koya spun to face the blinding beam, and his arm knocked against a bone. With that little tap, an entire pile of old bodies collapsed behind them, creating a landslide of skeletons that knocked Rosas and Enrique into a hole so deep they disappeared, leaving only the single beam of Rosas' headlamp shining up through the pile of corpses.

"Help us!" Rosas cried from within the hole. "Get help. I'll pay you. Get help. I can't move. A million dollars, get help. I'll give you a million dollars, ten million."

There was no way Rosas was ever getting out of there. Koya would have liked to look Rosas in the face as he suffered. He would have gladly sat there for days to hear his begging grow weaker. Being buried alive was not a bad way for the monster to die.

"Help us," Rosas pleaded. "My son is hurt. We need help. Have mercy."

"Eat dirt," Koya shouted.

He and Anta had to get out of this underground trap without a pile of bodies falling on them. He helped her crawl through the dark, finding their way with their hands, coughing in the dusty air, until ahead the barriers became easier to see. They squeezed under a slab of concrete punctured with twisted metal to where light shined on the stones. He helped Anta climb over a pile of bricks onto a ledge, and in the bright illumination of searchlights, saw that where the cathedral had stood was a big hole, and in the hole was a statue of *Tatya-Masi*.

CHAPTER TWENTY-TWO
I-GANG

He waited for two days for the chance to finish the job, to kill Rosas and loot the palace. Koya observed the soldiers and rescue workers digging at *Plaza de los Mártires*. Anta leaned on a pair of crutches beside him. The French doctor who'd fixed her up had told her she should stay in bed–as if she had a bed and he could ever keep his pesky sister from following him. The hoods of their rain ponchos drooped over their foreheads and blocked his side vision so he did not see the cop come up from behind.

"I told you two to get out of here." The cop kicked him so hard Koya landed on his knees.

Koya reached for the pistol beneath the poncho, ready to blast the pig no matter how many soldiers and cops were nearby.

Anta threw herself on him. "Please mister policeman no hurt I-brother," she begged while she wrestled with Koya to keep him from drawing the pistol.

"Get along. If I see you again, I'll feed you to the buzzards at Us'me."

"I'll feed you…" Koya tried to speak but Anta covered his mouth.

"What's that? What did you say?" The cop leaned over them, a black club in hand ready to beat them.

"He say, want help rescue Rosas," Anta said. She crawled to her metal crutches.

Koya stood, never taking his eyes off the cop. The skinny *mestizo* blinked at Koya's killer stare.

"Don't want to see you around here again," the cop said and stepped away.

Anta hobbled beside him. "Move, Koya," she said.

With one more hateful glare at the cop, Koya turned.

He wanted to kill that cop and every soldier that had shot his mother and little sister. He didn't care if he died. He would never let anyone kick him again. "Need I-gang," he said to Anta. "Need big I-gang."

* * *

Twelve days after being invaded by Rosas's army, a thousand poor remained in the muddy, charred ruins of Us'me. Marooned, with no trucks delivering to the dump, the survivors of the massacre decided as one it was time to leave. They packed what they could carry, wrapped in blankets tied to their backs or piled on carts. Those who could not walk were carried or pushed through the mud, past *señor* Vargas' brick house where the streets were paved and the buildings were built of wood and mortar. There, a dozen police, armed with heavy weapons, met them. Positioned behind two squad cars that blocked the road, the police told them they couldn't pass into the city. After much shouting, pleas, beatings and shots fired by the police, the slum residents withdrew up the slope of the dump to wait for a chance to escape.

* * *

The cops were lounging around their cars, guarding the entrance to the city. If there was any looting to be done of the abandoned houses and stores of Quesada, they'd do it themselves. They wanted no competition from the *indios* horde. When they saw the small tank motoring up the street behind them, they assumed that there was going to be some killing and the mob would be dispatched in a more forceful manner. So did the barrio residents, who stood up and fearfully began to retreat up the hillside.

The tank stopped a half-block from the barricade. The cannon barrel moved and dropped slightly. The cops looked at each other, curious as to why the barrel was pointed at them instead of up the hill at the Us'me mob.

"Boom!" The percussion echoed over the dump.

The two police cars blocking the road flew into the air. Those cops who weren't knocked out or killed by the blast stared in shock. Some of the residents of Us'me turned back and watched.

"Brrraaaat." Machine guns on the front of the tank threw lead at the police.

The bravest of the residents looked from atop trash heaps as the tank lurched forward and plowed aside the burning carcasses of the police cars.

The tank stopped at the entrance to the dump. A woman or child's voice broadcast from two speakers attached to the hood of the tank.

"Need-I fighters. Fight cops, fight soldiers. Go fight Rosas."

The residents exchanged glances. Nobody moved forward. Those who had not already run away leaned ready to escape.

The tank pivoted, smashing into cars parked on the side of the road, reversed direction and lumbered toward the center of the city.

Twenty Us'me men ran to catch up with the tank.

The voice continued to broadcast from speakers on the side of the tank. "Need-I fighters. Fight cops, fight soldiers. Go fight Rosas."

Two police cars, lights flashing and sirens squalling, tilted around the corner. The tank stopped. The cop cars slowed and cautiously approached the armored vehicle.

"Brrrraaaat." Machine gun bullets tore apart the police cars, leaving them burning in the middle of the street.

The Us'me residents cheered. When the tank pushed aside the cars with the bloody bodies of the cops sprawled across the seats, more of the poor followed.

"Need-I fighters. Fight cops, fight soldiers. Go fight Rosas."

By the time the tank rolled into the center of the city, the following mob of starving poor stretched for blocks. Some carried sticks. Others threw rocks, burned and looted.

When the tank reached the *Plaza de los Mártires* a group of cops began to fire from the top of a building.

The poor retreated in panic. The tank stopped. The barrel rose. Bullets plunked and ricocheted off the tank's armor.

"Boom! Boom!" The tank blasted repeatedly until it found the range. A shell exploded below the level of the roof and the building caught fire.

"Boom!" The tank gun spoke one more time and no more shots came from the roof.

Again, the horde cheered and surged ahead.

The tank drove into a small alley and stopped. The barrel swiveled and pointed to the street.

A small figure wearing a helmet with a white star in the center stuck his head out the top. A young girl arose beside him.

Koya pointed a box with buttons and a wall on the side of the building opened.

Anta spoke into a handheld transmitter. "Inside be guns. No touch I-car."

The leaders of the crowd peered into the space behind the raised wall, saw the sports car and crept inside. They entered through the blasted door of the passageway sloping beneath the palace. More of the curious pushed behind them.

It took two hours for the people of Us'me to carry the weapons from Rosas' bunker to the streets of Quesada.

"Have I-gang now," Koya said to Anta.

CHAPTER TWENTY-THREE
VICTORY ROAD

Ochoa stood in his command tent. One of his lieutenants handed him a report of the uprising in Quesada, something about the poor breaking into an armory and stealing a tank. Time to finish this business, he thought, and get back to the capital. He'd soon restore public order.

An aide stepped inside. Rain streamed off the open flap. "Sir, the rebels are approaching from the east."

Ochoa picked up a pair of field binoculars from the table and pulled his hood over his head. Outside, he looked across the plain. A half-mile to his east he saw a sight that made him refocus his binoculars. Moving toward him were a thousand jungle warriors from a distant age. Some of the prehistoric hostiles carried spears and blowguns, and some appeared to be flying over the heads of the others. An acid bile of panic rose in Ochoa's throat.

* * *

Quetzal the Plumed Serpent, in the skeleton body of Gabriel Ayala, pulled his jet out of the clouds to be the first to see the sun rise over the blighted land. He'd taken over the bodies of the pilots to get as close to the sun as possible. Below, *Inika's* clouds were drowning the planet. He imagined pushing the joystick forward and hurtling himself into the soggy earth. If there were a way he could die, he'd kill himself to escape this eternal imprisonment.

He banked the jet and looked down at the peak of the volcano Susuprina surrounded by clouds.

"Can you hear me, *Tatya-Masi?*" he whispered. "This time I will kill them all. Oh yes, I know where they are–your mother, MG, Kare, Norane. They are coming to me now. There will be no escape. Free me and I will use these bombs on their enemies. Free me, Du…I beg you, free me."

Quetzal was answered with silence. Defeat was bitter. To lose a world was the cost of a failed battle. To have to live on that world was to have to crawl when you could fly, to be blind when you could see the dew on the pedal, to have no taste when the sweetest honey was on the tongue.

The voice of *Kinchel* the Avenger in the body of *comandante* Ochoa came through his earpiece. "We have lost, *Quetzal*. The Sixth World will be a Water world."

"No. There's still hope," *Quetzal* pleaded. "*Tatya-Masi* has not obtained his full godhead. He loves this world and its human race. I sense this. I've always sensed this about him."

"I pity you having to stay on his world. I am truly sorry. *Mitnal* and I are leaving. Farewell, *Quetzal*. I hope that someday you might find the way to appease the Lordess and she will release you from your bondage."

Quetzal didn't respond. The other gods were already gone. A rage filled him. He would not appease *Inika*. He would unleash what power he had on this planet to destroy everything that was hers. She would regret ever trapping him in her domain. He rolled his jet and led the squadron toward the advancing La'ku.

* * *

Norane rode in the cab of a six-wheeler. Lilia sat beside him, her father at the wheel. The ancients, who needed no modes of transportation, flickered like fireflies alongside the truck. The moderns–La'ku from the jungle, villages and fields–followed in trucks and cars. They were heading to Quesada to reclaim their country.

The will to live when death was so close distracted Norane. The smell of the fields, the call of the birds, the drumming of rain and rush of water over rock spoke of peace as he led an army to war. Memories and regrets drew his thoughts to what might have been. He looked at Lilia's profile. Shrouded in the magic of the *Xucha,* she was as young and beautiful as the day of her wedding to Theodore Moss, nineteen years before. In the name of love, he'd selected her to be the Earthly Mother of *Tatya-Masi*. She'd suffered in so many ways for his cause.

He reached over and squeezed her hand, saw the jade light of *Xucha* in her eyes, and knew that it was *their* cause. The prophecy that all the rivers of man would flow into *Tatya-Masi* had come true. Castilian and *indio* had been united and now were on the verge of avenging the injustices of 500 years.

Their moment of intimacy was shattered when a shell exploded, opening a crater in the road in front of them. Don Carlos skidded to a stop and the battle began.

Tank and artillery shells exploded in the midst of the unarmed convoy. Vehicles blew up in flames. The cries of the injured were drowned in more explosions. The flooded fields offered no shelter to those who tried to run, as mutilated bodies were tossed up in geysers of mud.

Norane and Lilia stepped from the truck, and side-by-side, led the ancients toward the enemy. A tank round exploded in front of them, sending molten metal shards whistling past Norane's head.

He heard a gasp of pain behind him and turned to see Don Carlos on the ground, blood streaming from his scalp. Lilia knelt beside him and touched the side of his face. "I'll see you in Manoa."

She stood and faced Norane. Their eyes locked, and as the shells exploded around them, she leaned forward and kissed him. Above her shoulder, he saw twelve jets one hundred feet off the ground, flying straight for them.

"Move, move to *Tatya-Masi*," she said, lifted the *tunjo* over her head, and threw the necklace high into the air.

* * *

The *tunjo's* eyes flashed in the sky. Inside the lead jet, Ayala relaxed his finger on the trigger of the missile he was about to launch and spoke into the microphone in his headset.

"Abort. Pull up," he ordered the conquistadors in the eleven jets that followed him.

The noses of the A-37's, painted with the snarling jaws of jaguars, pointed skyward. Ayala rolled his jet.

His red-eyes in their hollow sockets followed the path of a ray of energy that beamed from the *tunjo*, refracted off the top of Susuprina, bounced off Ayala's jet, and back to the Jewels of Life. The rainbow-colored rays formed a triangle that turned onto a radial axis that spun over the peak, rose until it surrounded the globe in a pyramid. From that single point on the Earth, the clouds cleared and the rains stopped.

The golden figurine tumbled over and over, falling, falling. When the *tunjo* struck the ground, an 8.9 earthquake rumbled through New Granada. Tectonic plates violently ruptured with a roar that overpowered all the sounds of the tanks and exploding shells. No soldier or rebel could remain standing. A deep crevice split the ground at the base of the cliff. Tanks flipped forward. Soldiers and trucks were tossed and tumbled into the fissure like toys tipped from a table.

Buildings toppled all over the country. The mighty Palapi church spire crashed and fell across the steps onto the road.

At the *Plaza de los Mártires* in Quesada, deep within the earth, a mammoth slab of rock pushed over a minor fault line and lifted. Forced by unimaginable pressure, the debris of the Cathedral of the Apostles fell away as the ancient statue of *Tatya-Masi* rose out of the ground until it stood fully emerged, facing the Presidential Palace.

Inside the jet, Ayala raised his hands and the ancient flesh fell from his bones. "Du, you've released me."

He banked his jet toward the New Granada army lines and radioed the others. "Follow me to salvation."

Stripped of the scant covering of humanity that had cloaked them, the conquistadors, like Ayala, were now only skeletons, fulfilling the last tasks before release from their earthly bondage. Only bones and the remnants of sinews controlled the jets as they first blew the military helicopters out of the sky, then bombed and strafed the New Granadian ground forces.

* * *

A knee-bending weakness overwhelmed *comandante* Ochoa when *Kinchel* the Avenger left the Earth, abandoning him. He'd grown used to having the strength and intelligence of a god inside of him. Ochoa stared into the blue sky and cursed Ayala and the conquistadors. He understood that *Tatya-Masi* had made a deal with the *Plumed Serpent*. The Water god would stop the rains and release *Quetzal* from his bondage on the condition that *Quetzal* would protect his followers. Well, *Kinchel* the Avenger might no longer possess Ochoa, but the man, *comandante* Lisandro Ochoa, still had something to say. He had a responsibility to defend his nation. Defeat the rebels. Be the ruler of *Nueva* Granada, the new Rosas, the new god.

The *comandante* ran from his command post to where five tanks armed with antiaircraft missiles were parked. "The missiles! Launch the missiles."

With his order, the gunnery officers locked their radar on the twelve jets and pressed the buttons on their consoles. In rapid succession, twenty missiles leapt skyward, trailing flames and smoke.

* * *

At last, after 500 years of being trapped on the Earth, they could die. Ayala led the other conquistadors into the path of the missiles. His jaw clacked together as he saw the eleven jets burst into flames. "Death, come for me," he pleaded and released his last rocket at the tanks.

CHAPTER TWENTY-FOUR
RETREAT TO QUESADA

Norane had been able to beat the other Fire spirits, but not *Quetzal.*

The flaming descent of the conquistadors' jets traced black and white trails across the blue sky. The sun was out. The rains had stopped. *Inika* had lost. The truth was a poisonous potion for Norane to swallow. The battle for the Sixth and Final World was over. Fire had won.

On the verge of victory, *Tatya-Masi* had betrayed the forces of Water. The Sixth and Final World would be of Fire. When all the power of Manoa and the Jewels of Life had been united to lift *Tatya-Masi* to his godhead, the man Du, the god *Tatya-Masi,* had chosen Fire over Water.

The explosions and sounds of battle dimmed. Norane fought the urge to collapse. He would not leave in defeat.

The clouds had cleared from the peak of Susuprina. Lilia's body lay beside her father. Their spirits had returned to Manoa. Norane fell to his knees on the water-soaked ground. *Inika* was defeated and so was he.

He fell forward with his hand extended. Around him, the ancients melded into the oblivion from which *Inika* had summoned them.

"Cruuuuu."

The *tunjo* lay inches from Norane's outstretched arm but he lacked the mortal strength to answer its call.

With the last of his life, he looked up and saw Kare and the blonde *gringa,* MG.

MG picked up the necklace and stared into the animate Jewels of Life. "It called to me," she said.

A mortar shell exploded so close that the concussion knocked her down and the necklace fell by her feet.

Kare knelt beside her and placed his hand on her shoulder.

"Get me out of here," she begged. "Just get me out of here."

Kare picked up the *tunjo.*

Norane saw how the Jewels affected him. His brother's body expanded, his eyes cleared. The haggard look from hunger and fatigue was gone.

"I am done with gods," Kare said. "*Quetzal* is released and so am I." He knelt and placed the chain of woven hair and silver threads over Norane's head.

Instantly, Norane's weakness was gone. The mortality that had nearly claimed him was an obstacle he'd overcome. The Jewels of Life gleamed in the eyes of the pendant. The tattoos of the ancients expanded on their red skin. The jungle feathers were bright in the sun, and their weapons ready to use as they drew ranks around him waiting for his command. They had a war to fight. The La'ku could still reclaim their land.

Norane stood and stared into his brother's eyes. Without the *tunjo,* Kare's body was again beset by the physical toll of his days on the boat, the march, and the constant rain.

Norane clasped him by the forearm. "Karesito," he whispered.

"I am free now," Kare said.

"And Moss?"

"*Quetzal* protected him at the statue. He too is released."

Norane blinked at the pendant hanging from his neck and said, "I am not."

He lifted Lilia. One of the ancients bore Don Carlos in the same manner. The shapes of Norane and the warriors flickered. They took an upward step out of the physical realm and disappeared.

* * *

Comandante Ochoa had been knocked out by the concussion from *Quetzal*'s missile. When he regained consciousness he was on the ground. He could barely stand. One of his aides had to prop him up.

"What's the situation?" Ochoa demanded. His voice sounded hollow and distant. He wasn't sure the lieutenant had understood him. Ochoa saw the man's lips move. His voice was like someone oscillating a volume knob. Ochoa forced himself to stand on his own and compensated for his dizziness by locking his knees. He straightened his rain poncho and the twin holsters strapped around his waist. The lieutenant handed him his cap with the commander's star in the crown. Ochoa's ears rung and he thought he was going to vomit.

He concentrated on the battlefield and saw a horde of rebels moving on the road toward his lines. He didn't have much time to restore order to his ranks. The five tanks that had launched the missiles were burning. Three tanks had tumbled over a cliff created by the earthquake. Fuel trucks and troop carriers were in flames. His command post was destroyed along with his field staff and communications equipment.

Ochoa's mind cleared enough to realize that the sun was shining. *Tatya-Masi* had sided with the Lord of Fire. The thought gave him strength. The rebels were lightly armed. He still had his troops, artillery, mortars, and automatic weapons. With renewed confidence,

Ochoa ordered his forces to attack.

He pressed binoculars to his eyes, still having difficulty focusing. Shells from his field artillery landed on the rebel positions.

The "pop-pop" of small-arms fire alerted him that his position had been flanked. He turned to see a small force of rebels moving past the burning tanks. He pulled his pistols and began to fire. His men reversed their field of fire and repelled the assault. Another band approached from the right, and another from the left. The peasants seemed to be invisible until they were right on their positions. His troops' automatic rifles, grenades and mortars beat back each assault, but more came until Ochoa worried that his remaining stock of ammunition, food, water, and fuel would soon be depleted. The roads were blocked by fallen debris and there was no chance of reinforcements or supplies.

Reports starting coming in from around the country that rebels were taking advantage of the earthquake to rise up against police and citizens. Ochoa's head hurt and his body ached. He wanted to sleep, but forced himself to stay awake through a day of constant attacks from all sides on his position. At midnight, the *comandante* ordered a dawn withdrawal to Quesada.

When the sun rose, Ochoa was shocked to learn that half of his men had been killed or injured during the night, some with their throats cut, or with darts to the neck. With the attacks continuing, he was forced to abandon a quarter of his surviving tanks and vehicles. They loaded the dead in three trucks and the injured in five more and began an orderly repositioning.

The flood from the hurricane and the damage the earthquake had done to buildings and bridges made portions of the road impassable. Engineers, clearing the obstacles, were continuously harried, and they made little progress. What started as a controlled withdrawal turned into a chaotic daylong battle as the soldiers fought through ambushes launched from fields and earthquake-damaged buildings.

When they reached Pueblo, the fallen church spire blocked their passage. The battalion diverted along a rubble-filled street to the *Camionetas* Highway. When the column was nearly to the end of the four-block stretch of road, a mine exploded under the lead tank, and they started to take fire from the roofs and windows. Too late, Ochoa realized he'd been lured into a trap.

The battle in Pueblo lasted all afternoon. Ochoa had to abandon the trucks carrying the dead and fight his way out of town. It was not until night that six trucks carrying the *comandante* and a few hundred exhausted soldiers reached the edge of Quesada where they joined a combined force of police and armed citizens to bar the rebels from entering the capital.

The next morning, Ochoa repositioned the last of his anti-tank weapons and munitions to the top floor of a three-story building. From this vantage, he could fire on the mob approaching from the countryside and those moving toward him from within the city. By afternoon, Ochoa was fighting on both sides of the building.

CHAPTER TWENTY-FIVE
EL PRESIDENTE

"**M**ove by *Fierros* one time," Koya shouted down to Anta and swung the machine gun on top of the tank. She closed a metal flap over the viewing hole and steered by watching a small video screen, keeping the tank moving toward the bullets.

Battered by the hurricane, followed by the earthquake, and the decapitation of the ruling elite in calamity at the Church of the Founding Fathers, the social order of Quesada was gone. The poor took advantage of the chaos to rise up against the weakened hand of their oppressors. Every *La'ku* had been taught that when *Tatya-Masi* came the land would be returned to them. All believed the prophecy had come true.

The guns Koya had robbed from Rosas' Bat Cave had killed a lot of cops and soldiers. He and his gang fought for three days from the center of the city to its eastern edge, pushing against the final army position.

Anta steered the tank down a block that had already seen a lot of action and was met with a barrage of army bullets that clanked like cans off the side of the tank they'd taken from Rosas' garage.

Koya pointed the twin barrel .30 caliber machine gun at the sounds. "Brrraaaat. Ba-ba-ba-ba-ba." The gun pulled belts of shells from the ammo boxes by his feet. Puffs of dust exploded where the bullets hit.

An explosion that nearly turned the tank over followed a flash of fire on the third floor of the tallest building still standing. A blast of burning air blew him off the gun. His ears rang so loud he couldn't hear anything else. The world was blurred and the tank had stopped moving.

"Drive one time," he shouted at his sister. She pulled back on the handlebar. The engine whined but the tank would not move.

"Move one time." He dropped down to the controls for the big gun and turned the barrel until it was pointed at whatever *pinche burro* had broken his tank. When he shot the big gun, the tank recoiled but wouldn't move off the brick pile. The shell hit the building and sent up a big plume of smoke.

Another blast rocked the tank. The concussion shook him so hard his teeth hurt. "One big bullet," Koya shouted to Anta.

She pulled open the lever and the sewer-smelling smoke billowed around them. She loaded a shell half as big as she was, and shouted, "No I-more!"

He lowered his aim to the window below the roof and fired their last big bullet. The tank jumped and he imagined the big shell flying through the window and hitting the *guaricha* in the middle of his head. He must have hit their ammo because the building blew up from the inside, sending smoke and dirt into the air, and then fell down to join the rest of the buildings around them.

His gang kept firing for a couple of bursts, but then someone shouted, *"¡No más soldados!"* And everything quieted. They took a breath and just listened. That fight was over.

Koya picked up a rifle, stuck a pistol in his pants and climbed down. His gang gathered around the tank. Tough guys and *gamines,* good fighters when they were not robbing the stores and houses of the rich;

tattoos of devil horns, skulls, tears and names of girls and dead friends on their faces and bodies, flash jewelry, heavy gold necklaces, hoodies pulled over watch caps, two-hundred-dollar basketball sneakers, they called themselves the Mara Murciélagos, the *Bats*.

What was he going to do about his sister? Her leg was hurt too badly to walk and a tank was the only thing that could get through the violent and wreaked city. "Move I-sister one time," Koya ordered a Bat named Muñeco.

They put her in the bin of a wheelbarrow used to carry the boxes of bullets and rockets from Rosas' cave.

Twenty more Bats surrounded them–guns ready to use. It was fifty blocks back to the center of the city, and there were lots of cops and soldiers still trying to fight them.

Koya led the gang on a short run to the next alley. Smoke, burning rubber and dirt hung in the air and fires burned in knocked-down buildings. They spread out with guns pointed, looking for threats.

The distant growl of a tank sent the Bats to battle positions in the alleys and behind piles of rubble. A soldier ran around the corner and they shot him down. Then two, three more soldiers ran into their trap and they shot them, too. The sound of the tank grew louder. The Bats crouched ready to run, hide or fight. Then the tank rumbled down the street, followed by blocks of country La'ku on foot.

For the first time since they stole the *tunjo*, Koya saw happiness in his sister's eyes. "*Tatya-Masi!*" she said.

"Move, move to *Tatya-Masi*," the La'ku army cheered.

They were all heading to the *Plaza de los Mártires* to see the statue of *Tatya-Masi* that had risen out of the ground yesterday during the earthquake.

Koya was going there too, to see Rosas' body. He had to make sure that *chimba* was dead.

The Bats joined the long parade of *indios* moving through the city. When they met any lingering resistance, the rebels would take cover and fire back, and the fight would quickly be over.

Koya and the gang stayed with the cheering and singing La'ku fighters as they moved past the huge sign of the flaming snakebird that had made a solo flight down the charred side of the fire-gutted oil building. By the time they reached the center of the city, most of the cops and soldiers had taken off their uniforms or been killed.

There wasn't enough room in the *Plaza de los Mártires* for all the *indios* who wanted to see the statue of *Tatya-Masi*. The jade god, gold stick in one hand, a *tunjo* with emerald eyes carved on his chest, sat on a stone throne facing the palace.

Police and soldiers looked down from the roof and out the windows of the palace, but as long as they didn't shoot, the La'ku didn't fight them. That was OK by Koya. He didn't want the *indios* getting in and stealing the loot inside the palace.

Koya led his gang, pushing and shoving, to the center of the plaza where La'ku had set up tents and built cooking fires among the broken pieces of the cathedral.

Koya climbed down through the cement blocks and broken brick walls at the foot of the statue to the underground graveyard where he'd left Rosas begging for help. Koya squeezed between two slabs the earthquake had thrown together and looked into the dark hole.

¡Cabrón! He had to go back up to get lights and ropes before he could go any farther.

Above him, the crowd shouted that *Tatya-Masi* was here. "The god is here! Move, move to *Tatya-Masi!*"

Koya pulled himself back up to see what was happening.

Everyone was watching Rosas' palace. There on a balcony where governors, dictators, and presidents made speeches, the frog god waved and smiled at the La'ku.

The crowd chanted, "*Tatya-Masi*! *Tatya-Masi*!"

The god was holding a microphone and his lower jaw moved like a puppet. In the words and accent of a *rico quesadiano,* his voice trumpeted from large speakers.

"I can only stay among you for a brief moment. You have good leaders who will help you to have a happy, peaceful land. I ask you to follow one among you. Though he is not *indio*, he has lived, worked and fought at your side. I speak of your new *presidente*, Eduardo Morales. Eduardo Morales is *un hombre muy fuerte* . . ."

CHAPTER TWENTY-SIX
WE ARE ONE

Anta saw something rise up out of the rocks that made her feel sick. Rosas! She shouted a warning but it was too late. The RPG on Rosas' shoulder jumped and spit a stream of fire and smoke. The third floor balcony exploded and *Tatya-Masi*'s head came off and flipped backwards.

"We are one," Rosas chortled, looking like a half-human monster with goggles, bulletproof vest, and helmet.

Anta lifted her pistol to shoot him but he'd escaped back beneath the rubble of the cathedral.

Koya was after him like a cat after a rat. Anta's wounded leg wouldn't bend to climb through the bricks and broken glass. The staccato sound of gunfire echoed across the plaza. *Indios* shot at the soldiers in the palace while other La'ku ran or crouched behind piles of bricks. *La'ku* were getting shot all around Anta.

Koya and a group of Bats chased Rosas, firing into the dark, and then gave up trying to chase him underground. Anta leaned over the edge of the stone to see Koya climbing back out. "Take sister," he ordered, and led the Bats across the plaza.

Hopping on her good leg, Muñeco and a heavy Bat named Oso held her with one hand, their rifles in the other.

With a *"thunk"*, a bullet hit Muñeco in the chest. He groaned and fell, looking up at her like a little one wanting help. Another Bat, Yogi, pulled her away, lifting her through the panic.

The street in front of the palace was filled with fighting La'ku. The tank that had led the rebels into the city made a whining sound as its top turned and the barrel rose. "Boom!" The front of the palace was covered in smoke and dust and the firing stopped. A soldier on the roof shot something. Fire and smoke rose from beneath the turret. Flames spread around the metal sides of the tank before an explosion blew the top off.

The firing started again from the palace windows and roof. Anta hobbled past a La'ku man whose blood had formed a thick dark puddle where it had flowed out of him into the street.

Koya and the rest of the Bats shot their rifles at the palace as they ran down the block to the alley where they first went to steal from Rosas. Anta moved as fast as her hurt leg would permit, through the raised wall into the empty garage and steel door Koya had blasted open to rescue her. Other Bats ran past them down the tunnel to the Bat Cave. By the time Anta reached the cave, Koya was in the elevator with the card hanging from a chain around his neck.

"Koya!" she called.

"Watch door for Rosas one time!" he said to her as the elevator closed on him and a full load of Bats.

"What Little General say?" Oso asked.

"Rosas move by here one time," she said and pointed at the rear door to the passage under the plaza.

She doubted Rosas would still be there. That *rata* would have more than one escape hole. Using a rifle as a crutch, and holding her pistol in the other hand, Anta turned back toward the garage.

"Where go by, Little Sister?" Oso called to her.

"Kill-I Rosas, one time," she said.

* * *

Eduardo, in his best suit, a loaded pistol in the pocket, had been ready to be introduced as the next president of New Granada. He'd been standing inside the balcony room of the palace listening to the actor's performance as *Tatya-Masi* when a rifle-propelled-grenade launched from the crowd had taken Pacho **Núñez**'s head off.

The explosion had knocked Eduardo over a table. He'd awoken with his face pressed against the red bristle of a Turkish carpet. His first thought was that he was dying, but a quick inspection found that it was **Núñez**'s blood on him. General Ungo who had snuck them into the palace, had not fared as well, and was slumped against the wall with a bad stomach wound. The building shook from a large explosion and dust hung in the room with the strong scent of cordite.

Why had the La'ku shot their god? Did they know he was a fake? What was Eduardo to do now? He looked around the corner of the door into the hallway. Forty feet away, through a haze of dust and smoke, he saw two maids with black shawls over their heads, hurry through the door to the service stairs. A pair of soldiers with wide-eyed, ashen expressions of terror ran in the other direction down the hall.

"Get some help. There are wounded in there," Eduardo said and hurried after the maids.

The sound of the battle was louder as he descended the metal stairs that led to the kitchen. He ran past the stoves and refrigerators through the delivery door. Ahead, a metal gate blocked the service driveway. Shouts and sounds of the battle could be heard on the other side of a wall bordering the driveway. One of the maids pressed a button on the wall and the gate swung inward. Before the maid passed through the gate, she glanced back at him. Eduardo knew that crazy leer beneath the shawl.

"Rosas!" he called and raised his pistol, but the despot had already closed the gate behind him.

Eduardo pressed the button and ran into a chaotic scene of *indios* rebels engaged in a firefight with soldiers and police in the palace. Two rebels, the kind you would expect to see hustling a shoeshine on the street, raised rifles toward him. Eduardo ducked and squeezed his trigger. The sound of his gun and the reports from the rebels came as a blinding pain filled his body. The gun fell from his hand and his knees buckled beneath him.

Ahead, Rosas turned with a pistol in hand. Shots flew in both directions past Eduardo. His right side was numb and blood flowed from beneath his sleeve. He reached for his gun with his left hand as he pushed his back against the plaster wall to stand. Rosas had shot the two rebels who lay sprawled on the driveway. Eduardo squinted through his blurred vision. Rosas and the other maid were running a half-block away. Eduardo tried to aim his pistol, pulled the trigger, but his arm rose in the air. He couldn't focus. His arm wouldn't work. He staggered forward, fell to his knees, and breathed heavily, closing his mind to the pain, willing himself to rise.

He looked up to see Rosas' henchman, Major Bruto, reach down and easily pluck the pistol from his weak grip, then sling him over his shoulder as if he weighed no more than a child. The pain of bouncing against the giant's back drove Eduardo in and out of consciousness.

Inside an empty garage, a hand held Eduardo's face by the cheek and gave his head a quick shake. Hanging from Bruto's back, Eduardo opened his eyes to see Rosas and his son Enrique had dropped the shawls from around their heads. Both their faces were swollen and marked with scabs.

Rosas raged, "The filthy vandals. Animals. Look how they treat my property. Put him down."

When Bruto set him on his feet, Eduardo tried to stand, but

slipped to the cement floor.

The hem of Rosas' maid's uniform pulled up over his naked hairy legs as he knelt beside Eduardo. "Hey." Rosas touched the side of Eduardo's face with the cold steel of his gun barrel. "Wake up. We need each other. You understand? We've got to work together to beat this insurrection."

Eduardo weakly nodded.

Rosas stood. "OK. Let's get out of here. Take him."

* * *

Inside the palace, Koya was riding up to Rosas' room with an elevator full of Bats who would expect to do some robbing after the fighting was done. The problem with showing his gang the Bat Cave was that every thieving one of them now knew how to get into the palace.

The elevator door slid open in Rosas' closet. Koya crept into the room he'd only seen for a moment when Rosas had caught him last week. The Bats looked around at all the *rico* clothes and would have started robbing right then, if there hadn't been guns popping all over the place and a bullet hadn't come flying through a window, putting the Bats into a crouch with their guns ready, as he led them past a *rico* bed with a red silk crown, and out the door to a carpeted hallway that ran the length of the palace. The "pow-pow-pow" of guns going off came from rooms on both sides of the hallway. The Bats had learned how to fight together in the last four days and moved without words or directions. A Bat tossed a grenade through the first door. Following an explosion and a scream, the firing stopped from that room. Bats had already thrown grenades into the next two rooms when soldiers and a pack of cops ran up the stairs from the second floor. The lead soldier was immediately killed by a fusillade of bullets from the Bats. Other soldiers came from the rooms along the hallway. The gunfire doubled as the the Bats and soldiers battled.

Koya bolted across the hall. Bullets sang by him. He cut into a room with his gun ready to fire, crouched, his eyes searching for hiding soldiers. Two balcony doors had been blown away and two dead men lay on the floor. One of them was in a costume that made him look like he had green skin, webbed hands and feet. On the other side of a long polished table, fifteen feet from the costume, was *Tatya-Masi's* head. Koya's eyes went to the other dead man. He knelt beside him and quickly found a fat wallet in his *rico* blue suit.

From the hall came shouts of surrender. Just like on the street, the soldiers were not brave and only fought when nobody was shooting back at them. Koya stuffed the wallet in the front pocket of his cargo pants and with his rifle ready to shoot, stepped into the hall to see soldiers coming out of the rooms with their hands over their heads.

A quick drum of automatic fire came from the floor below. Koya pointed his gun in the back of a soldier with lots of colors and stripes on his uniform. "Move by street, one time," he said.

"I don't understand," the soldier said.

"Move one time." Koya jabbed the barrel into his back. The soldier understood him well enough to know that the next thing Koya was going to do was shoot him. He and the six remaining Bats walked behind the soldiers to where the stairs turned at tall windows.

The soldier shouted, "This is Colonel Girón. Cease fire! Cease Fire!"

Koya kept his rifle pressed in the colonel's back and stayed by the wall as he herded him and the others down to the second floor. No shots came from the lower parts of the palace as more soldiers quit. By the time they reached the first floor, Koya and the Bats had over fifty soldiers and cops crowded by the front door with their hands in the air. The problem was the La'ku were still shooting at the palace.

All the windows were shot up and the floor was littered with glass.

A soldier opened the door and waved a white sheet, and the rebels stopped shooting.

When the seven Bats marched enough soldiers and cops to fill a movie theater, out the front of the palace, the La'ku cheered and called, "Little General! Little General!"

A soldier on the roof took a shot at them. The colonel fell with an ugly wound in his head and the fighting started again.

Koya turned and ran back into the palace to take care of the *perros* on the roof who would shoot their own colonel, leaving the soldiers and cops they'd cleared from the palace with the La'ku. Some of the rebels tried to go with the Bats, but Koya turned, pointed his gun at them and shouted, "No move by Bat palace," before closing the door in their faces.

* * *

Anta knew where Rosas was going. He was going to the tailor shop she and Koya had broken into when they'd found the Bat Cave.

She limped out of the blasted door to the other side of the garage, and there he and Enrique were—disguised as women—moving down the hallway toward the shop. She had him now, but when she raised her pistol to pay him back for what he'd done to her family, a voice whispered in her ear. Naj, the old witch from the jungle, placed her bony hand on Anta's back where the jaguar had clawed her at the statue.

The *bruja's* breath was warm, her touch cold. "Are you *Xucha?* Use your forward sight," Naj said.

Anta turned back to finish the job, but the witch had cast a spell that froze Anta's finger on the trigger. The witches had stolen the necklace from her and now were keeping her from killing Rosas.

"Your life will end here if you continue down this path, Anta

Raymi. When you are ready, come to La'kuana and Naj will teach you the ways of the *Xucha*."

Anta didn't want to know anything about the ways of the *Xucha*. She just wanted to kill Rosas. She raised the gun again and aimed, but Rosas and Enrique had moved out of sight.

Anta tried to follow them, but the witch had also taken her strength. Dizzy, the wound from the jaguar burned on her shoulder and her leg wouldn't move. Cursing the witches, Anta slipped to the floor where she lay until Oso found her and carried her into the palace.

CHAPTER TWENTY-SEVEN
THE AFTERLIFE

The light on the other side of life was a red blur through Du's closed eyes. A disjointed clash of shrieks, wheezes, grunts, and slurps came to him as would imagined sounds, yet, at the same time, the bizarre cacophony clearly was emanating from distinct external sources. The audio split created an echo effect that made the voices and cries sound hollow and their locations difficult to determine. His vision expanded from the center in petals of sight. When his vision cleared, he was surprised to find himself on the shore of the Lake of the Frogs in the Sierra Nevada Mountains of California. Bleached corpses of trees lay washed up on a beach of rounded granite stones. The snowcapped shapes of familiar mountains in winter filled the distant horizon.

But he was not at Lake of the Frogs. Above him, stars and planets orbited in curved space over the pinnacle of a pyramid sky. Plants–some like lilies, others like miniature palm trees–floated on the lake that shimmered so brightly it appeared to be covered by reflective jewels. Behind him, meadow rocks and flowers strolled and spoke to each other. Du understood their thoughts in his mind, as if standing at the edge of a party hearing bits and pieces of many conversations.

A dragon walked on two hind legs from the forest. Du crouched in fear at the sight of the hundred-foot monster, flames shooting from his nostrils. Then, the dragon answered a question, barely formed in Du's thoughts, that the fire released the carbon he breathed.

Sights so unimaginable and immediate caused Du to wonder if he was having hallucinations brought on by eating the *Xucha's* mushroom. He was shirtless and his bare feet protruded from the bottom of his favorite bib overalls. He touched his face, felt the clammy cold of his skin, listened to his heartbeat and the faint whistle of his breath through his nose. No matter how inexplicable, this was real. He was dead and this was the afterlife.

"After, pre, inner, outer, time and space," a childlike voice said.

The comment on Du's thought appeared to have come from a caterpillar the size of a Dalmatian, leaving a trail of phosphorescent blood in its wake as it slithered over a rounded rock and into the iced grass of the meadow.

Du stepped away from the caterpillar.

"Watch it, moron!" A shrill squeak jumped in his thoughts.

Du stopped mid-step.

"Your foot, it was about to crush me."

Du could see nothing but forest floor. Concentrating, he became aware of microscopic groups of intelligence. One of the smallest, no bigger than an atom, was discussing with a cobweb the theory of irrational motion—whatever that was.

"Detect to see," a high-pitched voice said with a definite sarcastic tone.

Du was afraid to move. Eyes observed, tentacles sensed, noses smelled, antennae sent and received. An insect buzzed by and politely offered a greeting to which Du was too flustered to attempt a telepathic response.

An otter-like creature rose to the sparkling surface of the lake and floated on its back with head raised. As two clawed flippers lazily paddled, the way his fur spread out from the side of his skull, the rose color in his cheeks, the pursed lips and intelligence in the deep-set blue eyes reminded Du of his tutor Edgar Weinmann.

The otter chirped the kind of sound a whale or porpoise makes. In his mind, Du heard the otter speak in Edgar's German-accented English.

"Hello. New here, are you?"

Was it Edgar? Du had always hoped he'd find his dead loved one in heaven.

"If you wish me to be," the otter said.

Du had to be careful what he thought. There was no privacy here. But where was here?

"Excuse me, yes, I just arrived. I'm a bit lost, I'm afraid." Du's words hung in the air before being absorbed into the babble of other conversations. His voice sounded louder in his thoughts than in the atmosphere.

"Never been here before, then?"

"I'm sure I haven't, yet parts do seem like...where I come... came from."

The otter stood on the water. About four feet tall, in hiking boots, shorts, knee socks, and a felt hat, he was a miniature, otter version of the man who'd raised Du at the Lake of the Frogs.

Du heard Edgar's voice clearly in his mind. "You're where you discovered yourself to be. What we dream, what we remember, the things we all share, symbols and archetypes. We all create and apportion, then manifest ourselves as appropriate to our functions."

"Am I creating you?"

The otter stepped onto the shore. "This is not a dream or a hallucination. We create each other."

"I'm sorry. I didn't mean to imply that you're not real." He pressed his hands together and told himself to watch what he thought.

A long snake swam up and Du heard a warm feminine voice ask the otter, "Hey, baby, what do we have here?"

"I'm not quite sure yet, Azell. He seems to have just arrived with nobody to properly greet him."

Azell stood tail-first on the water and reached out with tiny arms. "Come here, baby. Let mama give you a big welcome hug." Her skin appeared to be shifting patterns of color.

Du hesitated, unsure how to reach the snake to hug her.

He need not have worried; she'd already wrapped herself around his legs and torso in a full body embrace. Her yellow serpentine eyes gazed at him with a loving maternal expression. "Welcome." Her head darted forward and she kissed Du on both cheeks.

"Thank you." Du blushed.

"Nice, Azell. Give him some love," Edgar said.

After another squeeze, she slipped off Du and rested her head on the limb of a weathered log on the beach. "What should we do with Du?"

"We could make rhymes with him, obviously, or just tell him what he wants to know," Edgar said. "He has many questions."

Azell's forked tongue flickered out of her mouth. "Ask away," she said.

"I don't know where to start," Du confessed.

"Think of something, we'll get it," Azell said.

"We're all very empathetic," Edgar said. "It's what makes us what we are."

And what *are* you? The thought was in Du's mind before he could stop it.

"Let me try, baby. Did they have religions where you came from?" the psychedelic snake asked.

"Yes, many."

"And gods?" Azell asked.

"Lots for each religion."

"Aren't you a god?" Edgar asked, staring up from the height of Du's waist.

Du looked at the familiar yet strange lake. "When I died, or whatever is happening to me, there were people calling me a god. But it was a mistake."

The otter and snake laughed in shrieks and chirps. Azell put her tail in her mouth and rolled around like a wheel. The otter did a knee-slapping dance and sang, "What are we gonna do with Du?"

"Never heard that before," the snake, Azell, said. "Usually when a novice shows up he's convinced he's the Supreme Being—quite a problem, usually. Shocking to them when they find out how common they are. Takes them a while to learn to be humble, appreciate the true order of things."

"The true order?"

"And untrue," Edgar said.

"And partially true," Edgar said.

Azell unwound herself and assumed a shape like a chair.

"Have a seat, baby, and mama will explain it to you."

Du was not sure if she meant for him to sit on her lap.

"Yes, that's right. Go ahead."

Du half sat, afraid his weight might harm her. "Go on, all the way. Make yourself comfortable. That's it."

Azell was surprisingly soft and supporting. She wrapped her comforting embrace around his body until her head was facing his and said, "You are a god to those *people*, as you call them. We are all gods somewhere, to someone. Here, let's start at the beginning. The universe is structured in a hierarchy of order from the lowliest creature on your planet. Understand—symmetry and balance? We are placed on these planets as the highest order there, but those that placed us are much higher than we are. And so it goes until you get to the Supreme Being, or S.B., as I like to call him."

Then the Supreme Being is masculine? Du thought.

Azell whooped. "Yeah and sexy, too."

Edgar waved his short furry arms. "There's also the untrue order and multiple variations. Try to think in a more elegant positional system."

"I'll try," Du said, but failed to suppress the thought that he had no idea what an elegant positional system was.

Edgar laughed his odd crossbred snort-cackle. "And they turned you loose on a world?"

"Excuse me." A woman interrupted with a hesitant tone. The Voice emanated somewhere above them where the stars and planets spun at the apex of the sky.

"Oh, my," Azell said. She straightened, forcing Du to stand, and then she stretched out flat on the ground, big eyes atop her flattened head, looking skyward.

"The Higher Beings," Edgar whispered. "We don't hear them very often, really never hear them. They like to use the invisible hand of fate and all that."

Although Du's empathy told him there were many Higher Beings speaking, he only heard the one feminine Voice.

"We appreciate your willingness to educate the novice but…" an embarrassed sound of a great throat clearing came from the Higher Beings. "I'm afraid that Du is correct. He is a mistake."

Gods big and small gasped. Excited murmuring spread throughout the crowd on the shore, in and atop the lake.

"Du!" The Voice silenced the gathering. "We owe you an

explanation. Existence is manifest in many planets and many more life forms. Early in the evolutionary cycle of each of these worlds, we select a specimen from that species of the world we determine will evolve to become dominant among its creatures. We grant the selectees extraordinary powers and preserve them so that when, as in the history of any planet, a moment of crisis arises, they can be used to affect the course of history."

"It is boring work, really," Edgar whispered. "One only gets to affect every so often."

"Would you please permit us to continue?" the Voice asked.

Edgar lowered his head and placed his otter paws behind his back. "Pardon," he murmured.

The Voice continued, "As we were saying, in approximately one out of every ten to the 194 zillionth power googol a mistake is made. In the case of Earth, we thought the dominant creature would be able to exist both in and out of water. Our agent discovered his error. He foolishly tried to cover up his mistake by combining the frog deity he had created with characteristics of Homo sapiens, the actual species of advanced development for your planet. He sought to limit the scope of the man-frog to a narrow cultural range."

I don't believe it, Du thought and bit his tongue to silence his careless mind.

"We do apologize," the Voice said, sounding hurt by his doubt. "We would like to work with you to try and undo or at least mitigate the damage we've caused."

Du stood straighter. He'd always known he wasn't a god. "Of course, I'll do what you want."

After a prolonged silence, while he waited for the Voice to tell him what they wanted, he asked, "What do you want me to do?"

"I'm afraid we can't tell you that."

If he were speaking to Higher Beings, or as close to the Higher Beings as he would get, and they wouldn't tell him what to do, did that mean he could do what he wanted? He looked to Edgar and Azell.

The snake rose up and met his stare. "You know what you are, don't you? You're an uncontrolled controller. We've never seen one before." Her eyes opened and closed rapidly in her excitement.

"What does that mean?" Du asked.

Edgar did a quick dance and bowed slightly. "What does it mean? It means you're free. They don't control you like they do us. There's nothing inevitable about your destiny, nothing preordained or path dependent. You can come and go when you want."

The Voice spoke again, "With one caveat: whatever you do will be replicated in the reciprocal planes. In other words, should you wish to do right, you are just as likely to cause wrong. If evil is your goal, blessings may well flow from your actions, unintended consequences, don't you know?"

He barely knew what they were talking about, but did understand that this might be his best chance to stop the rains.

"We'd like that too," the Voice said before he could verbalize the question.

"But how can I?"

"Not sure, really. It's pretty much up to you."

Du sensed the Higher Beings watching him, waiting. Lost and unsure of himself, he was now the center of attention. All the other gods wanted to be near him.

Several gods tried to engage him in discourse on mathematical and theoretical plotting of his potential, but he was unable to keep up with their thoughts. He felt horribly ignorant and outclassed.

"Wait, wait!" Edgar silenced the chatter. "You're confusing him. Keep it simple. Start with what you want. What is it that you want?"

Du studied the lake. He longed to sink to the bottom, to slow his heart and mind, and be whatever he was without thought or concern.

Azell slithered past him and entered the water. "That's right, sweetie. Will it with a sure and full heart."

Du jumped out as far as he could, landing with a splash forty feet from the shore.

If he was imagining the lake, the water was just like at home. He sank to the depths, where the light dimmed and the sand was soft. His breathing slowed. He crossed his legs and closed his eyes.

Visions came to him. In his upraised hand he held the golden beak and silver breast *Plumed Serpent*. "I release you," he thought.

The multi-colored feathers on *Quetzal's* tail spread into flaming clouds on a horizon through which the sun rose over Omagua. All that was and all that would be on the Earth was here. He had time to learn how to do good.

CHAPTER TWENTY-EIGHT
THE PASSAGE

Pain was his companion. His neck wrapped in a brace, Rosas lay on a double-king size bed, smoking a Havana. The more he rested, the more pain settled and claimed its own portion of his body and mind. Certain positions of his head, memories of his loss–these were the domains of pain.

Enrique sat beside his father. "Are you feeling better, Papa?" he asked.

The Lion in Recline rolled through a region of pain so he could see his son, who had his own share of injuries. Enrique's features were still distorted, his lips swollen and split, eyes bloodshot from being crushed by the landslide caused by the La'ku boy, Koya Raymi.

He told himself that he must try harder to be a more understanding father. "I want you to understand, *mi hijo*, we are in a battle that does not end, that ebbs and flows like the ocean, heh? Our tide is out, but will rise again."

"I want to go home, Papa."

"We will, *mio*, we will. I promise you."

"But when?" the brat complained.

The Missing Heart of His People found a position on the pillow where his neck was not in agony, and stared at a 60-inch flat screen on the wall broadcasting images of the worldwide damage caused by the twelve-day rain brought by the Water god. Even though *Mitnal* the Smoking Mirror was no longer with him, he marveled that the Fire Gods had stopped the rains.

"You must understand your adversary before you engage him in battle."

"But they are nothing, just Indians. They got lucky. They have nothing. They are poor and stupid."

He sighed at his son's ignorance. What was the use of protecting and training someone who could not survive on his own? He thought of the La'ku boy and girl. If only his son had half their cunning. Oh well, he had to work with what he had. "No, Enrique, it's not time. When it is your time, you will always beat the one whose time it is not."

"I don't understand you, Papa."

The Patron of the Just closed his eyes, nearly out of patience. He asked, "How do you think they beat us?"

"Luck. Whoever blew up the cathedral gave them their chance."

He'd never tell Enrique that it had been him who'd destroyed the Cathedral of the Apostles and killed his wife, Enrique's mother.

"But who gave them their luck?" he asked.

"I don't know."

"He who gave them luck is our enemy. Until you understand that enemy, you will be helpless against him."

"But who is it?"

"History."

"I still don't understand," the boy complained in his childish, feminine voice.

The Blessing That Goes Without Saying wondered if the Inca king Atahuallpa had a discussion like this with his son as a hundred Spaniards were conquering his empire. "Go read your history," he said, and laid back to rest and wonder when destiny might again favor him.

* * *

Eduardo sat at Moss' dining room table in Miami, along with the five remnants of the Morales family. A week since he'd been released from the hospital, his injured arm was still in a cast. At the end of the table, Eduardo's sister Matilde, Moss' wife, rang a small bell to call the Cuban servant to clear the first-course dishes. Was their sister, Lilia dead? Did that make Matilde something more than a putative wife? At the other end of the table, Moss sat with a passive expression, a dull sheen in his eyes.

Eduardo grudgingly accepted that he was indebted to his brother-in-law for arranging to have him medevac'd into the United States. Eduardo had wanted to kill Moss and Rosas for what they'd done to his family. Now they were working together again, united by their common goal of regaining their country.

His sister, her black hair done in a style that accented her high forehead and cheekbones, in a fashion favored by television reporters, leaned forward with an erect posture and said to him, "When you're feeling better, Eduardo, I have a friend from the club who has a brother who works for Senator Mathias, the chairman of the Foreign Relations Committee. She will be happy to arrange an introduction."

Matilde said the name of the chairman as if offering Eduardo an army.

"How interesting," he said and dragged a Cubano roll through the butter with his uninjured hand.

"You sound like your father when he wasn't paying attention," said their mother, Beatrice, seated across from him.

"I was paying attention," Eduardo said.

"And don't you think your sister brings promising news?" Beatrice asked.

"I do, yes. We must explore every avenue."

"And what, may I ask, is your opinion of this matter, Theodore?" She pronounced his name Tea-Adore. She despised her son-in-law ever since she'd discovered he was a polygamist who was married to both her daughters at the same time.

"I agree with Eduardo, Mama," Moss said in a lackadaisical manner.

Eduardo wondered if he called her Mama to infuriate her, but figured Moss, lately, was too docile to tease her. Ever since their adventure on the boat, Moss hadn't been the same. Couldn't blame him for that. The business with gods and goddesses would be enough to drive a stronger man mad.

Carli, Moss' ten-year-old son, always ready to liven things up with some mischief, asked, "Is my brother really a god?"

The twinkle in his nephew's eyes made Carli even more handsome.

"Don't call that thing your brother," Matilde corrected her son.

Carli would not give up his torment. "Do you know he's awesome famous? There are websites about him. He has over 100,000 friends on Facebook. They say he was in the band *Apokaful* before he blew up the Cathedral of the Apostles."

"¡*Válgame Dios!*" Aunt Tatua muttered and gripped the tablecloth with her liver-spotted hands.

"Carli, please," Matilde said with real distress.

"That will be enough, Carli." Moss snapped out of his lethargy enough to reprimand his son.

"You love him better than me," Carli said with feigned passion.

Moss' response surprised Eduardo.

Moss looked at his hands and then over their heads toward the kitchen. "He was a good boy."

After a moment of shocked silence, Matilde's voice shook with anger. "You will never mention that beast again in my presence."

Moss glared at her, and Eduardo thought his old verve might have surfaced, but Moss only nodded. "Yes, he is better forgotten."

His nephew squirmed with the urge to instigate more trouble, but remained silent. The women at the table could never stay mad at him. He was their avenging angel, who would make right everything the previous generation had done wrong.

Eduardo broke the tension. "I'd like to speak to the senator."

He doubted the senator would have time to concern himself with New Granada. The global deluge had wiped out whole agricultural regions, made more than half a billion people homeless, and destroyed countless factories and businesses. New Granada was not the only site of anarchy and lawless rampages. Everywhere, at every level, societies were mortally injured and struggling to recover with little external assistance.

The disruptions were not only in social order but thought. Carli was right. The story of the reappearance of an ancient rain god in New Granada had spread around the world. In times like this when so much had failed, there was a natural inclination of the weak to turn to mysticism and magic. More than ever, strong men of reason must now assert their control.

So what if *Tatya-Masi* was a god? This world was for the living to do with what they choose. No god could control human destiny. Whatever had caused the rain–be it nature or *chacs*–mankind had survived and would rebuild.

They finished dinner and Moss led Eduardo out sliding glass doors to the pool house. The wind rustled the palms and there were whitecaps on the ocean among the diamond reflections of moonlight. Inside the single flat-roof room he used for an office was a faint aroma of salt rot and chlorine.

"There's something I want you to have," Moss said, reaching inside his desk drawer. He pulled out the snake-wrapped cross and stared at the totem that had been the instrument of his possession by *Quetzal* the Plumed Serpent.

As the cross slowly twisted on the chain, the ruby eyes of the snake glinted with a brief flash of animation. Eduardo studied the necklace with suspicion. "Why?" he asked.

Moss looked up at him. "It haunts me. I thought you might… might understand after what we've seen together."

Eduardo scowled. "Give it to me." He reached for the silver chain. At the touch of the gold cross, he felt a slight, perhaps imaginary pulse of energy quicken his heart. "Come, I'll show you what we do with these gods."

He strode across the Bermuda grass to the seawall by the dock. Moss half-ran to keep up with him. Eduardo cocked his wrist to throw the cross into the ocean.

"No. Don't!" Moss reached for his arm.

Eduardo gave him a steely stare, arched his back and threw the necklace as far as he could toward the choppy sea.

A snowy egret flew over Eduardo's head, a gliding white ghost in the black sky. The long beak caught the necklace, flapped its wide wings and banked into the night.

Eduardo stared at the apparition with amazement.

Moss' eyes darted with a fearful expression.

Out of the dark came a faint sound that could have been a birdcall or branches rubbing together.

"Shraaaaaaaa."

CHAPTER TWENTY-NINE
KILLER

Koya couldn't go back to being a common thief. He was the leader of a gang that had formed to beat Rosas, and was now using Rosas' weapons to take over Quesada. In ten days, the Bats had become the most powerful and best-armed gang in the city, even challenging international gangs, like the Mara Malos. No cop, soldier, god, or dictator was ever going to oppress them again. And a whole country was waiting to be pillaged.

Koya knew that to stay on top of this band of killers, he had to be the coldest killer, the one who never stopped until all his enemies were dead. Rosas had done this to him. Koya fought only with an iron fist, without mercy or hesitation—the stronger and most ruthless wins. He'd learned that from Rosas' mistake of letting him live.

With the helmet low over his head, Koya sat hunched in the passenger seat of Rosas' red sports car. Seventy Bats followed him on foot for a daylight attack on the Malos' headquarters. An Uzi lay in his lap and an RPG leaned out his window. The remains of the head of the thief who'd stolen the car from Rosas' garage was tied to a rope and bounced behind the rear fender as a warning to anyone who might think of stealing from the Little General.

The driver, Cixao, a thin man with the growth of a new beard over his recessed chin, maneuvered the car around the bricks and wood of fallen buildings. Telephone and power wires hung low over water-filled potholes.

"Stop one-time," Koya ordered, waving a young Bat to the open window. "What be?"

The *gamín's* eyes were wide with fright and his voice shook. "Westside Malos on Concordia place, Little General, waiting."

The Malos must have been tipped off that they were coming and had set a trap for them. Somebody had to be the bait to start the fight. "Move fast one time by Concordia, " Koya told the driver.

Cixao hunched over the wheel, floored the gas, and took the car to full power, pushing Koya back in the seat. The tires squealed, and the skull bounced behind the car.

Six Westside Malos ran from a pile of twisted rebar and cement, firing their guns.

"Stop one time!" Koya ordered.

Cixao spun the wheel and hit the brakes so the car stopped crossways at the south end of the block, while the Bats closed in from the north. Koya jumped from the car, ignoring the bullets that punctured the door and wounded Cixao, and launched the grenade, taking out four Malos.

Forty Bats closed in from the east and west, driving the Malos into an apartment building where their boss lived and ran the operation.

"Burn building, one time," Koya ordered two Bats with incendiary grenades.

The RPG flew through the window. Flames engulfed the triplex and then rose higher when the Malos' weapons exploded.

A sound rose from the crackling flames, "Shraaaaa."

Heat prickled Koya's skin.

The flames rising from the building formed into the shape of a nine-headed dragon. Four heads on long necks bobbed and weaved on either side of a central serpent head. The head on the far right was his.

From that moment, something or someone was inside of him.

He left the wounded driver to be cared for by other Bats, had another Bat drive him back to the palace, rode the elevator from the Cave up to what had once been Rosas' bedroom, and was now his. He walked across the big room to the full-length mirror. The nine-headed monster looked back at him.

"Shraaaa." The call of the spirit tried to enslave him with fear.

He raised his gun and shot the mirror. In the shattered glass, he saw a twelve-year-old killer with blood on his arm. He stared at the shards of glass, went out in the hall where he'd battled four days ago, and opened the door to Anta's bedroom.

A tray with cold steak and fries lay on the empty bed. Old soft drink cans and bottles were scattered on the floor. A nurse, sitting at a table against the wall, rose quickly to her feet.

"Where I-sister?" Koya demanded.

The woman's voice stammered. "Little Sister said to tell you, Little General, she has gone to Omagua."

Koya ran to Rosas' room, his room, put on his helmet, and rode the elevator to the Bat Cave.

CHAPTER THIRTY
THE CALLING

The sun was bright and the city smelled cleaner and quieter than Anta remembered. There weren't many cars and no buses on the street in front of the palace. She limped to a parked taxi.

The driver's head lay back on the seat-rest, eyes closed. He was dirty and hadn't shaved.

When Anta opened the rear door and climbed in, the driver looked at her. "Yeah?"

"Drive by Omagua."

"Where?"

"By Palapi."

He twisted and laughed at her over the seat. "Don't you know the roads are all blocked? It's very dangerous. There's bandits everywhere and cops worse than the criminals."

"Go," Anta said firmly.

"You better have a lot of money. It's going to take some bribes."

Anta opened a purse made of alligator skin that had belonged to *señora* Rosas and pulled out a pistol. He glanced at the black gun. "You're Little Sister, aren't you?"

Anta frowned. She hadn't told her brother what she was doing because he wanted her to go to school, to act like a *rica* girl.

"The Little General know you're doing this?"

Anta laid the pistol on the seat beside her.

"Ok, I hope you know this is going to be hard." The driver started the cab and drove to where Koya's gang had built a wall of rubble across the width of the road.

Five armed Bats surrounded the taxi. Anta recognized three of them. One leaned in the open window on the driver's side and looked into the cab.

"Where go by?" he asked with his rifle ready.

"Taking Little Sister to doctor."

The gangster stared at her. "OK," he said. "Careful."

Bats had to lift truck tires to open a narrow passage through the barricade so the driver could move along the main avenue.

The city was changed, slower, fewer people on the street. Most of the stores had broken windows and doors. The few cars and trucks drove in stops and starts between spaces not blocked by fallen buildings, electric wires, or puddles.

A rapid series of gunfire caused the driver to lower his head and peek from side-to-side. "Why are you going so far?" He looked at her in his rearview mirror.

Anta didn't answer. Even if she'd wanted, she couldn't put into words the longing that she must find Naj. She wasn't sure she wanted to be *Xucha,* but did know that someday, somehow she must hold the *tunjo* again.

Another explosion rolled across the city.

The driver slowed at the beginning of every block before he sped forward. "You know there's no gas," he said. "I only have half a tank. We're going to have to get more gas."

She didn't respond to his increasingly desperate arguments.

"Even if I get you there, how am I going to get back? This is going to be very expensive."

"Have money, pay for one car," she said.

There was something familiar about the sight of a family on the curb with a pile of their belongings in front of a burning building. She'd seen it in a dream she'd had in the palace bedroom, waiting for her leg to get better.

They came to a line of stopped cars. Anta leaned to the side to see armed men had set up a checkpoint. They wore the uniforms and red hats of Rosas' *Fierros* in the street.

She held the pistol ready as a *Fierros* searched the truck in front of them. She could shoot this one but there were four more.

The back of the taxi driver's neck was red and he coughed as *Fierros* came to each side of the cab. There were shots and one of the *Fierros* fell wounded. The three others hid behind the hood of the taxi and opened up on whoever was attacking them.

A grenade hit the truck, shattering the window of the taxi, and sending glass showering over Anta.

As the driver lay on the seat, whimpering a prayer, Anta threw open the door and stepped onto the street. Pain made her flinch from trying to stretch her hurt leg too much. She took another short step, and a *Fierro* ran from the side of a building. She and the soldier stared at each other. She raised her pistol but was not fast enough. She saw a flash of light and then nothing.

* * *

When Koya and the Bats caught up with Anta, he couldn't stop the Bats from battling. There was no controlling them when they got into a fight, especially with *Fierros*. The truck in front of the taxi blew apart in flaming pieces.

Koya ran toward where his sister lay on the sidewalk, firing his AK-47, mindless of the bullets. Half a block away, a small figure, wearing a straw hat and a worn brown poncho, picked up the wounded girl and carried her away across her arms.

Koya didn't shoot the woman carrying his sister for fear of hitting Anta. The firefight lasted only a few minutes, but when it was over, the old woman and Anta were gone.

No matter how many houses and apartments he searched, no matter how many times he thought over what he'd seen, he couldn't find his sister. Without his sister, Koya saw the world only in darkness. When he killed, stole, tortured, if he thought of the sorrow, loss, or destruction he caused, it was only to mark how no other pain could match his own.

* * *

Anta's breaths couldn't pass the tightness that closed her throat. A scent of crushed jungle leaves and damp pressure on her chest awoke her to a numbing cold. She tried to open her eyes and was met by blinding light and stabbing pain. Voices spoke in a language that she remembered but couldn't understand. Hands lifted her head. Agony gurgled in her throat.

"Drink," a woman's voice said.

The two who had stolen her *tunjo* hovered over her.

"Drink," the witch Curratta repeated.

Anta swallowed a salty broth that broke the chill encasing her body, and her pain lessened its grip.

"Give I-*tunjo*," Anta gasped.

The strong *indio* Norane said, "When you are ready, brave *Xucha*. When you are ready."

* * *

Everything that was happening to her was in another place, as if she were watching a show. Norane carried her down the cliff to the statue where she'd lost the *tunjo*. At the bottom of the cliff, the jungle was burnt. Craters of disturbed earth, broken and burnt trees, marked where bombs had fallen. The statue of *Tatya-Masi,* still erect but dark with soot, looked down on birds and rats feeding on the dark bodies of dead La'ku, amongst their spears, guns, and clothes.

They went through a waterfall into a cave where the light was a dark blue and the air smelled of mud and mold.

"Cruuuuu."

The light of the *tunjo* flared in the rear of the cave.

Norane placed her on a narrow round stone table.

"Cruuuuu."

Twelve witches with long, white hair, hanging around skin so thin you could see the bones of their faces, walked from a dark hole in the cave wall. "*Tatya-Masi, Tatya-Masi,*" they chanted.

Curratta lifted Anta's head with one hand and picked up the necklace with the other. The Jewels danced with color and pulsated in the eyes of the frog god, as Curratta slipped the gold figure over Anta's head.

A verdant penumbra surrounded Anta. The bullet wounds closed. Muscles knit together. Her body warmed and pain changed to strength.

She knew what forward sight was, and with eyes that could see beyond the cave into a world she'd left, Anta saw her brother's frantic search for her. She sent him a dream where she whispered to him, "I am reborn. I am *Xucha.*"

EPILOGUE

It was hot and dusty in the foothills of the Sierras–a September day that buried deep memories of the great December floods. Kare banked the old Honda around a steep turn on the mountain road. His shoulder-length black hair was pulled into a ponytail. A green tee shirt lay tight over his thick muscles.

When MG had called him and asked him to come up to the lake, he'd felt rare joy. His abandonment by *Quetzal* on the New Granadian battlefield had left him devoid of purpose, wanting to be free, but thinking obsessively about his former master. Running had saved him from madness. What had started as a way of expelling pent up energy had turned into the life of a competitive marathon runner. Hundreds of miles and a careful diet had left him dark-skinned, lean, and strong.

He parked in the driveway of the house beside the Lake of the Frogs. He knocked on the frame of the open front door and peered through the screen.

"Come on in." A balding man walked through a tiled hallway to greet him.

"Ah, the errant knight." The man appeared uncomfortable that Kare did not return his smile. "MG said to bring you to the studio."

Tall windows overlooked the lake. Musical instruments and amplifiers rested on a stage. Shelves lined with disks and albums bordered a video screen and entertainment console.

Kare was led down a flight of stairs to a windowless basement and into a control room. A man and a woman sat beside a wide console covered with knobs and faders. A bank of computer monitors displayed vertical lines and boxes of sound waves.

MG, visible through a plate glass window, wore headphones and was singing into a microphone. Her voice, broadcast through monitors hung over the soundboard, reverberated with an echo as if she was singing in a stone chapel. The recorded background music included a flute, organ, and strings.

MG sang:

"Though the searchers seek him,

He is here but gone.

The criers long for him,

He does not ask why.

The man has become one,

He need seek no more.

Peace, lie still, beyond the door."

She sang along with a recorded chorus singing,

"Peace, lie still beyond the door."

When the song ended, MG closed her eyes.

The woman at the console spoke into a microphone. "Yeah, that's it. Deep."

MG took off her headphones and walked out the padded door into the control room.

"Kare!" She hugged him in a long, strong embrace, leaning her head against his chest.

He awkwardly held her. "He's my hero," she said. "Saved my life in the jungle. I never would have made it without him."

He remained stiff and unsmiling in the face of their friendliness and interest in him.

"Come on, let's go for a walk. I'll talk to you all later," MG said.

He was relieved to be away from the attention and out of the house. His shoulders relaxed and his arms swung more freely as they walked along a trail to the lake.

"Sorry about that," she said.

He nodded, still unable to find his voice.

"I guess that kind of answers my question," she said.

He glanced at her and then looked away.

"Keep you out of it," she said.

MG's fame was growing not only for her talent as a singer, but as a disciple of *Tatya-Masi*. The calamity of a completely shrouded planet, that no science or logic could explain, had engendered new levels of beliefs in spirits and metaphysical forces. She was right that he wanted no part of the spreading worship of ancient gods and goddesses.

They walked to the end of a boat dock. "I'm used to being in the spotlight. But there are ways that you can still have privacy, if you try." She took his hand.

His heart raced at her touch.

She gazed up at him. "I've got millions of people who think they know me, but they don't, not like you do."

She laid her hand on his shoulder and leaned into him.

He knew she wanted him to kiss her, and he wanted to, but didn't.

She stepped away. "This isn't over, Kare Kuwaru'wa."

"I know," he said.

As the shadows of the trees darkened the water's surface, there was a barely perceptible ripple. A bubble effervesced from the muddy depths, and among the rustle of the reeds, burst a faint sound.

"Croar!"

ABOUT THE AUTHOR

Jeffrey Marcus Oshins was born in Washington, DC and was educated in Europe. He has traveled extensively in Latin America where much of the inspiration for the 12 series arose.

ABOUT THE BAND

Apokaful is Kirsten Candy (vocals), Ian Stewart (guitar & percussion), Dennis Dragon (drums), and Jeff Oshins (keyboards).